The Mother Lode

After a lifetime of searching, the mother lode is finally within Amos' reach. But at what cost?

James Oliver Virmala

ACKNOWLEDGMENTS

When writing, we create many characters in our books that often become our friends. So many of these people in our books have names to match their involvement, but behind our mind's eye they are people we have met in our lives. Their unique characteristics have left an indelible impression on us and we bring them with us in the writing of books.

CONTENTS

BOOKS BY THE AUTHOR

Oli's Gold Book One
Search For Oli's Gold Book Two
Return To Oli's Gold Book Three
To Be A Mountain Man
Trouble On The Kansas Plains
Frontier Justice
Return Of The Mountain Man
The Tall Man
The Prospector
The Green Valley
Twilight Of The Mountain Man
The Mother Lode
Quest Of The Mountain Man
Journey's End
Rufus Pike
Rufus And The Pup
The Winding Trail Home
Rufus The Lost Years
The Kankakee Kid
Bogus Island
Tyler Tomas The Brothers' War
War of 1812 The Choice
Kyle Oliver The Next Horizon

DEDICATION

To my father and mother, who taught me values that have guided me throughout my life.

CHAPTER ONE

The spring morning was warm, with a soft breeze swaying new grass that was sprouting above the brown stubble from last year. An old man was riding out of the valley, a smile on his bearded face, his eyes glowing with anticipation. He stopped the buckskin and looked to the north. The buzzing of bees could be heard as they collected nectar and pollen from the prairie flowers. The mule he was leading cropped the succulent new grass.

It was May 1896, and Amos Mudd was feeling fine. The old prospector had spent the winter helping Dan and Mary August with their ranch in the green valley. As a thank you for helping Dan fight off some rustlers, the rancher and his two cousins had surprised Amos with a map that could lead him to gold. The map had originally been the property of Dan's grandfather, Oli.

It would now lead Amos to a cave which might still contain a leather scroll containing a map. When Dan and his cousins had been at the cave, they'd taken the gold left by the Spaniards. At the time they'd been dodging some questionable occupants in the area. Satisfied with the gold they'd found, the three cousins had left the leather scroll behind. While not sure what it contained, it might show the location of the Spaniards' mine. Just the possibility of a map leading him to gold was enough for Amos. He was on a quest for riches.

The buckskin snorted and bobbed its head, anxious to move on. The prospector's horse had been brought back from the rustlers' ranch. The mule was one of many that the prospector had had over his 65 years. They helped to remind him of the first Jenny, given to him by his father. Amos had named them all Jenny.

Touching the buckskin with his heels, the horse stepped out briskly. The mule shook its head in protest before following. There were two packs on the mule containing basic equipment Amos would need to reopen the cave and, hopefully, later work the Spanish mine. As he rode away from the towering walls at the mouth of the valley, Amos was humming a tune from his youth.

The old prospector was wearing his threadbare coat and had on well-worn wool trousers. His boots were low-heeled and his hat had a slouching brim. On his hip Amos had a well-oiled Colt .45, and in the scabbard a Winchester 73.

While the prospector's first love was finding gold, he also enjoyed being generous to those he met. He called it "doing good" when helping others. It made him feel warm inside. Dan August had first met the old prospector when carrying ransom money for a kidnapped boy. Without the help that Amos provided, things could have gone badly for Dan. Later, Amos had come to Casper and helped the rancher defeat a band of rustlers.

Amos reached back into his saddlebag and took out a fresh plug of tobacco. Tearing off a chew, he rolled it into his cheek and then put the plug into his shirt pocket. He chewed a couple of times and then spat at a boulder. As far as the prospector was concerned, life was good. He had spent his adult life in search of gold, helping others, or doing work for money when it was necessary to eat. Once again he rode with the potential of finally striking it rich.

Living in a fancy house or owning property others would envy had never been important to Amos. While he had often resembled a person who was down and out, in reality he had a rather impressive bank account in Cheyenne. When his father had died 47 years ago, he had left the potato farm to his only son. The proceeds of the property sale had been deposited into the Cheyenne bank and left to grow. The old prospector had always felt guilty about abandoning his father and had been unable to spend any of the money.

Instead, Amos had been determined to make his own way in the world with the dream of hitting a mother lode one day. The truth was, Amos had never thought much of the future or material things. There had been the promise to his father that he would return with gold and help him grow the farm. This had changed after his father's death, and Amos hadn't planned further than getting good whiskey and spending time with warm women.

The buckskin was a fast-walking horse and had a smooth gait. For years, Amos had traveled the west leading a mule. In the past few years his age made it necessary to ride the mule or, when available, a horse. The prospector's attention was drawn to some low brambles. A pheasant was suddenly flushed. With a smooth motion, Amos pulled the Colt and fired. The bird's wings flapped uselessly and it hit the prairie grass.

Placing the Colt back into his holster, Amos swung down from the buckskin and went to pick up the kill. Walking back, he said, "Look here, horse. I will be enjoying this fine bird for supper."

Amos was heading toward Casper, which was a day's hard ride, or two easy days from the valley. There was a spot Dan would stop and spend the night. It had a pond lined with oak trees to keep the weather off. The old prospector tied the pheasant to the saddle. Taking the reins and Jenny's lead rope, he walked for a while to loosen the muscles in his legs.

Spring was Amos' favorite time of year. Years ago, he had spent winters trapping to survive. He had partnered up with an old mountain man named Doo. The man had taught him much about wintering in the mountains, trapping, and hunting for fur. In the summers, they would search for gold. Amos had always looked forward to the summers and much preferred that to the rigors of winter. While trapping or prospecting in the mountains, he had built a dozen cabins. Within a year or two he would get the itch and be off to search for riches over the next horizon.

Since he had buried Doo, Amos had chased after silver or gold in the summer and then looked for work that would give him a warm place to sleep in the winter. Sometimes it was a logging camp cutting timber, or a line shack watching over cows. He had even done underground mining. Whatever he chose, it had to include a warm place to sleep and meals. He often thought back to the more successful summers that had allowed him to winter over a saloon, partaking in the rye and women it provided. Those were good memories.

A soft spring rain was falling when he reached the pond. Pulling the gear off the animals, he picketed them on a south-facing knoll with plentiful green grass. The new leaves of an oak kept some of the rain off his packs. By the time he had the bird cleaned and roasting over a fire, the sky had cleared. He marveled at the bright rainbow.

"God does nice work. That's a good sign for the start of the trip," he said, talking to himself. It was a habit he had taken up from years of wandering alone.

He sat on the log that had been put next to the fire pit by others. Reaching into his pocket, he pulled out some papers. It contained a copy of the original map and his notes. While working on Dan's ranch the past winter, he had spent hours looking at the pencil scratches he'd drawn. He had memorized every detail and no longer needed papers, but he enjoyed looking at them.

For the first time in his long life he actually had a map that could bring him gold. This wasn't just chasing a dream or rumor. There had been Spanish gold. He fingered the well-worn sheets and smiled. Amos recognized most of the landmarks and had a fair idea where the cave was located. The cousins' description of the canyon sounded like some he had once camped in. He may have even camped in the one where the cave was located.

Why none of the Augusts had taken the scroll left by the Spaniards made little sense to Amos. No doubt they lacked the burning desire to strike it rich and were satisfied with the gold they had in hand. While he tore the juicy meat from the bird, Amos made a mental list of additional items he would need from Hartwick's Mercantile. He also hoped to spend a little time with a sweet gal named Lizzy whom he had met on his last visit to Casper.

There were those who had told Amos that he'd wasted his life chasing dreams and spending everything he earned on selfish indulgences. To Amos, what they'd said made no sense. It was only natural to spend what a man panned out of a stream or was paid for by his labors. Unlike his father, who had lived a spartan existence only to die in his potato field, never having enjoyed what he had earned, Amos spent or shared what he made. He had no one to leave his life's work to. Odds were that he would die in the mountains on a quest for more gold and wild animals would receive the only benefit as they fed off his remains.

Amos didn't like thinking about the long past or his father's money in the Cheyenne bank. It always led the prospector to think about the Ojibwa woman he had met years ago. He had almost settled down with her, but would have had to give up his dream of going to the California gold fields. He had chosen to leave. As things turned out, Amos had never made it to California. But the mountains had come to provide him all that he needed to survive. Amos figured that should the day come when he was too crippled to search for gold anymore, he would then settle in Cheyenne and spend what he needed, leaving what was left of his father's money to the last woman who gave him comfort.

It was late afternoon when Amos reached Casper. He headed straight for the saloon and had the bartender, Lem, set him up with a room and a bottle of rye. The prospector sat at one of the tables and poured himself a good measure of the amber liquid. The bartender joined him with a cup of coffee.

"Harry survived the winter and the doc figures he will be good as new soon," Lem said.

The bartender was talking about the deputy who had taken over while Sheriff Winslow recovered from gunshot wounds. Dan and his cousins had brought three of the rustlers in to be tried and hung. The two brothers, Billy Bob and Slim, had been waiting for their hanging when they'd overpowered the deputy and shot him. The brothers had left Casper, hitching a ride on a coal train. Once in Cheyenne they had robbed a hardware store and disappeared. It was believed they'd gone south to join an outlaw uncle in Texas.

"I'm glad to hear the deputy's getting along," Amos said. "The only mistake I made was not shooting the brothers when they come to rustle cattle at the ranch. They give up damn quick once we put the leader down."

After a couple of drinks, Amos brought his saddlebags to the room. It was small, with a lumpy bed and a straight-backed chair. A lamp shared a small stand with a pitcher of water and a bowl for cleaning up. The prospector set his bags onto the bed and the partial bottle of rye onto the bed stand.

Heading back out of the saloon, Amos led the animals to the livery. The hostler, Pop, had sold him the mule. "If you're coming to get your money back for that fleabag animal, you can just git along," the man kidded Amos.

"Fleabag!" The prospector replied. "The damn mule will probably outlive both of us."

The bald-headed hostler smiled, revealing his missing upper teeth. He liked to tell the story of ducking too slow when an animal kicked out.

"I need both shoed before leaving Casper," Amos said. "Give them a good rubdown and some grain before taking them to the smithy."

"It'll be a couple days," Pop replied. "Ebert got him a job shoeing some army stock."

Amos was anxious to start on his search for the valley that held the Spanish leather scroll. Though disappointed at the delay, his first thought went to Lizzy. She would make his stay much nicer.

"I'm staying at the Casper Saloon," the prospector said. "Send word when the animals are ready."

Hitching up his worn trousers, Amos headed up the street, in search of the lady. "Hey, Amos."

The prospector turned toward the voice and saw Bert Hartwick waving hello. Deciding that it was as good a time as ever to order the things he would need, Amos waved back and headed for the mercantile. "I got a few things I'll need before heading out," he called to the merchant.

Standing at the counter, Amos breathed in the smells of the store. Bert carried about everything a rancher, miner, or mountain man could need. The coils of rope, leather goods, spices, soaps, and oiled metal made the store pleasant. There was another smell Amos recognized. Apple pie.

Bert's wife, Angie had been baking. "Your wife has been busy," Amos observed.

"She sure has," Bert replied. "She got a roast going, some potatoes, and a pie cooling on the window sill."

Amos' mouth watered at the thought of a home-cooked meal. He began to give Bert the list of supplies he would need. "It will be a couple days before I leave, so if you could hold the stuff here I would appreciate it."

"Not a problem," the merchant said. "When Dan was in last time, he mentioned you were complaining about your old rifle."

"That I was," Amos replied.

"I got in the Winchester 92s last week." Bert took a rifle down from pegs behind the counter. Handing it to the prospector, he said, "Seeing you're a friend of Dan August, I'll give you a good price."

Holding the rifle, Amos admired it, wondering if he could justify spending so much of his winter's pay on the Winchester. "I guess it would depend on how good a friend you figured I was of the rancher."

Bert wrote a price on a piece of paper and pushed it toward Amos. "I would need the worn-out 73 in trade." He was offering the new rifle at an attractive price. The old prospector continued admiring the Winchester.

"It also includes the meal Angie's cooking." Bert said, smiling.

"The older Winchester won't shoot the longer cartridge and I missed some wolves this winter because they was just a bit too far," Amos said. Finally, he shook his head no and handed the new Winchester back to Bert.

"I can shoot the same shell in the 73 and the spare old .44 revolver I carry," the old prospector said. "At my age, too many types of bullets could confuse me."

Hanging the Winchester back on the wall, Bert turned to the old man and said, "Not to mention the extra weight your old mule would have to carry with three types of shells. But you are still invited to have supper with us."

After adding a couple more items to the list, Amos bought some extra tobacco plugs to add to the one in his pocket. "Supper still at six?"

Smiling, Bert replied, "Six sharp."

As he left the mercantile, Amos called back, "I won't be late."

Standing in the street in front of the mercantile, Amos ran his hand down his stained beard. He liked the feel of the town. If he ended up finding the Spanish gold mine, he might settle right here and enjoy his golden years.

He had originally planned to go back to the saloon and have a few drinks and look up Lizzy, but Amos didn't want to arrive for supper feeling tipsy.

He remembered seeing a coffee pot at the livery. He headed up the street, toward the large open doors. As he entered, there was the sound of laughter. Pop was sharing a bottle with a slim black man. The hostler looked up at the prospector. "Come on in and set a spell. Join me and Hoss for a drink."

Smiling, Amos replied, "I got to taper off for the afternoon, but would like a cup of coffee."

Pop got up and took a mug off the nail it had been hanging from. Blowing the dust out of it, he handed it to the prospector. "Don't know how hot it'll be, but I can always pour a little adjuster from this bottle."

Pouring the inky black brew into the mug, Amos pulled over an empty chair and sat with the men. Turning to Hoss, he introduced himself, "You can call me Amos." Giving the man a close look, he added, "Your skin says your black, but your cheek bones tell me your ma or pa was Indian."

Giving the prospector a broad smile revealing nearly perfect teeth, Hoss replied, "You got a good eye. My mother was Flathead. She died giving me life. I spent most of my youth in the Bitterroot Valley. Reservation life wasn't for me, so I joined the army. They didn't notice the Flathead in me and let me join the 25th Infantry as one of the buffalo soldiers. We was up at Fort Missoula in Montana."

"Weren't it the soldiers from Fort Missoula that marched the Salish Flathead from the Bitterroot a few years ago?" Amos asked.

"They sure did," Hoss replied. "But I was long out of the army by that time and when I got out I had no desire to go back to no reservation. My father was a runaway slave in the '40s. The way he talked of life on the plantation was pretty much how I felt on the reservation."

Amos sipped the coffee. It was barely warm and stale. Holding it out for Pops, he said, "The coffee does need some doctoring."

"Hoss here was a sharpshooter in the army and knows more than I do about horse flesh," the hostler said.

"Sharpshooter," Amos replied. "Must have been hell shooting at your own people as a soldier."

"The Flathead tribes weren't hostile, but the Nez Perce and a few others were," Hoss replied. "I didn't have no trouble shooting at them."

The three men spent the rest of the afternoon telling stories and working on the bottle. Amos took a liking to the black man. He had almost as many stories as the old prospector and had seen a lot of the frontier. Just before the hour of six, Amos excused himself and headed for the mercantile. Mixing the rye with the stale coffee had kept his head clear enough to behave at supper.

CHAPTER TWO

Amos came down from the room above the saloon with his saddlebags over his shoulder and the rifle cradled in the crook of his elbow. His mouth was dry and his head had a dull ache from the rye he'd drank the night before. Only the memories of Miss Lizzy made the night worth the hangover.

"I got coffee on the stove," Lem called to the disheveled boarder. "After seeing the gal leave, I figured you'd be along shortly."

"You are a credit to barkeeps everywhere," Amos said, accepting the coffee. "I had planned to be gone before sunup, but who knows how long it will be before I have someone warm next to these old bones again."

Lem had buttered bread with honey and shared it with the old prospector. "I figured you'd forgotten that Pop told you your animals were ready. Which way you heading?"

"West," Amos said, taking a large bite of the bread. "I'll be travelling north of the Green River. Maybe even go into the Yellowstone."

"You going after silver tips?" Lem asked. "There are some big ones up that way."

"My rifle is a bit light for the big bears," Amos replied, "but if one comes my way, I will do my best to bring it down."

The prospector avoided talking about his true destination or about looking for gold. He didn't know if anyone in Casper knew of the gold that the August cousins had found, but most knew that he had spent the winter at their ranch. He had chased lots of strikes over the years and had even discovered a few streams with color. It never failed that when he would arrive in a town and visit an assayer with a little dust or some nuggets, he would be dogged by those wanting their share.

When Amos arrived at the livery, the hostler had the horse and mule ready for travel. Settling up with the man, Amos said, "When you see Hoss next, tell him I enjoyed visiting him."

"He come and got his bay an hour ago," Pops said. "He's headed north to Montana. Talking about family made him want to see his sisters. If you catch up to him, he'd be a good one to travel with."

"I don't travel as fast as I once did," the prospector said. "I figure to go west. I plan to look up an old friend that has been scratching a living out of the foothills."

Leaving the livery, Amos led his animals to the mercantile. Bert was stocking some shelves when the prospector entered. "I come to gather my supplies," he told the merchant.

"I got them near the back door," Bert replied. "By the look of them, it appears you'll be doing some mining. I figured you wouldn't want to advertise it to the town. Folks are peculiar and catch the fever mighty easy."

"I appreciate that, Bert." He went back out and brought the horse and mule to the back door. A few minutes later, the animals were packed and Amos was ready to start on his next adventure. He told Bert that he would miss Angie's meals and hoped to be back in the fall.

After adjusting the saddle on the buckskin, Amos tightened the cinch. Climbing onto the horse, he headed out of town with the mule following. He had traveled alone much of his life with nothing but a mule or horse to talk to. While he didn't mind it, he had always preferred having a partner who could share some of the camp chores and tell stories.

As Amos rode, he noticed that several drifters watched him with interest. Most men traveled by train when going any distance, not horseback. Everything about his rig identified him as a prospector. He hoped that the condition of his worn clothing and scarred saddle would discourage anyone from following him.

Riding west, Amos figured to throw off anyone following him. Should someone trail him, Amos knew lots of tricks to make tracking difficult. He thought about the map and notes in his pocket as he rode. The canyon with the cave would be in Montana. Amos was familiar with the Stinking River and the terrain north of it contained in the notes. Amos would be traveling between the Bighorn and Rocky Mountains a good part of the way. Maybe he would catch up with Hoss.

Independence Rock was just over a day's ride from Casper. Once he passed it, Amos would head northwest toward the Wind and Bighorn River, cutting across the Bridger Trail. A careful study of the notes given to him by the August cousins told him that the Bridger Trail would be the most direct route. An alternative would be following the Bighorn River north before cutting to the west.

Amos was familiar with other gold strikes in Montana. There had been strikes in Alder Gulch and Virginia City in 1860. The prospector might find that the scroll would show that the location of the Spanish mine was in that area. Any gold left in the Spaniards' mine would have been already taken out.

Once he had the scroll that was left in the cave, the question would be answered. Amos was in a good mood. He had learned long ago that it was the quest for the precious metal that he enjoyed the most. He would get a lot of satisfaction finding the original location of the Spanish mine.

Amos rested on a bluff overlooking the Sweetwater River. He had just passed Devils Gate and was chewing on biscuits that Angie had given him. With his clasp knife, he carved slices off a ball of aged cheese, adding flavor to his meal. Suddenly he felt a chill on the back of his neck. He set the biscuit and cheese down onto the lush green grass and picked up his canteen. While doing this he was slowly looking at his surroundings.

It was just a feeling, but the old prospector felt eyes on him. It might be nothing more than having the map to the cave and letting his imagination get the best of him, but he couldn't shake the feeling that he was being followed. While he could see landmarks miles away, the rolling plains he was traveling could easily conceal someone shadowing him.

"Well," Amos mumbled, "if you are out there I may as well make it easy for you."

What the old prospector was thinking of was leading whomever it might be to Fort Washakie near the Wind River. He would then watch for anyone coming into the fort a day or so after him and see if the person looked familiar. Laughing, he said, "While I'm there I can have a drink or two and if nobody shows, that will make the few extra miles worth the effort."

The horse and mule had stopped grazing and were staring at Amos having a conversation with himself. The old prospector tightened the cinch on his horse and climbed into the saddle. He rode toward the fort, keeping to high ground, making sure he could be seen. Tonight, he would begin looking for any campfires of fellow travelers. He thought about Hoss leaving suddenly just before him. Could that be who was giving him the uneasy feeling?

If Hoss should show up at the fort, or anyone else came that he was suspicious of, Amos would depart in the dark of night and then make sure his tracks couldn't be followed.

The prospector did some planning. On the Stinking Water River, or the Shoshone River, there was a small town called Cody located on the western side of the Bighorn basin. There Amos would spend a few days and watch. Should anyone he saw coming into Fort Washakie also show up there, that would confirm he was being followed. Amos would wait for them after leaving Cody and they would disappear into the mountains, never to follow another miner. Then again, if it was Hoss? The old prospector hoped it was not.

It was four days later, before Amos rode into the fort. It was located in the Wind River Indian Reservation and occupied by the army. There were Arapahoe and Shoshone tribes in the area. The fort had been named after a Shoshone chief. The Indian woman Sacajawea who had guided Louis and Clark was buried at the fort. The old prospector wasn't interested in the history of the fort. He rode up to a small saloon and tied his animals to the sagging rail. Hitching up his trousers and adjusting his gun belt, he ducked under the low door and entered the environment that always brought him pleasure.

The saloon had four lanterns burning, casting dark shadows through the dim room. The smell of tobacco smoke and rye filled his nostrils. Amos walked up to the bar, its planks polished by the elbows of countless patrons. A dark-haired man dressed in loose-fitting clothing stood behind the bar. He took the rag he had hanging over his shoulder and gave the bar a wipe in front of Amos.

"Got whiskey, tequila, and beer," he said. "What's your pleasure?"

"I'll take a bottle of the rye and a beer to chase it," Amos replied, noticing a dirty window behind him. "Bring it over to the table yonder."

From the window, Amos could see his backtrail. He was looking out when the bartender set the drinks on the table. "You waiting for someone? I can bring you another glass."

"Nope," Amos replied. "Just enjoying the afternoon sun. I imagine you get a lot of folks passing through here."

"Not here," the man said. "The fort's off the trails, and without the trappers or buffalo hunters of years past, things stay pretty quiet. Things do pick up when the army gets paid. I got some gals that draw them in."

"Gals you say," the old prospector replied. But the bartender had turned and was heading back behind the bar.

As the afternoon slowly went by, Amos nursed the bottle of rye. Twice he called the bartender over, once for another beer and the second time to order something to eat. The bartender brought over a bowl of lukewarm stew with two slices of day-old bread. Before the man could head back behind the bar, Amos asked, "What time do the gals come in?"

A look of surprise crossed the bartender's face. "It ain't payday at the fort."

The meal left Amos' stomach queasy. It was dark outside and a few of the locals had come in for a drink before heading home. Amos settled up with the saloon keeper and asked if there was anyplace he could get a room for the night.

"Your best bet is at the livery," the man told him. "Board your animals and Otis will let you sleep in the loft."

Carrying the bottle, Amos collected the horse and mule and followed the directions the bartender had given him. Leading the animals into the wide, gaping doors, he saw the hostler tossing hay to the horses. Otis turned and smiled. "The animals will cost a dollar for the night. Another four bits gets them some grain."

"I am hoping to sleep in the loft after you and I finish this bottle of rye," Amos told the man.

"Well, hell," the hostler replied. "That will get you a bunk in the tack room. Give me a minute to take care of your animals."

With his stomach still unsettled from the stew, Amos let the hostler drink most of what was left. Otis told the prospector the history of Fort Washakie and the Shoshone chief. During a brief pause, Amos asked, "Where do strangers usually spend the night?"

"Ain't many of them come to the fort," Otis replied, taking a swig from the bottle. "Most set up camp near the Wind River or trade for a bed and warm woman in one of the teepees. Of course, if you're on government business they put you up in the barracks or one of the officers' quarters."

Figuring that he could use an extra set of eyes, Amos said, "Maybe you could help me. I got the feeling that someone has been following me. If any strangers come around, I would appreciate you letting me know."

"It'll cost you another bottle tomorrow," Otis said, winking.

"It would be my pleasure," Amos replied. "I'll even help you drink it. My stomach don't feel so good after eating at the saloon."

"Sounds like you had Walley's stew," Otis said, laughing. "He makes a big pot once a week and keeps it on the back of the stove until it's et."

"Well. My guess is I was on the wrong side of the week," the prospector said. "Right now, I think I'll head for that cot."

Picking up his saddlebags and rifle, Amos went to the small tack room. Everything was covered with dust, including the cot. Shaking the dirt from the blanket, he pulled off his boots and laid down. He was sure that he'd be heading for the little house before the night was over.

* * *

Two days later, Amos rode in on the buckskin. He had been out on some high ground, watching the road south and east. Other than freight wagons or soldiers, he'd seen no other riders. He had three partridges hanging from the saddle horn. Patting the horse on the neck, he said, "Things are quiet in the hills around here."

Otis was taking care of a hard-ridden dun. "You was asking if any strangers come in. A hombre come in about an hour ago," the hostler said. "He come in on the north road, and looked like he'd been living out of his saddlebags for a while. He said he'd be in town for a couple days and asked for a good place to get a drink. I sent him to Walley's."

"I hope you warned him about the stew," Amos said, laughing.

Taking the reins from Amos, Otis said, "I didn't much like the looks of the fella. His eyes was kinda funny. They were too close and he had a weasel look about him."

"Sounds like someone I should look in on," the prospector said.

Eying the birds Amos was carrying, Otis suggested, "We should cook up them partridge first. I got some potatoes to toss in and we can have a fine meal."

Feeling the burn of hunger in his own stomach and with the prospect of potatoes, Amos replied, "Let's get to cleaning these birds."

Otis took care of the buckskin and set them a proper table while Amos did the cooking. It wasn't long after the meal was ready before they were picking the last of the meat off their partridge bones. Amos belched and stood up. While wiping his hands on his trousers, he said, "I best get over to the saloon and have a look at the man. I don't recall seeing anyone with funny eyes in Casper."

Otis pulled the cork from the bottle Amos has brought him the day before and poured a measure into his tin mug. "I plan to sit right here and enjoy this rye. If you want any later, you best bring another bottle back from Walley's."

It was just starting to get dark as Amos walked up the dusty street. Walley was hanging a lantern on the porch in front of his saloon. He waved at Amos and headed back inside. From within came the sounds of soldiers celebrating. The shrill laughter of women, the clinking of chips, and the music from an out of tune piano greeted him.

Smiling, Amos thought, *It must be payday*.

The few tables were occupied by card players, and several men crowded the bar. The prospector looked at the three women working the soldiers. Pushing his way to the bar, he nodded at Walley and the bartender brought him over a bottle and glass.

"Looks like a busy night," Amos said to the red-headed soldier next to him.

"By the time the weekend's over, most of these boys will be broke," the soldier replied.

"Do you include yourself in that?" the prospector asked, a twinkle in his eye.

"Not me, sir," the red-head replied. "I'm saving up to buy a small farm when I get out. Got a girl back east waiting for me."

"You're a smart man," Amos said. "When I was your age, I . . ."

The sound of smashing glass and a screaming woman interrupted Amos. A robust woman with tight curls in her brown hair, came running out of the back room wearing only torn undergarments. "You son-of-bitch, ripping my clothes!" she shrieked.

A man in long johns came out after her and as she turned to run, he grabbed hold of her hair with one hand and came around with the other, catching the woman in the side of the face. She wilted to the floor and he stood over her, bringing his foot back for a kick.

The prospector was only a couple steps away and caught the man by his shoulder and spun him around before he could deliver the blow. As the close-eyed weasel snarled and was about to object, Amos brought the barrel of his Colt across the man's skull, dropping him to the floor.

While a couple of the soldiers helped the disheveled woman up, Amos stood over her attacker. The man shook his head as got to his hands and knees. "You try and stand up, I'll give you another dose of this gun barrel," the prospector threatened. "You just crawl your ass out of this saloon and stay out. If I see you again tonight, I'll put a hurt on you that you just may not wake up from."

Followed by the jeers and hoots from the soldiers, the man crawled out of the saloon. Walley tossed his clothes out the door as the man attempted to stand with the help of the hitching rail. Setting a holster and revolver onto the bar, he said, "I best not give this to the bastard. He'd wait in the dark and back shoot you."

For the rest of the evening Amos was kept plied with drinks from the admiring soldiers. The red-headed soldier named Kelly stood next to the old prospector, letting everyone know they were friends. The soldiers had a midnight curfew and as they left the saloon they escorted the quite inebriated Amos to the livery. One of the men was carrying the bottle that was promised to Otis. After dumping Amos in the tack room, they told the hostler all about Amos coming to the lady's defense.

The next day, the sound of church bells woke the prospector. His head was pounding and his stomach was sour. It took him a bit to realize where he was. Otis was adding wood to the stove and putting on coffee. "You going to sleep all day?" he called to Amos.

His inquiry got only a groan in response. As the prospector staggered from the tack room, Otis let him know that the funny-eyed man had come for his horse earlier and was sporting a bruise and cut on the side of his forehead. After settling up, he'd led the horse to the saloon and knocked on the barred doors. There was a short wait and Walley had opened them, handing the man his revolver and holster. Without a word, the man had climbed onto his dun and headed away from the fort.

"The gal he roughed up told the soldiers his name was Soot," Otis told Amos. "One other thing, they said the drinks are on them if you come back tonight."

The years showed on the old prospector and he sat holding the cup of steaming coffee. "I best stay away from the saloon tonight. Hard drinking is for the young. Another night just might kill me." After taking a sip of coffee, he asked, "Did you get a bottle last night?"

After a moment, Otis grinned. "Your room is still paid for."

"Have my horse and mule ready for me tonight," Amos said. "I'll be leaving the bottle on the books in case I come back by here again."

CHAPTER THREE

Daylight found Amos miles from Fort Washakie. He was about a half-day's ride from the Bridger Trail. The trail wound north between the Rocky Mountains and the Bighorn Mountains. It was a route that the prospector had taken many times since it was blazed by Jim Bridger in 1864. Amos had once followed it to the gold strike in Montana, finding only enough for groceries and winter lodging.

He sat under a scrub oak below a red rock ridge and was brewing a pot of coffee. Amos had attempted to sleep for a while after stopping, but the confrontation with Soot and the desire to put distance between the fort and himself wouldn't allow his thoughts to shut down enough to go to sleep.

Amos had decided he would follow the Big Horn River north and then cut west when he reached the Stinking Water River, rather than take the more traveled Bridger Trail. It would be more difficult than the trail, but anyone who was following him wouldn't expect him to do so. The truth was, Amos could have made most of the trip by train leaving right out of Casper, but he felt that following the original route taken by the August cousins' grandfather would make finding the canyon easier.

By now, Amos was fairly sure that the canyon was in or near the Crazy Mountain. They had been named after an emigrant woman who had gone mad after her family had been killed by the Crow. The Crow believed that the mountains had mystical powers. His first goal was Red Lodge, Montana. The cousins had stopped there before continuing north.

After eating a couple of biscuits he had gotten from the fort, Amos saddled the buckskin and put his packs onto the mule. He was looking forward to the trip along the Big Horn River. He still got a great deal of pleasure traveling through the high country cut by winding rivers. The river would provide fresh fish, waterfowl, and other wildlife that came out of the hills to drink. Amos would pass the occasional cabin or small ranch that could provide a bed off the ground and news along the river.

The prospector spent a few moments looking at the basin in front of him, watching for any movement. Satisfied that it was safe to travel, he climbed onto the buckskin and, taking the mule's lead rope, he headed north. The rough, winding road was void of any travelers. Amos had his eye on a pass that would bring him to the Wind River just before it joined with the Bighorn River.

It was getting dark when Amos reached the Wind River. He was exhausted from riding. Both of his animals were showing signs of the rigorous travel. He made camp in a grove of cottonwoods. After a meal of hard bread and water, he rolled out his bedroll and fell into welcome sleep.

It began to rain during the night. The cottonwood protected the sleeping prospector from most of it, with only a few large drops working their way through the leaves. Amos pulled the blanket over his head, ignoring the change in weather. Fog shrouded the world around him when he awoke.

After relieving himself, Amos moved the horse and mule to fresh grass. Patting the buckskin on the shoulder he said, "This is good weather for a fellow looking to lose folks following him."

The old prospector couldn't be sure if he was being followed. For all he knew, Soot was just a rowdy, passing through the territory. Again, he reminded himself that it could just be having the map that was causing the feeling he was being followed.

Amos dug through his possible bag and fished out a flint and steel. Searching out some tinder and dry sticks under the cottonwood, he put them together and got his fire going. He rinsed the coffee pot in the river before filling it with water. He caught the flash of the white belly of a trout.

Setting the water to heat, he got some line and a hook. Using his knife, he cut a stick and rigged it for fishing. He found some worms under rocks next to the river and was soon sitting on the foggy bank, waiting for breakfast to find its way to his bait. By the time he had caught three fish, the coffee was done and the fog was lifting. Amos put a little side meat into the blackened frying pan and placed the cleaned trout to fry.

Once the meal was finished, Amos got the animals ready and headed north along the river. The

Wind River would join up with the Big Horn River near some thermal springs and the Big Horn would eventually flow into the Yellowstone River in Montana. Amos was looking forward to enjoying fish for many of his meals. He was following a trail and wound back and forth, crossing the river several times before he reached the Stinking Water River.

Amos was a week away from reaching the Stinking Water River. He was in the high desert between the mountains and there were trees along the rivers or in the foot hills of the mountains. He liked the openness of the route. He knew that there were ravines and ridges that someone could hide behind for a short time, but traveling through would force them to come into the open, making them easy to spot.

He stopped at the thermal springs and enjoyed a good soak in the warm water. The area had been purchased from the Arapahoe and there was talk of making it a state park. The thought saddened Amos. He had been in the mountains when there were only trappers, the tribes and wilderness, unspoiled and unreachable by civilized folks. It seemed like the states and the government wanted to grab up all the beautiful areas and make them into parks.

Amos' body felt rejuvenated when he rode away from the springs the next morning. Ahead of him was the Big Horn River. He spotted a few buffalo grazing on a hillside and near a waterhole were some pronghorn. Shooting buffalo was a thing of the past. Hunting them for hides had just about wiped the herds out.

Suddenly, Amos smiled, making a decision. Whether he found gold or not, it was time to stop living the life he had enjoyed for the past 40 some years. Come winter he would settle down near a town. He would build a cabin and maybe find a woman to share it with.

The prospector wasn't in any hurry, so he stopped at Owl Creek. The fish he had had for the prior breakfast were on his mind, and there was a nice pool on the creek before it reached the Wind River. Loosening the cinch on the buckskin, he picketed it on a patch of grass. He thought about pulling the packs off the mule, but changed his mind and put it on the same grass with the horse.

Amos had the fishing rig from the other morning on his packs. He took it and was soon tempting the fat fish to take his bait. The water in front of him splashed and for a second he thought he had hooked a big one. Then there was the report of a rifle! Amos dove ahead over the creek bank and crouched below the bank in knee-deep water, his Colt in his hand.

Two more shots clipped the bank above his head. Amos moved along the creek bank, looking for an area to work his way to high ground, hoping to return fire at the bushwhacker. He heard the sound of running horses leaving the area. In desperation, he looked above the bank just in time to see Soot leading the buckskin and mule behind his dun and riding north They disappeared beyond a rise.

"That son-of-bitch!" Amos shouted. His heart was pounding and he was short of breath as anger surged through him. "I should have killed the bastard," he growled. The anger was quickly replaced by cold determination. A man on foot can travel as fast as one on horseback, and a determined man even faster. He would see Soot again.

The first thing the prospector had to do was take stock of what he had. His coat lay near the spot where he had planned to make his meal. His rifle and saddlebags were on the buckskin, he suddenly realized, so was the sketch of the map. He picked up the coat and felt the notes in its inside pocket. He looked in the direction that Soot had gone.

"At least he doesn't have these," Amos said.

Chances were that Soot had stolen the animals to get back at the way Amos had treated him. The sketch of the map would mean nothing to him. The prospector knew he could find the cave without the map. He had memorized both the notes and the map and was pretty sure he knew the area where the canyon was located.

He had his coat to keep him warm in the high country and everything he needed to survive, along with his winter wages in the possible bag slung over his shoulder. With the Colt and knife to hunt and clean game with, he would be just fine. Amos looked down at his worn boots. They should take him to the Stinking Water River, where there was a small town. He'd get another pair there. Amos retrieved the fishing pole that had gotten tangled in some brambles on the creek bank and found that he had caught a nice-sized trout. He smiled. Things were looking up.

Making a quick meal of the fish, Amos took after Soot. The trail was easy enough to follow in the sandy trails along the river. The prospector was determined to walk from first light until dark, only taking time to shoot game of opportunity. He had a limited number of shells for the Colt. The possible bag had a dozen extra cartridges. Again, he could get more when he reached the next town.

Amos continued walking until it was too dark to be sure of Soot's tracks. He then curled up just off the trail, using his coat for a blanket. His legs were cramping from the stress of the pace he had set for himself. He stretched them to try and get the muscles to relax. He finally fell asleep, thinking of Soot in the sights of his Colt.

Like manna from heaven, Amos opened his eyes and saw a large jackrabbit not 30 feet away. His holster was rolled up near his stomach with the Colt. Slowly, he pulled the revolver and fired. The rabbit jumped to the side and kicked a few times before expiring. Throwing the coat aside, he went over and picked up the animal by its ears.

The prospector looked around, wondering if Soot could have heard the shot. He half hoped the son-of-a-bitch did and came to investigate. The next shot would be through the man's scrawny body.

Amos was stiff from walking the day before. He recalled days gone by when he would lead his mule for days with no effect on his body. He cussed his old bones as he cleaned the rabbit. The fire he had started was ready and he put the animal on to roast. He didn't have time to spare to cook it properly, but would put a little char on the outside before eating it.

After an hour of walking, the prospector's muscles warmed up and, with a full stomach, he kept a good pace as he followed the trail. Soot was also making good time, swapping back and forth from the dun to the buckskin. On the third day, Amos came to Soot's camp where he had been met by two other riders.

The prospector broke into a cold sweat at what he saw. Scratched into the dirt was a map much like the sketch Amos had in his saddlebags. Wracking his brain, Amos went over what he had in the stolen gear. Nowhere had he left a note about the cave or gold. Even the notes in his coat only listed distances and landmarks. It was possible that they had found the map and had drawn it during a discussion of what it might be.

He wondered, *Could one of the riders be Hoss?* He thought about the visits with Hoss and Pop. Again, he was sure that he'd never mentioned looking for gold. Bert, who had sold him the supplies, had guessed, and the cousins might have said something in the past that might have gotten to Hoss.

All of a sudden, he remembered Billy Bob and Slim. They had been tied up in the ranch house when the cousins had told him about the map. While they had tried to keep their voices down, maybe they had overheard enough. He had heard that they'd headed for Texas. All Amos was sure of was that the men he was following had seen the map, and he would have to assume they knew it would lead to gold.

Amos put his hand on the butt of the Colt. He would need more shells when he got to that town. The three riders' tracks led away from the river. They were headed straight to the town on the Stinking Water River. He would have to be careful. They just might lie in wait for him, or he might overtake them. The shells he had for the Colt wouldn't get him far in a firefight.

The prospector figured that he was three, maybe four days from the town. He wondered if he'd be able to get a horse or mule. If the men stopped there, he would deal with them right after getting some cartridges. He hoped he would find them there. If they passed through without stopping, they might be bent on finding the canyon.

It was near dark when Amos came to the Greybull River. It had been a day since he'd last eaten, so he decided to spend the night and try for a trout. He was in luck. They were hungry and he soon had two nice cutthroat trout lying on the bank. In the dusk, Amos put together a fire, his mouth watering at the prospect of the fresh fish. The first one was near raw when he ate it. The second had more time to broil over his fire.

The next morning, Amos found some currant bushes on the other side of the river. For a half-hour he ate the nearly ripe berries. He realized that this might be the only food he found today. He was no longer worried about following the three men's trail. He had lost it the day before when they were crossing shale. He didn't want to waste time trying to pick it up, because it was now a race between him and the three men to find the canyon with the cave.

After he had the leather scroll in hand, he would then deal with Billy Bob, Slim, and Soot. He would save the law the cost of a hanging. As he thought about sweet revenge, Amos plodded along, having to stop and rest every hour or so. Sitting on a low rock ledge, he fumed at his slow pace. It was probably caused by the missed meals. His time had to be devoted to putting miles behind him, or hunting. Right now, the prospector was driven by the need for distance.

That night, Amos made a dry camp. His canteen had gone with the buckskin. He chewed on some currants he'd saved from the morning. The tart fruit did little to quench his thirst, but helped the dryness in his mouth and throat. He was up and walking well before daylight, taking advantage of the cool morning air. Sunrise found him trudging across the high desert.

Amos shaded his eyes and surveyed the sage brush and rock-covered land around him. He had placed a small stone into his mouth to stimulate the saliva glands. In the distance, he could see a tree line through the heat waves rising from the high desert floor. There should be a stream running into the Stinking Water River. It would be another three hours before he reached it.

A dust devil swirled across the basin in front of Amos. His eyes followed it, and then stopped. The prospector blinked several times. For a moment, he had thought the swirling dust had moved some distant brush, but it wasn't brush. It looked like a rider, maybe two! Then what he was trying to make out disappeared. Amos squinted, trying to focus on the area, but there was nothing.

Standing up, he began stiffly walking again. "Damn old bones," he muttered. As he trekked on, Amos kept glancing in the direction that he thought he'd seen the riders. It would do him little good anyway. If it was someone who could help, they were at least five miles to the east. There was no way he was going to walk that far out of his way for a drink of water.

Other than a few berries, the prospector hadn't eaten or drank since yesterday morning. The tree line kept wavering in the distance. "Best not be a damn mirage. By God, I'll drink the sand when I catch up to it."

The sun blazed in the June sky and Amos was forced to stop again and rest. He slid down a ridge and sat leaning against the red rock. The only saving grace was that he could now see the tree line clearly. Even if the stream or creek was dry, it would offer some protected pools this early in the summer. His throat was dry and it hurt to swallow. To the west he could see mountains. Some of the higher peaks had snow cover.

"Them damn mountains are just taunting me," he complained.

Then he heard a hoof strike stone. Someone was riding toward him from behind. Weak, tired, and thirsty, Amos closed his eyes and mustered his strength as he listened to the sounds. It was more than one rider. It could be Soot and the others looking to finish him off. The prospector gripped the butt of the Colt. Slowly, he pulled it as he rolled to his hand and knees. Grabbing the drooping brim of his hat, Amos placed it onto the ground beside him.

Taking his time, Amos worked his way back up the ridge. By the sound, the riders were still a distance away. Reaching the crest, he slowly came up, using some sage brush to conceal himself. It was one rider and he was leading a second horse. It was his buckskin! Amos squinted, trying to make out the rider, but he knew it wasn't Soot.

Then he recognized the man leading his horse. It was Hoss. Amos held the Colt at the ready. He had no idea if the man riding toward him was friend or foe. The black man should have been in Montana by now. Amos didn't know why he should be in this area and why he was leading the buckskin?

Amos was thankful that Hoss was riding directly toward him. The prospector wasn't sure he'd have had the energy to chase the man down, had he been passing further away. Then Hoss pulled up. He was looking at the ground, at Amos' tracks. Was this the rider who had passed him several miles to the east? He could have cut back and followed the prospector's trail. Could it be that the three men had split up to find and kill him?

Amos was hot and thirsty. His mind was racing and he was having trouble focusing. All he knew for sure was that he was going to stop Hoss and get water and his horse back, even if he had to kill the man. The rider slowed down as he approached the ridge. He started to turn east to find a way down.

"Stop where you are, or I'll shoot you right out of that saddle," Amos croaked, trying his best to shout.

"Amos? Is that you?" Hoss asked.

Standing on unsteady legs and fighting not to slip down the ridge, the prospector leveled the Colt at Hoss. "It is. Why are you following me?" he demanded.

Hoss smiled. "I ain't following you. I am looking for you," he explained. "I heard you was shot out near the Greybull."

Hoss swung off the gray, removing the canteen from his saddle. "I'll bet you could use a drink about now."

Amos' mind was anything but clear. He lowered the Colt and kept his eyes on the black man. It could be a trick. When Amos reached for the canteen, the man might draw his revolver and shoot. The prospector was punchy. Amos did not know what to believe. Seeing the state of the prospector, Hoss set the canteen down and stepped back, keeping his hand in plain sight.

Amos stepped over the ridge and stooped to retrieve the canteen. He attempted to spit the stone out of his mouth, but his tongue felt thick. Finally, it fell from his lips, rolling off his beard. Suddenly, Amos did not care if Hoss shot him. He couldn't open the canteen with the Colt in his shaking hands, so he put it into the holster and then finally drank the life-giving water.

The prospector had trouble swallowing and coughed. "Take your time, Amos," Hoss cautioned him.

After a few swallows, Amos stopped. He was so thirsty that he could have gulped the whole canteen down, but knew he had to take small drinks. He looked at Hoss. "What brings you out here?"

The black tied the horses to some scrub and looked at the prospector. "You scared me, Mr. Mudd," Hoss admitted. "I am glad to see your wild eyes have settled down. Like I said, I come looking for you."

"Why . . . how?" Amos stammered.

Hoss replied, "I was in a saloon north of here and was having a few drinks. These three hombres come in and they was talking about having shot someone. A fellow with close eyes was telling the other two he was sure he'd got a bullet into some fellow back on the trail. He said it was where Owl Creek meets the Wind River."

Amos sat on the ground while listening to Hoss. He still held the canteen. The man continued. "Well, I'd had a drink or two more than I should have and was in no shape to do any more than listen what they was saying. One of the other men said he had found a map in the saddlebags. Things they were saying didn't make no sense to me."

"What did the men the funny-eyed man was talking to look like?" Amos asked.

"They was young and had sandy color hair, might have been brothers," Hoss replied.

"Sounds like Slim and Billy Bob," the prospector said. "Me and some others brought them in to be hung for rustling. I figured to let the law take care of them. They broke jail. I should have shot them right off. I damn sure should have."

Hoss watched Amos, waiting for him to take another drink. Then he continued. "Figuring it was none of my business, I ordered another drink. Then the fellow they called Soot was kind of cussing you for what you done at the fort."

"I kept listening. The skinny brother kept asking Soot if he was sure he got you. The funny-eyed bastard said he was sure because when he fired you went over the creek bank and didn't come back up. I finished the drink and figured I better leave and ponder on what they'd said. I stepped out and saw your buckskin, still saddled, with your gear on it."

"Realizing it was you, I got to thinking, what if he didn't kill you? You could be lying near the creek, wounded and in need of help. Without thinking, I got my horse and headed out of town leading the buckskin. If I didn't get to you in time, I could at least bury you."

The water was making Amos feel better and clearing his head. "I am damn glad you did. His shot was a clear miss, but my old age might have killed me before I got to the next town."

"It was just luck that I saw you," Hoss told him. "I was looking at the mountains and caught your movement. I damn near went right by you."

Amos dug into the saddlebags on the buckskin. The map was gone. He brought out a plug of tobacco. Cutting a chew off for himself, he then offered some to Hoss. Shortly the two men were riding back toward the town. The prospector noticed that his Winchester was also missing from the scabbard.

CHAPTER FOUR

It was noon the next day when the two men rode into the small town on the Stinking Water River. They headed straight for the livery. A tall, stoop-shouldered man with thin silver hair took the animals from them. Hoss and Amos followed him toward the stalls.

Amos was about to ask him about the horse that Soot rode when he spotted a dun tearing at some fresh hay. Then he stopped in mid-step and looked toward the back of the livery. It was his mule! The hostler tied the two animals near some open stalls.

"It'll be six bits per day, two more if you want grain," the livery man said.

Hoss dug into his pocket for coins while Amos stared, unaware of what the hostler had said. Clearing his throat, the silver-haired man said, "Did you want grain for the buckskin?"

Realizing the man was talking to him, Amos replied, "Yes, some grain. How much did you say?"

"Eights bits for the night with grain," the hostler said, somewhat impatient.

As the prospector handed the coins to the man, he said, "I was looking at the mule you got there."

Breaking into a broad smile, the livery man said, "It's a fine animal. Got it yesterday. Lots of demand at the canals. I should get a good price for it."

"Wouldn't have been the fellow that owns the dun that you got it from?" Amos asked.

Suddenly, the smiling hostler's face went cold. "Ain't your business where I got it. I paid good money for the mule and got paper to prove it."

Hoss stepped back, giving the two men some room. The hostler was a good six inches taller than Amos and had the reach on the old prospector. Of course, Amos had his Colt as an equalizer.

"Did the mule come with packs and a Winchester rifle?" Amos asked.

The liveryman was suddenly looking uncertain. "It had a pack saddle. I did hear that the man sold some stuff at the mercantile. He said he was selling his gear and going to Oregon."

"Seems to me a man could use a pack animal to go over the mountains to Oregon," Hoss commented.

"We'll be back," Amos said. "The mule's name is Jenny and it best still be here."

The two men left the livery and headed for the mercantile. It was a weathered clapboard building with a porch cluttered with items for sale. A sign on the front said, "Johnson's Supplies." Amos recognized some of his mining gear still in his canvas packs. A rosy-cheeked, portly man was cutting some cheese for a woman dressed in a gingham dress.

Amos waited for them to complete their transaction and then stepped up to the counter. The owner cut a sliver of cheese and held it out to the prospector. "Take a taste of the cheese. Hadley just brung it in."

Evidently, Hadley was the local cheese maker. Amos took the slice and was pleased with the flavor. Once he settled with the merchant, he figured to buy some. Behind the counter in a rack was a Winchester 73. The prospector was willing to bet his initials were carved on the other side of the stock.

"Thank you for the cheese," Amos said. "Unfortunately, you've come into possession of some stolen gear."

"And that would be?" the merchant asked.

"The packs out front and the rifle behind your counter," the prospector replied.

Once again, Hoss stood ready if Amos needed him. The rosy-cheeked man turned to take the rifle down, "Anything particular that would identify it as yours?" he asked.

"Amos Mudd is my name, and my initials are on the stock," the prospector replied. "I was ambushed near Owl Creek. The back-shooter thought he got me and took off with my animals and gear. I found my mule down at the livery."

"I give $10 for the rifle and another for the gear," the owner said, concern on his face. "We're a small town and that's a week's earning for me. Most folks around Cody buy on credit. Some never seem to catch up. I had a little money put away and used it to buy the stuff, hoping to get a bit ahead."

The rifle was set onto the counter with Amos' initials plain to see. "You wouldn't happen to know where the man that sold you the items is right now?" the prospector asked.

"More than likely, he's at the saloon. Probably lost the money playing cards with Ace by now."

Both men saw the merchant's wife standing wide-eyed near a doorway at the back of the store. Amos looked at Hoss. "Do you think we should go and get Mr. Johnson's money back?"

"Sounds like a fine plan to me," Hoss said.

Turning to the merchant, Amos said, "I will need a box of .45 shells."

Placing a box of .45's along with a box of .44's, the owner pushed the shells and the rifle toward Amos. "You may need both," Mr. Johnson said. "Watch Ace. He has a small gun in his sleeve."

Loaded for bear, Amos and Hoss left the mercantile. Standing in the middle of the street was a short, stocky, barrel-chested man with a badge pinned to his vest. He was tearing a chew off a tobacco plug. "Ansel at the livery told me you two are making a claim on a mule he paid hard cash for."

Amos stepped off the porch and faced the law officer. "Not only the mule, sheriff, but also this here rifle and packs at Johnson's place."

"Seems like a lot of your stuff has shown up in other folk's businesses," the sheriff replied.

Sizing up the sheriff, the prospector decided he was a no-nonsense lawman. He only hoped that he was also fair. "There was a polecat named Soot that took a shot at me and then stole my animals and gear. Trusting his aim, he didn't come and check if I was dead," Amos explained. "I surely wish he had, because if so, he'd be rotting near Owl Creek and I'd be on my way to Red Lodge."

"You figure this here Soot is here in Cody?" the sheriff asked.

"His horse is and that seems like the only thing he hasn't sold," Hoss volunteered.

"Well," the sheriff said, "Owl Creek is out of my authority. This Soot ain't committed any crime around here. It is your word against his whether the stuff was stolen or not. Hell, you ain't even wounded. Now, it is your right to find the man and work it out with him. If he kills you, I'll hang him. If you kill him, you best be out of my territory before I find the body."

The sheriff then looked at Hoss. "You got any stake in this?"

"No, but you could call me a witness to western justice," Hoss replied.

Snorting, the sheriff rolled his chew and spat. Muttering, he walked away toward his office. Stopping suddenly, he turned. "Watch out for Ace's hidden gun."

Amos handed the rifle and .44 shells to Hoss. "You take this and back me up. If by chance I get killed, send Soot to Hell and then get out of Cody. You are welcome to my buckskin."

They walked down the dusty street. The town was quiet in the heat of the day. As they approached the saloon, Amos heard the sound of coins clinking together. Looking into the dim saloon, he saw a bartender reading a paper at the end of the bar. He held a fly swatter and swung at any insect that landed close by.

Pushing open the batwing doors, the two men stepped inside and walked to the bar. There were three men playing cards. Two had bottles of rye next to them. A well-dressed man with greased back hair and a carefully trimmed moustache was not drinking. Amos guessed that he was Ace. The man with his back to them had the build and look of Soot. The third man appeared to be a local businessman.

"A bottle and two glasses," Amos called to the bartender as he placed some coins onto the bar. While waiting for the drinks he kept his eyes on the card players.

Ace glanced up momentarily and then began dealing. "We got room for two more players, next hand," he said.

The bartender brought the bottle and poured the drinks, then picked up the money before heading back to his paper. The two men tossed them down. Amos liked the burn of the liquor in his throat and refilled the glasses. Taking a sip, he said, "We're looking for a fellow name Soot that owes folks some money."

He saw the man with his back to them tense. Setting the drink down, Amos walked up behind him and saw he held aces and eights. "You got a dead man's hand, Soot. You're in luck, you've got a choice."

There was a slight movement of Ace's arm and Hoss warned him, "Keep your arm still or I shoot you through the elbow and you'll be dealing one handed from now on!"

Soot turned slowly and looked up at Amos, his eyes wide with fear. The businessman threw his cards down and moved away from the table. "You got . . . you got the wrong man," Soot blubbered. "You want Billy Bob and Slim."

Grabbing him by the collar, Amos pulled Soot backwards, sending him crashing to the floor, the chair splintering. The cold eyes of Ace narrowed, realizing that Amos was costing him his afternoon pigeons. Stepping away, the prospector pulled his Colt. There was the sound of two men coming into the saloon. They pushed open the batwings and, seeing Amos standing over the cowering Soot, changed their minds and they left.

"You know your way out," Amos ordered. "Crawl like you did at the fort."

"It ain't me you want, it's them Leeson boys," he pleaded.

Picking up the pot and the money that was in front of Soot, Amos stuffed it into his possible bag. Ace's face was red with anger as he sat, helpless to stop events in front of him. Then, shoving the crawling man with his boot, Amos followed Soot out of the saloon. Hoss kept the rifle on Ace and an eye on the bartender, who had little interest in the events.

A small crowd of townspeople had gathered in front of the saloon. Amos addressed them. "This man is a back shooter and thief. With the blessings of your sheriff, I will be escorting him out of your town."

The prospector had barely stopped talking when Soot pulled a gun hidden under his coat. Amos shifted the Colt and fired, sending a .45 slug through Soot's arm, shattering his wrist. Screaming, the back shooter rolled into the fetal position, hugging his bleeding limb.

The townspeople scattered, fearing being hit by a stray bullet. Hoss and Amos grabbed Soot under the arms and dragged the sobbing man toward the mercantile. Mr. Johnson stood on the porch watching the men approach.

Seeing the mangled arm, he said, "Set him on the porch. I'll get the doc. Try not to let him get blood on my goods."

Hoss was grinning. "I told that gambler that I'd shoot him in the elbow, so you decide to aim for this coward's arm?"

"Hell, I planned to shoot him plumb center and let him die slow from a belly wound," Amos replied. "It must be age that made me miss."

Amos settled with the merchant, using the money from the poker table while Hoss watched Soot being cared for. The town dentist, who was the closest thing to a doctor, did his best to stop the bleeding and bandage the arm. Washing his hands at the pump, the doc said, "I should cut it off now. It will never heal right and may go sour."

Soot sat crying on the edge of the porch. Amos went over and sat next to him, "You ain't cut out for this bad guy stuff."

Sniffling, the wounded man said, "I done what they asked. Billy Bob and Slim said they'd take me with them and we'd all be rich. I brung your stuff back to them and then I wake up yesterday and they were gone. It weren't right what they done to me."

Up the street they saw the sheriff coming toward them. "No one was killed," Amos called to him.

Puffing his chest up, the sheriff asked, "Who started the shooting?"

"Soot here pulled his gun and I had to shoot him," Amos explained.

"It's against the law in Cody to pull a gun and start people shooting," the lawman replied. "Bystanders can be hurt."

"I was defending myself," the prospector objected.

"Oh, you ain't in trouble. This here funny-eyed fellow is," the sheriff explained. "He started the gunplay. Of course, I'll have to ask you to leave Cody so no friends of this here fellow come looking for you."

He looked at Hoss. "If you weren't involved, you are welcome to stay."

The sheriff took Soot off to jail and Amos and Hoss headed for the livery. It took the rest of Soot's money to buy the mule back. The silver-haired hostler ranted about losing money and the added cost of feeding the mule. Finally worn down by the determination of the prospector and having heard that Amos had shot the man who'd sold them to him, he settled.

The sun was just over the mountains in the west when the two men rode north, the majority of Amos' gear intact. They rode for two hours before stopping near a swiftly flowing stream, choosing a spot under some cottonwoods to camp. Hoss took care of the stock while Amos got the fire going for their meal.

Shortly, the coffee water was heating and the blackened frying pan was crackling with side meat. "Tomorrow I'll make us some sourdough biscuits," Amos called to his friend.

Hoss came back carrying their blanket rolls and saddlebags. "I do like biscuits," he replied. He placed the gear near the fire. "Soot said he stole your stuff to get rich. How was he going to do that?"

Amos thought for a moment, tending to the frying pan. A decision made, he turned to his friend. "I had a map in the saddlebags showing me where gold had been stored. I was told that there was something in the cave with the gold that might lead to the mine."

"Another map?" Hoss asked. "You said you had the map."

Amos explained that a Spanish expedition had traveled from the south to search for gold. They'd found gold and planned to take it back but ran into trouble, and all but one of the Spaniards ended up dead. The lone survivor was unable to carry the treasure back south and had hidden it in a cave. He'd traveled back south with a map showing the location of the gold. He was ill when he reached the Spanish settlement and ended up on a ship back to Spain, still in the possession of the map.

Years later one of his descendants gave it to a sailor heading for the Americas. He'd died before making it to the west and had given it to Oli August. The cave was found and all the gold was removed. All that was left was a leather scroll that might have the location of the mine.

Amos then told Hoss about helping Dan August fight some rustlers and Dan had given him a sketch of the original map that Oli, his grandfather, had gotten. Dan and his cousins had regretted leaving the scroll, but due to the haste of their visit to get the last of the gold, they had left it along with three gold coins. All three had been successful investing their shares of the gold and had never gone back to the cave.

By the time the story was finished their meals had been eaten and they sat drinking the last of the coffee. Amos could see the excitement in Hoss' eyes as the firelight flickered off his face.

"Do you think the leather scroll will show where the mine is?" Hoss asked.

Amos smiled. "I am not even sure if it is a map at all. I have spent my life looking for the mother lode. I'm not young anymore and this search will be my last."

"Was it your map of the cave that Soot was after?" his black friend asked.

"I don't know if he knew what he was after, but by getting my gear, Soot was successful. Billy Bob and Slim ended up with my map," Amos replied.

"So, you don't know where the cave is?" Hoss inquired.

The prospector tossed out the dregs from his tin cup. "I have been wandering these mountains for over 40 years and have seen my share of valleys and canyons. While my age might have slowed me down a little, the mind is still sharp. I don't need the scrap of paper the map was drawn on. I know every detail it showed and believe I have spent time in the very canyon."

As the fire died down, the two men rolled out their blankets and turned in. Hoss lay for a long time looking at the stars and thinking. Listening to Amos, he had felt true excitement at the prospect of riches. The prospector had not promised him any, but he wondered what it must be like finding gold.

The next morning Amos was mixing up some sourdough and talking about the saloons and women in Red Lodge. Hoss finished checking on the animals and was in a thoughtful mood. The prospector finished putting the biscuits into the Dutch oven. The coffee was ready, so he poured two cups and handed one to Hoss.

"You are mighty quiet this morning," Amos told his friend.

"I didn't sleep too good," Hoss admitted.

"I can understand that," Amos said. "The shooting in Cody can leave a person unsettled."

"It's not that, Amos," Hoss replied. "I went to my blankets thinking about being rich. Having stacks of gold so I could buy anything I could want."

"Well, I would caution you about having stacks of gold," Amos said, chuckling. "I have been looking for those stacks all my life and they are still somewhere out of my reach."

"I don't want them," Hoss answered. "Did I tell you my father was a slave?" Without waiting for an answer, he continued. "He often spoke of the plantation owners back in Arkansas. They had money, but most weren't happy. When he was serving their meals, they would talk of being worried about losing their crops, cattle, or slaves. They had family troubles with relatives wanting their share. Nope, I got me a good life without worrying about having gold and then having someone take it. Just like the map you had taken. Even the possibility of riches had almost got you killed."

"I must agree with you," Amos said. "Gold is a blessing and to some a curse. I figure I am somewhere in between the two." Laughing, he said, "I have never been blessed with too much and that has prevented it from becoming a curse."

The men sat eating biscuits with their coffee. The sun was warm and the sound of the stream was pleasant to listen to. Like so many of the camps Amos had spent time in, it quickly felt like home. He was surrounded by everything he needed to be comfortable. With the meal finished they got the animals ready to travel.

"I'll travel with you to Red Lodge," Hoss said. "Then I'll be off to visit my sister."

Amos climbed onto the buckskin. "I could use a partner in this venture, and would be pleased if you would stay."

"No, I best not," the black friend replied. "If I hear you found the mother lode, I will be sure to look you up and let you buy me a drink."

"It's a deal then," Amos said. "But I wouldn't start wetting my lips in anticipation of that drink. This is just one of a hundred hunts I have made and all I got to show for it is a horse, a mule, and this threadbare coat."

With the worry of finding gold gone, Hoss' mood improved and he talked of his life and loves for the next two days traveling to Red Lodge. They rode into the town to the smell of coal fires and the sounds of trains pulling out, loaded with the black rock taken from the mines. Immigrants from around the world had come to Red Lodge to work in the mines. To keep the hard-working miners happy the town had twenty saloons offering anything a working man with money in his pockets wanted to spend it on.

They passed men with their faces blackened by coal dust heading for their homes, all carrying lunch pails and many carrying a pail of beer to wash the dust out of their throats when they got there. The two men stopped at the livery and were met by a skinny, bent old man with a chronic cough.

He smiled, exposing yellowed and chipped teeth. "Tie the cayuses and mule to the rail. I got a rack just inside to put your saddles on." After a fit of coughing, he continued. "Too damn many years in the mines. A dollar will get them brushed and fed each day. If your lookin' for fun, take the first street to the right and stop at Goldie's. Tell her Kelly sent you and she'll take care of you."

"I thank you," Amos told the hostler. "We could use a drink and someone to help shake the trail dust off us."

"You haven't seen a couple of pock-faced kids with straw-colored hair come through lately?" Hoss asked.

Kelly coughed and shook his head. "Be hard to tell. This here town has lots of folks come through. Some come for fun, some for work, and others for trouble. I don't much take notice. Ask Goldie. Her business is to take notice of folks."

With that, the old hostler went back into the livery, his coughing echoing in the large building. The two men put their saddles onto the rack along with the packs from the mule. Leaving, they trusted Kelly to take the animals in and feed them. The streets were a combination of cobblestone and dirt, with ruts or potholes to trip a man up if he wasn't careful.

Following the hostler's directions, the two men made a right and walked down the street carrying their saddlebags over their shoulders. They could see a weathered sign advertising Goldie's saloon and rooming house.

"I went through here in '70 when gold was struck in the area. Even then it was a place to have fun. In '86 the train come in and with it a whole lot of places a man can get in trouble," Amos said, reminiscing.

Hoss looked over at his friend and saw the glow of anticipation. "I take it this is your kind of place."

"Oh, yes!" Amos replied. "My kind of place."

It was early afternoon and already the saloon was busy. Several tables had men playing cards. There was a Faro table toward the back, as well as a roulette wheel. A long bar ran along the right side, with a well-stocked back bar offering liquor from near and far. Two men in white shirts and vests were busy making drinks for the card players. There was a small stage to the left, with a man playing piano. The oak floor was blackened from the coal dust on the patrons' boots. Several gaudily dressed women walked among the tables, offering their charms or soliciting drinks.

Amos noticed a cage at the far end of the bar with a large-bosomed woman with blond hair. She sat at a small desk supplying clay chips and counting money. He and Hoss headed for the bar and ordered a bottle of rye. Pointing to a table, the nearest bartender said, "Have some seats, gents. You might want to try our Scotch. It just come in from Scotland."

"Make it rye and we'll drink at the bar, thank you," Amos replied. "Later, I'd be pleased to buy Miss Goldie a Scotch if that's her drink."

Hoss tossed down his drink and told Amos, "I going to go up the street and get a room. I need to get rid of this saddlebag."

Picking up the bottle, Amos said, "Sounds like a plan. Later I will ask the lady in the cage about Billy Bob and Slim."

Grinning, Hoss said, "I got this friend I stay with when I'm in Red Lodge. I'll meet you tomorrow for breakfast at the Carbon Café at the head of the street."

The old prospector stood with a bottle in his hand, watching his friend head out the door. "I'll be damned," he muttered. "I think Hoss has him a gal."

"Ted said you'd buy me a Scotch whiskey," a sweet voice said, startling Amos. Turning, he was nose to nose with Miss Goldie.

The smell of her perfume filled his nostrils. Her makeup was tastefully done and her lips were pouting while her eyes smiled. "Miss Goldie, it would be my pleasure," Amos replied after an awkward pause.

"I don't drink Scotch, but I have an excellent French cognac that I do drink," she teased him.

Without looking away, Amos said, "Ted. The lady and I will have the cognac. Make it French."

Leaving the rye on the bar, Amos followed the blond woman toward the back to a round table that would serve six. The cage was just a few feet away. The bartender, Ted, came with the cognac and two snifters. Removing the cork, he poured a measure into each glass and returned to the bar.

Goldie cupped the snifter in her hands, warming the amber liquid. She smiled at the prospector and asked, "What is your name?"

Holding his glass, unsure if he should drink, he replied, "Amos. My name is Amos Mudd."

"Warm it in your hands," she instructed. "It makes the drink much better, Amos Mudd."

The smell of the warming cognac and the expensive perfume worn by Goldie were almost overwhelming to the old prospector. "Now," she said, "swirl it and breathe in as you take a sip."

For the next few minutes the old prospector allowed his senses to be caressed by the scent of the cognac and perfume. The lady said something but he missed it.

"I apologize, Miss Goldie, but my mind was overcome by the moment and I missed what you told me." Amos said, sorry that the spell had been broken.

"Ted heard you speak of Billy Bob and Slim Leeson," she repeated.

"Ah, . . . yes," Amos stammered. "I had planned to ask about them." Surprised that she knew their full names, the prospector became cautious.

"They have visited here in the past," she said.

Amos tried to read her face, but was unable to see anything more than her precocious smile. "I have some business with them and was hoping to catch up with them here in Red Lodge," he told her.

"Have you come to pay their bill?" she asked, her expression remaining the same.

The prospector was in the process of taking a sip of the cognac and stopped, his mouth hanging open. Recovering, he said, "Not exactly. In fact, if I am successful in finding them, you may never get paid. I intend to have them hung, or kill them myself."

"I would consider it a favor if you were to kill them," she said, moving closer to Amos. "They hurt two of my girls and skipped out on their bill."

It turned out they had been in Red Lodge a month ago and had caused Miss Goldie problems. It was said that they had killed a man in another saloon before leaving town with some coal miners in hot pursuit.

Having a common interest in the Leeson boys turned out to be a bonus for Amos. Not only did he have a most pleasant night with Miss Goldie, but he was not charged for the French cognac he was sure he couldn't afford. The next morning when he left, he was given the unfinished bottle of rye.

Hoss was just finishing his breakfast when Amos entered the Carbon Café. "I was fearful you might have gotten lost at Goldie's," he called out.

Sitting heavily in the chair across from Hoss, Amos ran his hand down his beard. "It was a night of French cognac, a warm woman, and a common enemy of the Leeson boys."

"You sure do smell pretty," Hoss said, kidding.

Amos ordered potatoes and eggs for breakfast. The freckle-faced waitress brought him a cup of steaming coffee and refilled Hoss' cup. While waiting for his meal, the prospector told his friend about what he had learned about Billy Bob and Slim.

Hoss had also found out that others had had trouble with the boys. They had been seen in town within the last couple of days. They had stolen two horses on their way out. It was doubtful that they would return to Red Lodge any time soon.

"It is too bad Goldie didn't know," Amos lamented. "They'd be hanging right now."

Using a piece of bread to wipe up the last of the egg yoke and grease from this plate, Amos stuffed it into his mouth and then asked Hoss while still chewing, "When are you leaving town?"

Hoss smiled as he watched the old prospector enjoy his food. "I plan to leave around noon."

Wiping his mouth with the back of his hand, Amos pushed his chair back a bit. "I would like to take you on as a partner in this venture. I can't promise you anything more than the enjoyment of the prospect of finding gold. I'll be honest. I am getting too old to take these things on alone and I could use . . . I need your help."

Hoss sat toying with his cup. Finally, he looked up. "I'll come with you as your partner. I also realize that the Leeson boys may be a problem."

"They are my problem and I don't expect you to go against them," Amos said.

Smiling, Hoss replied, "I think we can take them."

CHAPTER FIVE

While Amos liked the pleasures of Red Lodge, he was happy to be away in the fresh air. He was now three days, maybe four, away from the valley with the cave. Hoss volunteered to range out ahead and watch for Billy Bob or Slim. If they spotted him, they wouldn't consider him a threat and let him go. With luck, Hoss would see them first.

The terrain was getting more mountainous. To the east there was rolling grassland, but they were traveling along the foothills of the Rocky Mountains. Amos was impressed with his partner. Hoss had the moves and looks of an army scout. He would find a defendable place to camp and have a fire going by the time the prospector caught up.

Amos sat near the fire, looking at the notes he had on the canyon with the cave. He had little need for his sketch of the map which the Leeson boys now possessed. Hoss came in with an armload of wood. "Should be enough to take the chill off come morning," he said.

"Now that we're partners, I may as well let you know what I know," Amos said.

While a pot of beans bubbled on the fire, the prospector shared the notes and drew a rough outline of the Spaniards' map in the dirt. Hoss was quick to pick out some of the landmarks. "It ain't too far from Crazy Woman Mountains."

"Yep, just a bit south," Amos replied. "There was a strike in Virginia City just a week's walk west. That may be where they mined the gold and the cave may have been along the route back to their settlements. The scroll should let us know in a hurry."

"Well if it was mined in Virginia City, that's okay with me," Hoss said. Then, frowning, he asked, "Why would they leave the gold?"

"The map showed three graves," Amos told him. "Could be they run into some hostiles and they were all killed except for the one that carried the map back. Any horses they'd had would've have been run off or stolen. I figure being the only one left, he cached the gold with intentions of coming back some day with horses and soldiers to get it."

The sound of an axe biting into wood stopped the conversation. Amos quickly brushed out the map in the dirt and the two men moved away from their fire.

They hunkered down behind some wild plum bushes and listened. There were several more thuds of the axe. "Our woodsman ain't too far away," Hoss said.

"And he don't care about being heard," Amos added. "I think we should look the fellow up."

"We got us a pot of beans about done," his partner said. "If the fellow is friendly, we could invite him in to have a bite."

Dusk was settling in and the two men headed toward the sound of the axe. While Amos had some years on him, he could still move through the trees as quietly as any of the Indians he had met. Hoss moved away to one side around 30 paces and made no more sound than the fog that rolls in over a hillside into a valley.

The chopping stopped and then there was the sound of someone stacking wood. They broke into the edge of a clearing and there in the middle was a modest log cabin with a barn to the back. They were just able to make out a young man stacking the wood onto a sledge pulled by a donkey.

Amos stepped out and said, "We heard you chopping and thought you could use a bit of help."

The startled boy leaped over his load of wood and brought up a double barrel shotgun, "You best come out and show yourself clear!" he demanded. "I ain't afraid to use this here gun!"

"Take it easy son," Hoss said. "We won't hurt you."

Realizing that there were two of them and they were a distance apart, he crouched down behind the wood. "I warn you, I'll shoot and this here shotgun will make sure I don't miss."

"Young man, my name is Amos Mudd and I am coming out into the open. Nobody is going to hurt you. We got us a big meal cooking yonder and just wanted to invite you to share some."

"Both of you come out slow and I won't shoot," the young man said.

"Would you be willing to point that scatter gun toward the sky in case it goes off by accident?" Hoss requested.

Feeling in control of the situation, the young man stood up and pointed the gun away from the two men. Amos walked out first. "That's a fine-looking burro you got there. It must make hauling wood a bit easier."

"I'm coming out too," Hoss said. "Had me one of those critters when I was young."

The two men came out with both hands in plain sight. The young man cradled the shotgun in the crook of his arm and slapped the donkey on the butt to get it going. Keeping his distance alongside the men, he said, "They call me Chip. Real name's Andrew, after my pa."

"Is your pa home? We're looking for a couple of men and figured he might have seen them," Amos inquired.

"Pa's dead. Mining accident near Red Lodge," the boy said.

"Sorry to hear that, Chip," Hoss replied.

"Me and ma are working the place now," Chip explained. "My sister Elly is too young to be much help, but she tries."

Amos was impressed with the young man. He couldn't be more than 12 years old and was taking on a man's job. They reached the cabin and the open doorway cast light onto the front porch. Chip leaned the shotgun against his load and began stacking the wood against the cabin wall. The gun slipped and fell, causing both Amos and Hoss to jump away.

"It can't hurt you," Chis said. "I run out of shells a while back. It was my pa's and I get comfort carrying it."

"Who are you talking to?" a female voice called out.

"It's two men that invited us to share a big meal they're cooking," the young man replied.

A young woman who had the look of hard times stepped out. Clinging to her skirts was a little curly-haired girl about three or four years-old. "Share a meal?" she asked.

Seeing the two men with her son, a look of surprise crossed her face and she exclaimed, "Oh!"

"Don't worry ma'am," Amos said. "We run across your son back on the wood lot and sort of followed him here. We got a pot of beans cooking back yonder and would be pleased to share with you."

"You said a big meal," Chip contended.

"That I did," Amos replied. "It *is* a pretty big pot."

"Chip! Where are your manners?" the mother scolded. Then to Amos, "You and your friend are welcome to bed down near the cabin, or in the barn."

"Thanks. Give us a few minutes and we'll get our gear and the beans and be back," Hoss told the woman.

Turning away, the two men went to move their camp near the cabin. Chip called after them, "Wait a minute and I'll have the wood unloaded. We can carry your gear and the *big meal* on the sledge."

Shortly the packs and pot of beans were loaded onto the sledge. The two men walked with their animals while Chip drove the donkey. "What kind of farm does your mother have?" Amos asked.

"We grow potatoes," the young man said, his chest puffing up with pride. "We got four acres planted this year and we're clearing two more for next year."

"I know a little about growing potatoes, son," the prospector said. "Must be hard work without the help of your pa."

"It was my pa's dream of building the best potato farm in this area. Me and ma will do it for him."

They had reached the cabin and Hoss brought the pot of beans into the cabin. Amos moved away, busied himself unloading their packs and tending to the animals. Suddenly, his throat hurt and his eyes stung. It had been years since he'd thought about his own father's potato farm in Maine, how he had refused to stay and farm, the confrontation with his father the night before he left to find gold in California, and the promises he'd made about coming back with gold to share with his father.

He remembered reading the letter telling him that his father had died working the fields, found by a neighbor days later. Here was a young man who wanted to fulfill his father's dream rather than run from it.

Hoss came out to help his partner. "Mrs. Williams fried up some potatoes to go with the beans." He then noticed the look on Amos' face. "Is something wrong?"

The old prospector forced a smile. "Just some old memories coming up. My father grew potatoes in Maine."

When Amos was putting the horse and mule into a corral, he noticed two milk cows and a team of horses in the barn. He and Hoss washed up at the pump before going into the cabin.

Lucia Williams had a sparsely furnished and very clean home. What furniture she had had been brought west when she and her husband had relocated. There were two rooms and a loft over the second room. Chip said he and Elly slept in the loft. The table was set for five with the beans and potatoes served in stoneware bowls. A wood cutting board held freshly sliced bread and butter.

Sitting at the table in the cabin had a comfortable feel. Amos was sure that he had not felt so at peace since his mother had died when he was about Chip's age. Mrs. Williams had changed her dress and put her hair up. The long hours working in the sun showed on her face, but she was still a handsome woman. The potatoes were perfect and even the beans tasted better at Mrs. Williams' table. Once the meal was done and the dishes finished, the two men and Mrs. Williams drank coffee while sitting on rockers on the front porch.

A soft breeze was blowing, bringing the smell of fresh plowed dirt from the fields. The children had been sent to bed and the animals had been fed and watered. "You have a fine place here, Mrs. Williams," Amos said.

"Call me Lucia, Mr. Mudd," she said.

"Okay Lucia, but you must call me Amos and my partner here is Hoss," the prospector said, staring into the dark.

For a couple of minutes, the only sound was creaking as the three of them rocked slowly. Amos cleared his throat. "Mrs. . . . I mean, Lucia. Have you had any strangers come through in the past few days?"

"Maybe pock faced-boys with straw colored hair?" Hoss added.

"There were two men that rode by and used our pump to water their horses. I was in the barn milking and heard them work the pump. By the time I got back to the cabin they had gone. They rode right through the freshly planted field," the young woman said. "I didn't get a good look at them."

Amos would have liked to take a chew but didn't feel it would be right if he spat off her porch. He was sure it was the Leesons who had used the pump. They had the disregard for other people and would ride through the field. "It is just as well they left before you saw them. They might have brought harm to you," Amos said.

After a bit the two men excused themselves and headed to the barn to sleep. One side had hay stacked in it and would make a soft place to sleep. "Mrs. Williams sure is a nice lady," Hoss said.

"It does take a special woman to run a place like this," Amos agreed. "She mentioned a town a few miles north that she does business in. When we go through, I want to send a few food items and some shells for the shotgun to them as a thank you for their hospitality."

The next morning, Amos insisted on making pancakes for breakfast. He had what he needed in his packs, including some maple syrup. He enjoyed fresh milk with the meal. It had been a long time since he'd drank milk. Again, it brought back memories of his youth.

It was mid-morning when they rode away. Chip followed along, talking a mile a minute until they reached the edge of their property. He then stood calling goodbye until they were out of sight. Amos found it important to know that the Leesons were a couple days ahead of them. He was sure that they were intent on finding the cave. He was also sure that they would have difficulty finding the canyon without a lot of searching.

They stopped in Absarokee to buy a few things. After sending the items back to Mrs. Williams, the two men left, avoiding any other farms and villages. They had been riding for a couple of days searching the foot hills when Amos pulled up. They had another two hours of daylight and near them was a grove of beechnut trees. A broad grin spread on the prospector's face.

"Well, Hoss. We are here," he said.

Looking around, the partner said, "This ain't no canyon."

"You're right my friend," Amos said. "The canyon is a mile, maybe two from here. Oli August was the first to find the cave and the night before he ate beechnuts. I did some prospecting in this area several years back. I remember the canyon and this grove. I figure we can spend the night and get an early start in the morning."

"You don't want to spend the night in the canyon?" Hoss asked.

"Unless someone has been using it regular, the trail in is easy to miss," Amos replied. "Let's hope nobody has taken up living in the canyon."

Both of the men were excited about being near the end of their quest. They realized that this would also be the goal of Billy Bob and Slim, so they moved back into the trees and set up a small camp. They talked quietly through the evening about finding the scroll and possibly the location of the mine.

Even though it was early July, the mornings were still cool. Amos didn't want to make a fire that morning and had been up long before sunrise, watching and listening. He climbed down from the rock outcrop and held the threadbare coat tight around him.

Still speaking quietly, he called to Hoss, "Let's get the animals packed and go find the canyon."

"Did you see anything this morning?" he asked Amos.

"All was quiet," he replied. "If anyone had been close by they'd been starting a fire to ward off the morning chill."

Neither man had slept well and were anxious to leave the grove to find the canyon. They slowly rode north, watching for breaks into the foothills. Twice they rode in a short distance only to have the cut they followed end.

Amos suddenly pointed to what appeared to be an animal trail. "That's it!"

They rode in, searching the hills on both sides and the brush-filled trail in front of them. Both men held their rifles across their saddles. The rocky side rose up on both sides of the riders and the cut became wider. The brush disappeared and the sandy soil showed evidence of past riders and wild animals passing.

They passed scattered, charred remains of a camp fire from past years. Then they turned into the canyon. Amos pulled up. Across the canyon he could see the two jagged peaks and round top mountain in the distance. What they could see of the canyon was about 40 acres with a small pond to the right. Water flowed from the pond, running back into the canyon. The appearance of the men had startled some deer that had disappeared in that direction, giving the promise that the canyon might continue to wind further back.

Amos swung off the buckskin. "This is the canyon."

Hoss looked at the grass-covered floor and the pine trees that grew up on the south side. Several maples and aspen grew above the walls of the canyon. "This looks like a fine place to make a home."

Near the pond there was a rotting lean-to. Hoss trotted his bay over and swung down near it. "Looks like someone lived here for a while." Grabbing one of the punky logs, he pulled and the side collapsed.

Amos walked up, leading his horse. "Well, I'm glad they went and left the canyon to us. There are supposed to be some graves on the south side. The cousins said you could see the quartz crescent shown on the map from them."

Loosening the cinches, they watered the animals before picketing them on the lush grass and then went to explore the rest of the canyon. Amos frowned at what he saw. The graves had been dug up. A few bones and a skull lay on the surface.

"Someone looking for valuables left on the dead bugger's body," the prospector said.

Hoss rolled a boulder over and saw three crosses chiseled into the stone. "At least someone respected the dead," Hoss replied.

Looking around, the prospector saw the crescent in the rock wall. Pointing, he said, "The cave is behind the rubble below that quartz."

"What do we do first?" Hoss asked.

"First, we rebury these dead Spaniards," Amos said. "Then we will set up our camp. It will take some time to dig through the rocks and find the cave. That work we will save for tomorrow."

While the prospector didn't tell Hoss how he felt, the scavenged graves bothered him a great deal. They would be following in the footsteps of the deceased Spaniards, and he didn't need their restless ghosts causing bad dreams and making the search more difficult.

Hoss had assumed that they would go to digging for the cave right off, but he wasn't against putting the dead back at rest. "I suggest we pick a spot for our camp and make us a pot of hot coffee and a bite to eat before attending to the graves."

For several minutes Amos stared across the canyon. Finally, his partner interrupted his thoughts. "What are you thinking, Amos? Do you agree with some hot coffee?"

"I was just picturing my cabin under the trees below the pond," he replied. "Yes, coffee it is."

They decided to set up their camp near the pond. Trees offered shade from the sun and a defensible position should the Leesons show up. They found remnants of several past fires near the spot. Someone had even chiseled a shelf into the rock and had built a stone fire pit near it. The two men decided that they would make this their makeshift kitchen.

They let the horses and mule graze without a picket rope. If they tended to wander too far they could always hobble them. With a pick and two shovels in hand, they went to the graves. Amos said a quick prayer to the departed, then picked up all the exposed bones and placed them into the indentions of the graves. He and Hoss then filled them with dirt. Then, taking stones, they piled them high on what they figured was the location of the original graves. Hoss placed the boulder with the crosses at the foot of the mounds.

Amos removed his tattered hat and said a prayer for the departed. He condemned those who had dishonored the graves and assured them that he was pleased to make things right again. Finishing, he heard Hoss say, "That goes for me too. Amen."

CHAPTER SIX

Amos and Hoss sat near the camp, satisfied that they had put the spirits of the Spaniards back at rest. It was mid-afternoon and they stared at the rubble covering the cave. "I think we should dig just a little," Hoss said.

Glancing at the sun, Amos replied, "We got about five more hours before dark. I think you have a good idea."

The two men hurried to the rock and rubble below the quartz crescent. Long experienced in digging for gold and mining, Amos looked at the pile. He pointed to a dip in one section. "When Dan and his cousins were here getting the rest of the gold, they had to hurry because of some robbers that were using the canyon. I figure they didn't pile extra rock closing it."

In agreement, the two men attacked the rubble, tossing it away from the stone wall. The coolness of the morning was long gone and the sun burned down on the men. Amos rinsed his mouth with the canteen and then took a drink.

Sweat glistening on his forehead, Hoss said, "We got us a nice, cool pool of water over there. We been at this for an hour. I figure if we don't hit the cave soon, I am going to get me a cold drink."

By this time, Amos was stripped to his long john top and Hoss was stripped to the waist. They grunted and pulled at the rocks. They had just about decided to go take a break at the pool when they heard a stone fall somewhere under the pile. They were close to the cave!

In another hour they were looking into the narrow cave. The Spaniards had cut the cave into the sedimentary rock. Amos ran his fingers along the tool marks near the opening. "I'll go get us a candle," Hoss offered.

While his partner was gone, the prospector marveled at the work that had been done to store the gold. It was unlikely that anyone would have ever dug under the several feet of rock and rubble to discover the cave if the lone Spaniard hadn't carried the map back with him. Now, a second map might be just feet away and could reveal the source of the gold.

Amos and Hoss could not both fit into the opening at the same time, so Amos took the lit candle and crawled in. It felt cool in the cave. He had not gone far before he came upon the shelf. He could see the hand prints of the Augusts that had been here before him. He collected the three coins they had left behind. The three coins would pay for a winter's food if sold to a collector.

Behind the shelf was the leather scroll. Amos picked it up carefully. The leather was old, but due to the dryness and constant temperature of the cave it appeared in good condition. Slowly he searched the area behind the cave to see if there was anything else. A fine dust from time had settled. As he rubbed his fingers across it, felt something move. With care he worked the object loose. It was a cross, . . . a gold cross! It was slender, about an eighth-inch thick. It was two inches wide and four inches high.

He continued to feel around and noticed that there was quartz on the back wall. It would have made digging the cave somewhat easier. Satisfied that he had found everything left in the cave, Amos crawled out backwards, into the sunlight. Squinting in the brightness, he looked at his partner. "We got the map and three coins. I also found a gold cross."

"Do you mind if I crawl into the cave?" Hoss asked.

"Please do," Amos replied.

For several minutes Hoss remained in the hollow. Finally, Amos heard the scraping of his clothing as he crawled out. Emerging, he snuffed out the candle. "It is good medicine to be as one with the spirits. I could feel them in the cave. I felt their energy and a happiness that we had made this trip."

"I need something cold to drink," Amos said.

"I agree," Hoss said, "and then we can have a drink to success. I have some rye in my bags."

As they walked back to the camp, Amos tested the stiff leather map. It had been rolled into a smooth five-inch scroll. Any writing or sketches were on the inside. He estimated that it was 12 inches wide and about 30 inches long. The prospector knew that he would have to take care unrolling the map.

The leather would have been tanned using animal brains and possibly urine to remove the hair. Thinking of the deer they had seen earlier, Amos figured that the leather had come from their ancestors.

Once back at camp, Amos gave the three coins to Hoss. "If it is okay with you, you can have the three coins and I will keep the cross."

His black friend smiled. "That is fair. Money meant little to my people, but the coins will be good medicine."

Amos wrapped the leather scroll in a blanket. "After supper we can attempt to unroll the map. Now, I think we should have a drink of that rye."

The men had rigged a fly tarp to keep the weather off their supplies. The map was given a special place in the middle of the shelter to make sure it stayed dry. The men talked and watched their animals graze in the canyon. Suddenly, Hoss sat up. "The deer are back," he said. "I could go for some venison steaks tonight."

Amos looked across the canyon. "Can you hit one from here?"

Hoss smiled and got his rifle out. "I was one of the best in the army. I ain't lost my touch."

The ex-army man carried a Springfield Model 1884. The trapdoor, or breech-loading rifle used a .45 caliber shell and the rear sight was rack and pinion and could be adjusted from 200 to 1400 yards. Hoss looked across the canyon, estimating the distance to the deer. He fussed for a minute with the elevation. Then, in a sitting position, he rested the barrel on his knee and forearm.

The rifle shot shattered the stillness of the canyon, echoing off its walls. The deer wheeled around, with two running and the third dropping. Brushing his knuckle across his nose, Hoss said, "That is supper lying down there."

While Hoss skinned the deer, Amos brought the map out. "I'll take a peek at what we have here," he told his friend.

"Don't be rushing it," Hoss warned the prospector. "That's an old hunk of leather and it might crack and ruin the map."

Amos didn't have to be told. He had once tried to soften an old pair of boots, without much success. Unlike the boots, all they wanted was whatever information that was imprinted on the leather. The prospector spread a blanket and sat on it with the map. Slowly, he unrolled the first couple of inches. The leather resisted having the curve taken out and Amos knew that at best he would only be able to open it enough to read.

After dropping some steaks into a sizzling frying pan, Hoss call over, "What do you see so far?"

Shaking his head, Amos replied, "Not much so far. Just some kind of writing that I can't read."

"You may as well eat and then the two of us can try and unroll more."

The fry pan was heaped with juicy venison and there was a pot of hot coffee. Sitting with their loaded plates, they picked up the meat with their fingers and ripped chunks off with their teeth. Juice ran down Amos' beard and Hoss' whisker-covered chin.

After the meal was eaten they added a portion of rye to their coffee and went back to the map on the blanket. Care was taken to clean any venison juice or fat from their hands. With the map between them, they were able to unroll it into a 10-inch diameter tube.

The inner end of the piece of leather had a six by six-inch piece cut out.

It was now too dark to see inside the tube, so they let it coil back up and wrapped it in the blanket to store until morning. Hoss had shot a good-sized doe and they decided to make some into jerky. In the light of their campfire, the two men sliced the meat and hung it onto aspen sticks near the fire. While Amos cut the meat, he had a thought. "Hoss, I want to close the opening of the cave again. It just doesn't feel right leaving it open."

"It will also prevent the Leeson boys from knowing we found the map, just in case they stumble on this canyon someday."

The next morning found the two men piling rocks and rubble onto the opening. Once they were finished, Hoss brushed out their tracks and other evidence that they had worked in the area. They walked back toward the camp and saw the horses and mule drinking at the pond. They were pleased that the animals hadn't wandered out of sight further into the canyon. Despite the fact that they hadn't wandered, the men planned to bring them in that night.

After checking the venison jerky, they spread the blanket to look at the map. Once again, they were able to unroll the leather into a tube. The bright noon sun made it possible to see what was inside. Both men were disappointed. The side of the leather was covered with writing which they figured would be Spanish. Neither read the language and that left what it said a mystery. Amos noticed marking that reminded him of the mountains shown on the original map along the edge of the notched-out area.

"If there was a map, the Spaniard cut it out and took it with him," Amos said, disappointment heavy in his voice.

"Maybe the writing will tell us where the gold was mined," Hoss said, sounding hopeful.

Smiling, the prospector said, "You are probably right. Our only problem will be finding someone we can trust to let us know what it says."

Both men sat thinking about who they could trust who not only spoke Spanish but could also read it. Unrolling the leather into a tube did not crack any of the inside with the writing, but if they tried to do any more the inner surface might crack, taking out some of the writing.

Leaving the leather in a tube, Amos wrapped it in a blanket and headed for the fly tarp. He moved the gear to make more room for the leather tube. Amos felt a stab of pain in his upper shoulder and then the sound of a rifle. He went down, flat on his stomach. Grabbing his Winchester, which lay under the tarp, he rolled out and regained his feet in time to follow Hoss into the trees.

"Damn, Amos! I thought you was dead! You went flat down right when I heard the shot!"

The back of his shoulder throbbed and Amos felt something warm soaking his shirt. Then there was a second shot. The two men saw their animals running away from the pool heading toward the back of the canyon. The buckskin stumbled and fell. "Some son-of-a-bitch shot your horse," Hoss growled.

"I think that Billy Bob and Slim have found us," Amos said, swearing under his breath.

"It appears they plan to put us afoot," Hoss said. "If I get a glimpse of them, this Springfield will make short work of their plan."

The men were thankful that the bay and mule were to the far side of the canyon and out of range of the shooter's rifle. Regardless, several shots were sent in the animal's direction, all falling short of the intended target.

The prospector was sweating in the midday sun. He tried moving his left arm and found it painful due to the wound. He squinted, searching the rim around the canyon. He would have plenty of time to worry about the wound if they got out of this alive. Right now, he just wanted to strike back.

"In the rocks above the graves," Amos said, "I saw a flash of light near the edge."

Both men lined their rifles on the low brambles just back from the edge and fired. There was a cry, followed by several shots that kicked up dirt and struck things in their camp. Amos and Hoss fired several more times into the brush above the rim. All was quiet from the rim.

"I think we hit something with our first shot," Hoss said.

The prospector crouched near his friend and was breathing heavily, struggling to endure the pain in the upper left part of his back. "We got to go after them," he whispered.

"I'll go," Hoss said. "First let me check where the bullet hit you."

He helped Amos remove his shirt and then used a knife to cut the long johns open to expose the wound. Using the shirt, Hoss fashioned a bandage, tying it tight to help stop the bleeding.

"That will stop you from bleeding to death," the friend said. "You got a bullet in you that has to come out. I'll be back as quickly as I can."

Scooping up the rifle, Hoss moved through the trees, circling toward the direction that the shooting had come from. He was also armed with the knife and his Colt stuffed into his waist band. Amos sat in the trees, feeling light-headed. He lay back on the ground and looked up through the trees. If the bullet had struck something inside and caused it to bleed, he might be looking at the sky for the last time. He listened for the sound of anyone moving around him.

Suddenly, he thought about the buckskin. It had been a good horse and he would miss it. He would be riding a mule again. To keep the throbbing wound off his mind, Amos tried to think about what he could discard now that he had only one animal. Slowly darkness enveloped the old prospector and he lay still, hardly breathing.

* * *

His mouth and throat were dry. He had to get up and keep going. *How much farther to water?* Amos wondered. He tried to sit up and fell back. Pain shot through his left shoulder. It forced the fuzziness of his mind to clear. He wasn't out on the high desert anymore. Memories of being shot came back.

He opened his eyes to darkness, only this darkness had stars in the sky. He heard Hoss near the fire. Then he was coming toward him. "I see you're awake. I got some venison broth for you to drink."

He put a saddle and blanket roll under Amos to help him sit up a little. With a shaky hand, the prospector took the tin cup and sipped the hot broth. He felt weak. It was all he could do to hold the cup to his mouth. The liquid made his throat feel better.

With a raspy voice he asked, "Did you get them?"

"They were gone when I got to the rim. We hit one of them good. There was lots of blood. I followed it to where they had their horses. The wounded man was still bleeding when they rode away," Hoss told him. "I would have continued after them, but I worried about you. You were out when I got back and looked more dead than alive. I figured you'd die with the bullet in you and could die if I tried to get it out. Either way, you'd be just as dead. So, I took advantage of you being unconscious and got it out."

Amos attempted to move the left arm but the pain prevented it. "In the morning I want you to leave me here and go after those son-of-a-back shooters."

"I ain't going anywhere, partner. First we get you back on your feet and then we will go after them together," Hoss said.

"Well, at least take your bay and go and scout which way they went before the sign is gone. I'm afraid it might be a few days before these old bones will be up again."

"I want you to know," Hoss said, "bending down saved you. They was aiming at the middle of your back and fired a second too late. The bullet lodged just under the skin, near the top of your shoulder. I figure the long johns and shirt stopped it from breaking back through."

Unable to comprehend what his friend was telling him, Amos insisted, "We can't just wait for them to come back. You got to find out where they've gone."

Finally, Hoss agreed with Amos. But he would not go until he was sure the prospector was out of danger. And to Hoss that meant sitting up. By noon the next day, Amos was sitting against an aspen, gritting his teeth against the pain. He feared falling to one side, because he knew he wouldn't be able to catch himself and then Hoss wouldn't leave.

With a canteen, his rifle, some jerky at his side, Amos convinced Hoss to go. The mule had been brought in and was tied and saddled nearby. "You sure you're okay enough for me to leave?" Hoss asked.

"I am feeling much better," Amos lied. "Now go find out where the bastards went. I will be waiting right here for you when you get back."

A blanket was folded under Amos to sit on, and a second one was over his legs within easy reach to pull up if he felt cold. He could feel the bulky bandage on his back. Hoss rode away on the bay, keeping to the trees for cover as best he could in case the Leesons had come back to finish the job.

He had barely gotten out of sight when Amos' eyelids became too heavy to keep open and he lost the battle to stay awake. It was dusk when he awoke. He had shifted to the left and was leaning over, close to falling. His left arm was too weak to push himself back up. His shoulder throbbed and he was shivering. The blanket on his legs was only inches from his right hand, but he didn't dare reach out for it, afraid it would cause him to go over.

"You are in damn sorry shape, Amos Mudd," he muttered.

He looked toward the fly tarp. He wondered if one of the shots the Leesons had put into the camp had hit the leather tube. His thoughts then came to more immediate problems. Amos' bottom ached from sitting up too long. He wasn't sure which hurt more, his bottom or his shoulder. If he let himself fall sideways his bottom would feel better, but the shoulder would take the impact and hurt a lot more. It might even start bleeding again. Then his legs started to cramp. Amos was in his own personal hell.

The sound of a horse coming caught his attention. As it entered the canyon, he saw that it was Hoss. He wanted to holler at him to hurry up and do something to relieve some of his pain, but he didn't want to admit that his friend was right.

Hoss swung down from the bay and came over to Amos. Seeing his friend slumping to one side, he reached down and helped him sit up. "You're soaking wet and shaking!" Hoss exclaimed. "I shouldn't have left you."

Through chattering teeth, Amos replied, "I'm just fine . . . What, what did you find?"

His friend pulled the blanket up and tucked it around the prospector. "First, I am going to make something warm for you."

"Coffee and rye," Amos said, his voice weak.

With the fire started and the water heating, Hoss came back to the prospector. "I followed the two boys out into the foothills. They was heading south. About an hour further on, the wounded one fell from his horse. He must have died because I found where he was buried. Just a sand bank caved over him."

"Were you able to tell which one we hit?" Amos asked.

"No, I couldn't," his friend said. "I even thought about digging him out for a minute, but then I would have had to mutilate him or bury him proper."

The prospector hesitated before nodded in agreement. Hoss had grown up with the Flathead and they feared meeting those that they had killed on the other side. Mutilating the body would leave your enemies defenseless in the afterlife. If you showed respect with a proper grave, then the dead would feel no need to come after you.

Hoss helped the prospector up so he could relieve himself before adding coffee to the hot water. After standing for a few minutes Amos' head cleared and the dizziness passed. Using a broken branch to steady himself, the prospector joined Hoss at the fire. With a little help from his friend he sat on the stone ledge. The coffee with rye tasted good and spread a warmth through Amos' body.

"One thing I can't figure," Hoss said. "When the brother left he rode to the northeast."

Amos took a sip of the hot brew and thought for a minute. "There's a few small towns a day or two in that direction. Maybe they got friends that way."

"After a day or two of rest, we best ride out of here," Hoss suggested. "It's too easy for someone to sneak up on us."

"I agree, it is a good place to hide but damn hard to defend," Amos replied. Sitting on the ledge drinking coffee laced with rye, the prospector already felt better.

Over the next couple of days, Hoss managed to bring down another deer. Amos was getting around better. He still had little power in his left arm and the shoulder would throb whenever he exerted himself.

He had finished sorting through his gear, having decided what he had to leave behind. Hoss came back from watching the entryway for any sign of life. Amos looked up at his friend and muttered, "What the hell do I do with the leftover stuff?"

"Had us a pretty good cave a while back," Hoss replied, chuckling.

Amos snorted, "I ain't going to dig that open again."

"I saw a deep cut in the canyon wall when I was fetching the deer. Looks like the weather will stay out for most part," his friend told him.

The cut was a good place to cache the gear. There was an overhang in the rock wall and at an earlier time water had carved a decent-sized gorge to the back of it. It was high and dry now and would protect the gear until a future time when Amos could return for it.

The place had been used in the past by other people. The rock in front was blackened by ancient fires. Someone had painted pictures of animals on the roof of the hollow. Amos felt a kinship to the prior wanders and figured it would be a good place to camp when he came back.

With the leather scroll wrapped in his blanket roll and his saddlebags filled with items that he would need, Amos climbed onto the mule. Hoss led the way out of the canyon with his Springfield across his saddle. The prospector couldn't carry his rifle, so it was in a scabbard. Amos stopped for a minute and turned the mule to look back at the grass-covered canyon. He would be back and just maybe to stay.

CHAPTER SEVEN

Amos was running a fever when they reached Red Lodge. The wound pulsed with every step the mule took. It was a week and a half since he had been shot. Amos figured that a bottle of rye or maybe cognac would cure what ailed him. Hoss had noticed that it was getting warm and red around the wound and had put together a poultice the day before. He led the way into the town and rode straight to a white clapboard building with a sign: *Doctor Jennings*.

The doctor was a young man, maybe in his 30s. He had come with the railroad to Red Lodge 10 years earlier when he was just starting out. The lifestyle of the coal town had made him an expert in bullet wounds. Despite the objections of the old prospector, Hoss and the doctor got him into one of the back rooms and stripped to his waist.

"Just let me go down to Goldie's and she'll have me up and around in no time," he complained.

Doc Jennings felt around the wound, causing Amos to wince from the tenderness. "We got a little infection going on in there," the doc said.

"I done the best I could," Hoss said. "I used almost a half-bottle of rye cleaning my knife and the wound."

"Damn waste of good rye," Amos muttered.

"I'll have to open the wound again and clean it out," the doc said. "Could be just a little piece of his clothing." Turning to Hoss, he continued, "I am going to give him some valerian to put him in a half-sleep. I'll need you to hold him still."

"Give me my shirt," Amos demanded. "I don't need this youngster cutting me open."

"Now Amos," Hoss said sternly. "We got us a partnership here. If you up and die from the wound going sour, I will be left alone. Now one can't be a partner by his self."

While Amos debated with Hoss, the doctor got a strong cup of tea for the prospector. "This will make you feel tired."

Sipping the brew, Amos exclaimed, "What the hell is this?"

"Just drink the tea," Doc Jennings urged him. "You don't want me to cut on you without something to dull the pain."

"Just get me some damn rye." As the prospector muttered, his words became more slurred.

The doctor gently turned Amos onto his stomach and said to Hoss, "Let's get to it."

* * *

Sometime later, Amos awoke. His head ached worse than his shoulder. "What the hell!" he demanded, struggling to get his bearings. "Let me out of here!"

"Hush, Amos," a soft voice said.

The prospector blinked rapidly, breathing in the familiar smell of perfume. He turned his head and looked into the gentle face of Goldie. "The doctor said you might be feeling a bit confused when the valerian wore off and asked me to be here for you."

Amos tried to sit up and she pushed him back gently. "You just lie there for a little longer. The doc says I can move you to my place after you're a little stronger."

A smile broke across Amos' bearded face. "By God, I feel plenty strong right now."

"It's late and I have to go back to work," she said. "You rest and I'll be back tomorrow to see you."

The doctor came into the room. "I see you're awake. Your partner went to the café to get you some soup."

"That tea snuck up on me," Amos growled.

"That it did," the doc replied. He held out a small bottle with something small and bloody in it. "You see that. It is a small piece of your shirt. If it had been left in, the infection would have gotten worse, and more than likely you would have died."

Amos snorted, but before he could say anything, Goldie whispered in his ear, "If you had died, I would have been left without one of my favorite acquaintances. Now thank the doctor and do what he says."

"Because you asked me, I will do it." Then the prospector looked at the young doctor and said, "Thank you for what you did."

Goldie gave him a quick kiss on the cheek and said, "I'll see you tomorrow."

Before he could reply she got up and left the room. Doc Jennings helped Amos sit up and checked the wound. Much of the heat had left it and other than the ugly bruise from the impact of the bullet, it was looking better.

While he was doing this, Hoss came in with the soup. "It's chicken. That'll cure you fast."

"Your stomach might act up for a bit, and the headache will pass soon," the doc said. "The soup will help both. I set up another bed so Hoss can spend the night and help you if you need anything."

The two men watched the doc leave the building. "Well, let me help you with the soup," Hoss said.

"Yes, I'd like that," Amos replied. "I want to thank you for bringing me here, Hoss."

"You're welcome, Amos Mudd," his friend replied. "It's what any good partner would have done."

After eating a serving of the soup, Amos suddenly chuckled, "I guess I've kept you from your friend here in Red Lodge."

"Not a problem, Amos," Hoss replied. "It didn't take no time to get the soup and you was asleep for some time."

It was two days before Amos was able to move into Goldie's. The doctor promised to stop in and see him every few days. The prospector, other than feeling a bit weak, was in good spirits and preferred to spend his evening watching the goings on in the saloon and partaking in some cognac. The doctor wanted him to keep the arm in a sling for a while and Amos had decided to do whatever the smart young doctor wanted.

The leather scroll and Amos' gear was stowed under Goldie's large bed. The prospector figured it was safer and better guarded than most banks. The saloon owner was pleased to hear that one of the Leeson boys had been sent to his grave. She hoped it was Billy Bob. He was the worse of the two.

Amos and Hoss would meet each day at the Carbon Café for lunch. The prospector was healing fast and the wound had completely closed. Other than stiffness, he felt he was ready to travel. It was now August and the two men had lost too much time from Amos being shot.

It was a drizzly day when Amos came in shaking the rain off his hat. Hoss had beat him to the café. The prospector sat down heavily and placed his hat onto the floor beside the chair. Their waitress had a quick smile and came to the table with some hot coffee. "The special today is pork roast. One of the owner's pigs was hit by a wagon and they couldn't see wasting good meat."

"As long as it didn't lay in the road too long," Amos said, "I'll have the special." Hoss nodded that he would also.

The prospector leaned close to his friend. "I thought of someone that knows Spanish. I told you about Dan August. Well, he knows a Mexican named Juan Torres. He is a good man and a man we can trust. We got to go back to Casper to look him up."

They were interrupted by the pert waitress returning with two plates of the special. She placed them in front of the men, her thumb in Amos' gravy. "Careful, it's hot," she said as she licked the gravy from her thumb.

Amos watched her go and smiled. "She'll make a man a good wife someday."

"As long as it's a forgiving man," Hoss replied.

As they enjoyed the meal, Amos told his friend what he knew about the Torres family. Juan had two daughters, a son, and a wife who made the best goat cheese.

"I can wire Dan that we are coming and we can take the train. We'd be there is two to three days," Amos told his friend.

"Has the doc said it is okay for you to travel?" Hoss asked.

"He has cautioned me to take it easy," the prospector said, "and what could be easier than riding a soft cushion on a train?"

"I'll need a couple days to get ready," Hoss said. "My sister came down to visit and will be leaving for home the day after tomorrow."

"Then it's settled," the prospector said. "I will make arrangements with the livery to take care of our animals, and I still have to settle up with the doctor and, of course, Goldie."

With a spring in his step, Amos left the saloon the next morning and headed for the doctor's. Finally having a plan to figure out what was written on the leather made him feel good. Doctor Jennings was in the back room with a patient when Amos arrived. He sat down on a straight chair near the door and waited. The doc came out with a young woman, heavy with child. He was assuring her that all was well and he would be seeing her again soon.

The two men stood in the open door and watched her husband help her into their buggy. "She's a good girl," Doctor Jennings said. "It's her first and she is a bit scared."

Shifting his attention, he looked at Amos. "Come in the back and take off your shirt."

The prospector sat quietly while the doctor checked the wounded area. He then listened to Amos' heart and lungs. Finishing with the exam, Doc Jennings went to a small table and picked up a folder. Returning, he sat next to the prospector, concern on his face. "Why the face, Doc? I am feeling great."

"When you climb the stairs to Miss Goldie's room, how is your wind?"

"Funny you should ask me about my wind. Shouldn't you be asking about another part of my body?" Amos kidded.

"My guess was if I asked you about that, you'd only give me some version of the truth," the doc said, returning the jab at his patient. Getting serious again, he repeated, "Do you get tired climbing stairs or walking fast?"

Amos thought about hurrying to the café in the rain and having trouble catching his breath. "No more than would be expected at my age."

The doctor opened the folder and looked at the notes scribbled inside. Without looking up he said, "Hoss tells me you two are going to Casper."

"You spoke to Hoss?" Amos asked, confused.

"He brought his sister by yesterday," he explained. "The coal smoke has given her a cough."

"I didn't know," the prospector said.

Shaking his head, Doctor Jennings continued, frustrated for having to explain. "Hoss' sister is not important or how I learned that you're going to Casper. I heard something in your chest, in your heart and lungs, that isn't right."

Amos had gained a great deal of respect for the doctor in the past weeks. He felt a bit of alarm seeing the concern on the man's face. "What do you mean by 'isn't right'?"

"I like you, Amos, and I don't want to scare you unnecessarily. I heard something in the beat of your heart that wasn't . . . isn't normal. Also, you have some fluid in your lungs."

"Are you telling me I'm dying?" Amos asked.

"No!" the doc said sharply, then more softly, "No, I am not. But it might be the start of a longer-term problem. I want to give you this folder and have you see the doctor in Casper. For all I know, what I'm hearing could be caused by the bullet wound and the bad air in Red Lodge."

Suddenly, Amos laughed. "Doc, I am well into my sixties. I've had a good life and never expected to live forever. You have been good to me and fixed me up proper. When I get to Casper, I'll visit Doc Morgan and let him have a listen."

"That's all I ask, and when you get back in this area stop by and we'll go to Goldie's for some cognac," the young doctor replied.

The spring was gone from Amos' step and the folder in his hand burned. He thought of all the times he'd had close calls and survived. He had always found a way to get through and go forward. He thought of the trek across the high desert earlier this year. He remembered the frustration at how tired he was getting and having difficulty keeping on going.

He entered the saloon, went straight to his room and put the folder with his gear. His hand rested on the leather scroll. *I am so close to the mother lode*, he thought. He heard the door open behind him, "Ted told me you came in, Amos. You didn't stop and say hello."

He turned and looked at the big-bosomed blond. "I am sorry, I wasn't thinking."

They sat together on the edge of the bed. "Is something bothering you, Amos?" she asked.

"You sure know how to read what a person's thinking, Goldie," the prospector said, trying to smile. "The doc just told me I wasn't going to live forever."

Putting her arm around him, concern came over her face. "He didn't tell you that you were going to die today?"

Chuckling, Amos said, "No, not today, or tomorrow either."

* * *

Hoss and Amos were sitting at the café eating their supper when the pert waitress came by with two cups of coffee. "So, is this your last meal here?"

"It will be until we come back," Hoss said, tasting his coffee. "I will miss this weak brew your boss makes."

Patting the train tickets in his coat pocket, Amos told the girl, "We'll be leaving before daylight on the freight and then switch to a passenger in Billings. A couple more transfers and we will be in Casper."

"Everyone is always leaving," she complained. "But, Lucy is still stuck here in Red Lodge."

"Well, Lucy, your time will come," Amos assured her.

"You are right. Maybe Billy Bob will surprise me and send a ticket." Then, frowning, she added, "That won't happen."

As if struck by lightning, the two men froze and stared at the young waitress. "This Billy Bob," Amos asked, "didn't he run into a little trouble here in Red Lodge?"

"It wasn't his fault," she said. "He had a brother Slim, and he done it. He took the horses and Billy Bob couldn't bring them back without being blamed."

"I can understand that," Hoss said, and then, fishing for more information, he asked, "Did Billy Bob himself tell you that?"

"He sure did," she replied. "Slim got his, though. Billy Bob told me someone shot Slim for no reason. Isn't that awful?"

Amos was dumbstruck. Billy Bob had been in Red Lodge since he'd been shot! "Yes, yes, it is awful," Hoss said. "If Billy Bob needs help going after the shooter, we could do that."

The waitress smiled sweetly. "But that wouldn't work. You're leaving in the morning."

The prospector got his wits about him. Cocking his head, he looked up at her. "These tickets would be good most any day. We're not in any hurry to get to Casper."

"It wouldn't do any good anyway," she said. "He's headed for Virginia City to meet some friends. They know . . ." Suddenly, she whispered, "They know about a big gold strike. He got a map right to it."

The owner hollered from the kitchen, "Lucy quit your visitin' and get these orders!"

She smiled and winked. "Excuse me, I got to go."

The two men sat in silence, their coffee getting cold. Finally, Hoss said, "We ain't going to catch the train in the morning, are we?"

"Hoss, I was just told that my ticker ain't quite right, by the doc. It don't seem right take a chance and leave this Billy Bob business unfinished."

"I'll be ready come daylight," his friend said.

Hoss got to the livery first the next morning. When Amos arrived the bay and mule were saddled and ready to go. "Took some time to say goodbye?"

"I give the leather scroll to Goldie for safe keeping," Amos told him. "Only me or you can get it out of her safe. I also told her if we never come back or she hears we were killed, it becomes hers."

"I doubt it will do much good without the rest of the story of the cave and gold," Hoss replied.

"I agree," the prospector said. The two men climbed into the saddle and left Red Lodge at a trot. Virginia City was a week away. They had gotten extra ammunition and supplies the night before. Billy Bob had the habit of leaving a trail of trouble wherever he went, so the two men hoped to keep track of him by his bad deeds.

An hour down the trail, Hoss looked at the old prospector. "You said something in the café and as your partner, I got to know more."

Amos thought back. "I don't recall saying anything that needed more talking."

"You said something about your heart," his friend reminded him. "You said the doc told you."

"He said my ticker sounded wrong and something about my lungs," Amos explained. "You can't trust them young doctors. I think they work hand in hand with the grave digger and try to scare you to death."

Hoss rode in silence for a mile and then spoke softly, "If Doc Morgan is still in Casper you could go and see him. They say he's good and has been around a good many years."

Frowning, Amos stared at the trail ahead. Begrudgingly he admitted, "That's what the young doctor suggested."

They stopped in a small town that was rapidly disappearing into history. The saloon was also the local store. The livery had closed, but the building with a broken-down corral still remained. They had a drink at the saloon while deciding if they wanted to ride on for a couple more hours.

Sipping on the watered-down, pepper-laced rye, Amos asked the bartender, "I wonder if you've seen a friend of ours. Pock-faced kid with sandy yellow hair?"

"I'll take your guns, gentlemen," a raspy voice said.

The two men turned and stared into a Colt leveled at them by a man wearing a tarnished star. "I may have misspoke calling the kid our friend," Amos said. "He is more of an acquaintance and not a good one."

The lawman squinted at the two men. "Explain yourself."

Hoss spoke up, "The blond kid back shot my friend here a month back. We are looking to bring him back to Red Lodge to stand trial."

"Yet you first called him your friend," the sheriff said.

"The kid has friends and they are just as low as he is," Amos explained. "I was just being careful by calling *him* my friend."

After a couple of tense minutes, the lawman put his gun back into the holster. "He was here yesterday. You see the bump on Paulo's head? The kid hit him and took his money box and two bottles of rye."

"It was three, ah, four bottles, sheriff, and a week's sales in the money box," the bartender recounted.

"We are sorry for the trouble he caused you," Amos said. "When we catch him, we will add your charges to his other crimes."

"Are you men deputized?" the lawman asked.

"No," the prospector replied. "We're more like concerned citizens that want to see justice done."

The decision was made not to stay in the small town and the two men rode on. After a bit Hoss said, "Damn it!"

"Damn it what?" Amos asked, surprised by the outburst.

"If Billy Bob drinks four bottles of that rotgut he'll be dead before we can find him," Hoss replied, laughing.

They stopped short of Virginia City in the late afternoon and decided to set up camp rather than ride in to town unaware of where Billy Bob might be. Their camp overlooked piles of tailings and rubble showing evidence of years of mining. At one time small towns stretched about 14 miles along the gulch and there had been 10,000 residents. Like many of the boom towns,

Virginia City was now down to about 600 people. Most of the towns still had an ample number of drinking establishments.

The next morning the two men were riding along the gulch when a group of riders came their way. In just moments they were surrounded by what turned out to be a posse. "It ain't them," the leader shouted.

"Who you looking for?" Amos called to the man.

"A kid named Billy Bob and a couple of his pals. They killed an old miner and stole his gold," the leader said.

"We're after them too," Amos said. "We'll come with you."

In a cloud of dust, the posse swept by with Amos and Hoss following. It was an unorganized mess. At one point part of the riders took off on a trail that Amos knew he and Hoss had made. It was impossible to let the leader know.

Jenny began to falter and Amos fell back. Hoss pulled up and waited. "I guess my mule is getting old just like me," the prospector said.

"It don't matter," Hoss assured him. "We know if Billy Bob gets away, he is headed for the canyon."

Following the disappearing posse with their animals at a walk, Amos said with regret, "We rode a long way for nothing only to have to chase the bugger back to the canyon."

"Don't be talking like that," his friend responded. "Now we know where Leeson is and, by God, we'll get him."

The sound of the posse faded into the distance and the two men followed, saving their animals. A mood had come over Amos. The words of the young doctor haunted him. It seemed everything he did now reminded him that things weren't quite right inside.

He moved his wounded shoulder. Much of the stiffness was gone. He slid the Winchester out of the scabbard and held it across the saddle. He figured that if he could no longer do all the things he wanted, at least he could look like he was able.

Gunshots ahead let the two men know that the posse had caught up with the thieves. They urged their animals to a trot and approached a wide cut. The gunfire was just beyond the edge. Pointing to the right, Hoss said, "We best go to high ground. It don't make sense riding downhill into a firefight."

Leaving their animals just short of a cluster of boulders, the two men climbed them to get a view of the fight. The posse was pinned down in the cut while Billy Bob and his friends shot at them from the far ridge. One of the men from the posse lay in the bottom, wounded or dead. The posse horses had scattered when the men took cover.

"It's like a turkey shoot," Amos said. "They can take their time picking them off at the bottom. After they wound or kill a couple more they'll ride off free."

"Not if I have something to say about it," Hoss replied. "The bullet will drop about 12 to 18 inches from here. Let's give Billy Bob something to think about."

Hoss set the cartridges onto the rock next to him while Amos checked the loads in the Winchester. "Let's give them hell," the prospector said.

From their elevation some of the thieves were exposed. "You take one on the left, I'll go after those on the right," Hoss told his friend.

The two men chose their targets. "Now," Amos said.

As one, fire belched from the two men's rifles and then they continued to shoot as fast as they could pick out another target. Hoss dropped a thief with his first shot. Amos sprayed chards of rock on his man. His second shot hit its target. As they shot, scattering Billy Bob's men, the rest of the posse arrived riding hard. Within minutes the death sentence for the men pinned down below turned into victory, and the gang was surrounded and forced to give up.

Retrieving their animals, the two men rode to join the victorious posse. Billy Bob sat on the ground with a leg wound and two additional survivors stood with their hands in the air.

The leader came up to Amos and Hoss. "You guys saved our bacon. I was sure my next stop would be the pearly gates."

Billy Bob looked up and shouted, "You boys want to get rich! These men have a map to a gold mine and if you let me go, I'll take you there!"

"Billy Bob, there ain't no map and all you're going to get is a rope around your scrawny neck," Amos snapped at him.

As the posse trussed up the men to ready them for the ride back to Virginia City, Billy Bob began to kick and scream, spurting blood from his wound. The posse leader turned out to be a deputy from Alder Gulch.

The men stood around waiting for the scattered horses to be rounded up. The deputy asked

Amos, "All that babbling about a gold mine. Any truth to that?"

"I am afraid not," the prospector lied. Then Amos told the deputy of the other bad deeds that Billy Bob had done, including eluding the hangman's noose in Casper.

"I can promise you he won't miss his date with justice in Virginia City," the deputy assured him. "This time next week he'll hardly be a memory."

"Would you do me a favor?" Amos asked. "Let Goldie in Red Lodge know when he's hung."

A broad grin of recognition spread across the deputy's face. "I spent some happy hours in that saloon. I'd be glad to. I might even bring the word personally."

Amos and Hoss stood and watched the posse ride away with their prisoners and the bodies. Billy Bob twisted and kicked on the horse he was tied to, cussing and crying.

"I have never seen a man that feared the gallows as much as that kid," Amos said.

"I had him in my sights when the rest of the posse rode in," Hoss admitted. "I should have squeezed the trigger."

The days of riding back to Red Lodge were quiet. Both men seemed to be in their own thoughts as they rode through foothills and rolling plains. Finally, Hoss said, "We ain't been very good company the last couple of days."

"Well, I been thinking over my life and am not sure what to make of it," Amos replied. "The problem is, I can't think of anything I'd want to change."

"Just look at me," Hoss said. "I am well into my 30s and haven't even started living yet. I got the years on the reservation, those in the army, and the rest has been just searching for something more."

"Maybe that is enough," Amos concluded. "Maybe it is the looking that men like us want. The finding would ruin the looking." Both men laughed at the absurdity of the statement, yet it was probably true.

When Amos walked into Goldie's Saloon to let her know about the capture of Billy Bob, he was surprised when she said, "I just got a telegram. Billy Bob met his maker!"

"That is one man that won't be missed," Amos replied, thankful for the news. The kid had seemed like a cat with nine lives, but finally his luck had ran out.

"I wouldn't let the little gal at the café know," the prospector warned her. "She had kind of a shine on the kid and was helpful in bringing on his end."

"Youth and blind love, it's a poor mixture," she said. "Would you join me for some cognac to drink to Billy Bob's end?"

After two days of rest and recreation, Amos and Hoss finally climbed onto the train and headed for Casper.

CHAPTER EIGHT

Amos boarded the train with a feeling of anticipation. In a carpet bag he had a change of clothes, a few essentials, and the leather scroll. Hoss carried his belongings in his saddlebags and laughed when he saw Amos. "All you need now is a couple of kids hanging on you and you'd look perfect."

"The fellow that sold me this said it would last me a lifetime," Amos said, chuckling. "I sure hope he doesn't know something I don't."

It was September and the nights were cold and the days comfortable. Amos thought back to riding away from the August ranch and thinking that he'd be mining gold by now. The trouble with the Leeson boys and Soot had cost him most of the summer. Now he was headed back to Casper and to friends.

They rode in the caboose of the freight train, drank coffee and told stories with the brakeman. When they reached Billings, Montana, they caught a train that had passenger cars. The clacking of the wheels on the tracks lulled Amos to sleep. It took two days with layovers to arrive in Casper.

When Amos stepped off the train, Dan August and Bert Hartwick met him. Introductions to Hoss were made and they headed for the mercantile to enjoy one of Angie's suppers. Mrs. Hartwick's rosy face was all smiles. She loved to cook and she knew Amos loved to eat.

After the meal was over, the men went to a small room that Bert used for an office. They all had cigars and glasses of brandy. Dan was the first to speak. "I imagine you have the map in your bag there."

"I have, only it isn't a map," Amos answered. "There is a leather scroll with lots of Spanish writing on it. It might tell of the location they mined, but we'll have to wait until someone can read what it says."

"Have you got anyone in mind?" the broad-shouldered rancher asked.

"Juan Torres," Amos replied. "If he reads Spanish, I believe he is a man we can trust."

Smiling, Dan agreed. "I know he does read Spanish and English. I would trust him with my life."

Amos could tell that Dan and Bert wanted to see the scroll. He opened the carpet bag, then he and Hoss opened it into a tube on the desk. Each man in turn, picked it up and looked at the words pressed into the inside of the leather.

Bert's face flushed with excitement as he held it. He pointed to the notch on one corner. "Looks like a piece had been cut off."

"I think it was a map of some kind that the Spaniard decided to take with him," Amos explained.

"It's too small to be the map my grandfather received from Jolly," Dan observed.

All of a sudden, Bert had an idea. He left the office and returned with a piece of packaging paper and a pencil. He placed the paper inside the tube and ran the pencil back and forth making an imprint of the markings. Taking the paper out, he looked at the results. On the packaging paper some of the letters could be seen, but most did not transfer well.

The others looked at the result and shook their heads. "If one took their time, it might work," Hoss surmised. "But the indentions are too uneven to make it work well."

"Can it be rolled out more?" Dan asked.

"We can try that when Juan is reading it," Amos replied, "but right now we're afraid that the inside would crack, destroying the writing."

The men sat staring at the leather scroll, each wondering what it might tell them. Suddenly, Amos slapped his knee. "I almost forgot. Billy Bob and his brother Slim have met justice."

"That's good news," Dan replied, smiling. "I'll let the sheriff know."

"Slim got off easy with a bullet, but Billy Bob kicked and cried all the way to the gallows," Amos said, laughing.

"He liked to run with a rough crowd but had little spine when the cards were against him," the rancher replied.

They decided to leave Casper the next day. Amos and Hoss would travel with Dan part-way to the ranch before splitting off toward Juan's. Dan spent the night at Hartwick's while Amos and Hoss chose the Casper Saloon.

"You are welcome to spend the night here," Bert offered.

"I appreciate the offer, but there was a little lady at the saloon that I might look up," Amos replied.

Amos and Hoss left the mercantile, heading for the saloon. After the door shut Dan turned to Bert. "I didn't have the heart to tell him that Lizzy got married and left town."

* * *

With two horses rented from the livery, Amos and Hoss met Dan at the mercantile. Looking over the animals, Dan concluded, "Pop gave you a couple of good horses. Out-of-towners usually get his scrubs."

"I brung him a bottle to help with his aches and pains," the prospector replied. "He made sure we had the best."

Riding out of town, Amos squirmed a bit, trying to get comfortable. The livery saddle didn't fit his bottom nearly as good as the one he'd left in Red Lodge. The two men accompanied Dan the first day. Just over a year before, he and Dan had stopped at the same pond and shot a couple of ducks.

Dan notice three mallards near the cattails on the far side. Pointing at the ducks, he asked, "Feel like another challenge for supper?"

Hoss asked, "Can anyone get in on this?"

Loosening the Colt in his holster, Amos set the rules. "The worst hit cleans the ducks, and if you miss it's a meal of jerky. Hoss, you take the left one, I'll take the center and Dan gets the one to the right."

Dan picked up a good-sized rock and threw it into the pond, flushing the birds. As one they drew and fired. Two ducks tumbled as Hoss fired again at his bird. It then fell into the brown grass on the far side of the pond, flapping its last.

Sliding the Colt .45 back into its holster, Amos said matter-of-factly, "I'll get the fire going while you clean the birds, Hoss." Then the three men burst into laughter.

While cleaning the birds, Hoss was able to point out with satisfaction that he had grazed his bird with the first shot and the second took off most of its head. In the brisk air of the night, the three men enjoyed the juicy waterfowl with some strong coffee. Mrs. Hartwick had given Dan some biscuits to go with their meal.

After eating they sat around the fire, gazing at the night sky, pointing at shooting stars from a meteor shower. "Do you think we'll ever run out of stars with all them ones falling down?" Hoss wondered.

"I used to think they was stars until I read about the one in 1833. Turns out it was dust from what they called a comet," Amos said. "Don't ask me any more than that. Most of what I read didn't make much sense."

"Whatever they are," Dan concluded, "they sure make the night more interesting."

The next morning Amos and Hoss said their goodbyes to Dan and headed for the Torres farm. The prospector had told his friend about the wonderful cheese that Juan's wife made, which Hoss was looking forward to. To one side there were endless grass plains and on the other purple mountains. They rode past Circle A cattle grazing on the plain.

"These are the cows that the rustlers took," Amos explained. "Billy Bob and his brother were part of the gang."

They caught sight of a rider pushing some animals out of a draw. It was Curly, one of Dan's ranch hands. The two men rode up and helped him convince some of the stubborn cows to leave their summer home.

With the cattle headed toward the main herd, the men stopped and shared tobacco. Amos looked the ranch hand over. "Is the leg you broke giving you any problem?"

"This cool weather makes it ache a might," Curly said. "You come back here looking for work?"

"Not me," Amos said. "We're off to visit the Torres ranch and then we head back for Red Lodge."

"No sign of rustlers this year and the cows are in good shape," Curly said as he spat onto the brown grass.

"They hung Billy Bob in Virginia City and his brother died shortly before that," Hoss said.

"Damn good to hear," Curly replied. "He was the one that shot my horse out from under me, causing me to break my leg."

A steer turned back toward the draw and Curly waved goodbye as he wheeled his horse to go after it. Hoss and Amos trotted across the golden grass on their way to find out what was written on the leather.

* * *

The balding Juan Torres welcomed the two men as they rode into the farm yard. "You are just in time for supper."

Juan's wife Teresa quickly added two more settings to the table. His daughters Karla and Diana helped their mother, excited to have unexpected company. Amos looked around. "Where is Ricardo?"

Juan shook his head. "He is happier working for Senior Dan at the ranch." Then a look of pride came across his face. "I am told he is a top hand."

The prospector sat next to Hoss and said, "At least you have your daughters to help with the farm."

"Soon Karla will marry," Teresa informed him. "She will be moving to Casper."

Amos understood wanting to leave the farm only too well as he thought about his father's potato farm in Maine. "As long as your children aren't too far away, that is what's important."

Fresh bread, cheese, meat, and vegetables made up the meal. Hoss complimented Teresa on the cheese. "Amos told me you made a good cheese and he was being modest. This is the best I have eaten."

Teresa blushed at the compliment. "She learned from her mother," Juan said, "and we hope Diana will carry it on."

The prospector caught the roll of the girl's eyes. The daughter might have other plans than to spend a life making cheese. "It would be a shame to lose fine cheese like this," Amos said.

With the meal finished, Amos explained the reason for their visit. Taking the leather scroll out, the prospector placed it onto the table. Juan pulled back the edge of the leather, exposing some of the words. "His name was Salvador Ximenez," he said.

Juan sat back and let the leather close. "I can read it. Some words won't be familiar to me, but you will have an idea of what it says."

"I ask no more," Amos assured Juan.

The father motioned to Diana. "Bring paper and pencil."

With extra lamps lit, Amos and Hoss sat across from each other and unrolled the map until Juan held up his hand to let them know he could see it. Juan began to read in Spanish while Diana wrote the words down. Several times he read a part over several times to figure out an unfamiliar word, or one that had been too damaged to see. Only a line or two were in a crease that couldn't be read.

It took most of an hour to put the words from the leather to paper. Juan had read in Spanish and his daughter had written it in Spanish, leaving Amos and Hoss unaware of what was written on the scroll. The prospector looked at Juan's wife, who had tears in her eyes. She said something to her husband in Spanish.

Juan sat back. "Like Teresa says, it is a very sad letter. It is something a man who does not expect to live would write."

With almost reverence, Juan closed the scroll and set it in front of Amos. "Give me a moment and I will write what it says in English. While doing this, Teresa served the men strong coffee with milk and sugar, along with some sweet bread.

Hoss and Amos looked at each other. They now surmised that it wasn't directions to the gold mine. In much less time that it took to copy the leather scroll, Juan had it translated to English. He set the paper in front of Amos.

My name is Salvador Ximenez. I with 20 men, 10 horses and 10 Yaqui Indians traveled north to explore and map the new land. We left April 1764. Our exploration was to last two years. We mapped our route and claimed the mountains and plains to be the property of New Spain. A second party was to follow in six months and establish a fort 70 days march north to protect settlers in the territory. In May, 2 men were lost crossing a river. We marched 155 days north and found gold. We built shelters near the gold and worked through the winter. Meat was provided by the many wooly beasts roaming the plains. In the spring we had 4 horses and many tools taken by other Indians. 6 men and 2 Yaqui were killed getting 2 horses back. We built defenses and continued to mine and smelt the gold. Some in bars and some in coins for use at the fort for trade. In June, the Yaqui left us taking 2 horses. When taking horses to water or hunting we are often attacked. Five men were lost. July, food is scarce and we ate two horses. The rest will be needed to carry the gold south.

The ground shook and the mine flooded. 3 men drowned leaving only 4 of us to bring back the gold. We were attacked getting wood for smelting the last of the ore. We must leave soon. We are preparing to bring the gold to the new settlement. August, I am now alone. The others were killed while hunting meat. The horses have been taken. I will find a safe place to store the gold and then I will walk south with a map showing its location. May God guide me and protect me.

"The expedition was a year after France gave the land to Spain," Juan explained. "It was after the Seven Year's War. They were there to make sure the French left. It was probably just good fortune that they discovered the gold."

Shaking his head, Amos replied, "All the years of traveling the area, I never had that kind of fortune."

"Dan has told me of gold," Juan said. "The map and this gold, is that what his grandfather found?"

"It was," Amos replied. "We had hoped that this was a map or directions to the mine. The lower corner that was cut off may have contained information about the mine, but that will be lost forever."

Smiling, Juan replied, "It is just as well, my friend. As beautiful as the shine of gold is, it will make men do evil things."

"Amen," Hoss said. "Our reward will be to allow this Salvador Ximenez to speak and tell his story."

All agreed and toasted with their coffee. The scroll and the pages were put away and the conversation changed over to how the crops had been and Juan's plans for the future with fewer children to help with the farm.

Another day was spent before the two men left the Torres farm. Teresa and the daughters treated Amos and Hoss to many culinary delights, while Juan walked them around the farm, showing off the late vegetables and Teresa's goats. Once again, Amos was exposed to a happy family and pangs of regret went through him.

The two men rode back by way of the ranch, bringing cheese and vegetables from Juan, before returning to Casper. Dan had read and re-read the contents of the leather scroll and agreed with Juan's assessment. He told the story of his grandfather spending the winter in the cabin of Don Sikes, who had died attempting to remove his own broken leg. His grandfather had found a note with the last words and thoughts of the dying man.

CHAPTER NINE

The leaves were beginning to change when the two men returned to Casper. They headed straight for the saloon. In the dim light they saw that Lem was eating a bowl of soup at the end of the bar. Two patrons sat at one of the tables, playing small stakes poker. The familiar smell of working men, lingering perfume, and spilt rye greeted them.

"Welcome back, gentlemen," Lem called out. "I got some extra soup in the back if you'd like a bowl."

"Sounds good," Amos replied. "I'd also like a beer and a shot."

"Make mine just the soup and a beer," Hoss added.

The hot soup had just arrived at the table, along with several slices of day-old bread, when Sheriff Winslow came in, his large frame blocking out the sunlight from the door. "Join us for some soup?" Amos invited.

"Just had a meal at the café," he replied. "Bring us a bottle, Lem."

"Everything quiet?" Hoss asked.

"Had to throw a hothead in jail that thought Pop charged too much for oats," the sheriff said. "I figured he had a chip on his shoulder over something else and took it out on old Pop."

"Did Dan tell you about Billy Bob and Slim?" Amos asked.

"He did," Sheriff Winslow replied. "I been wanting to talk to you about that. Each boy had a $500 reward on them, dead or alive. I understand you and Hoss killed Slim, but you were part of a posse when Billy Bob was caught, so there is no payment for him. The sheriff in Virginia City vouched that Slim was dead from what his brother told him. I'll have the money in my office tomorrow."

The sheriff paused for a moment and then added, "I would have liked to have been there to watch Billy Bob kick at the end of a rope."

"It was a fitting end. I figure one reward is more than fair, sheriff," the prospector said. "Me and my partner can use the extra money."

"I thank you, sheriff," Hoss said. "If you ever need to visit Slim's grave, I'd be happy to take you to it."

Amos dunked a piece of bread into the hearty soup. Stuffing the sopped end into his mouth, he bit it off and wiped drops from his beard with the back of his hand. "Hey Lem, damn good soup!"

"Thank Shirley at the café," he replied. "She brings me something different each day."

"Soup was the special at the café today," the sheriff acknowledged.

"Does Doc Morgan still have an office in Casper?" Hoss asked.

"Sure does," Ben Winslow said. "The white-haired old sawbones is still keeping us fixed up. You feeling sick?"

"Not me," Hoss replied. "Amos here is supposed to see him. The doc in Red Lodge suggested it."

"It that right, Amos?" the sheriff asked, looking over the prospector.

"I been getting tired easily and he said things sounded funny inside," Amos responded. "Hell, I'm in my sixties. I am supposed to get tired."

"The doc is good at what he does," the sheriff replied. "Wouldn't hurt to visit him."

With the soup eaten, the prospector grabbed the sheriff's bottle and refilled his glass. Tossing down the drink, he poured a second. "This will fix whatever ails me."

The sheriff left to make rounds and Hoss announced that he was going up to the room. Amos placed his drooping hat on his head and told his friend he needed to get some air.

Amos walked along the street, deep in thought. Too many people were worrying about his health. He found himself in front of the doctor's, next to Hartwick's Mercantile. He was looking up the stairs when Angie came out onto the porch. "I think Doc Morgan is in."

"Thank you, Mrs. Hartwick. I been meaning to visit him," Amos said.

"I got a ham in the oven. Supper will be at six. Bring your friend," Angie told him before heading back in to the mercantile.

Taking a deep breath, Amos slowly climbed the stairs, muttering to himself, "For Christ's sake, you ain't climbing some damn gallows." With that, he hurried up the last couple of steps and knocked on the door.

The doctor called for him to come in. He was busy at his desk, reading an official-looking paper. Turning to the prospector, he said, "What can I do for you?"

Amos told Doc Morgan that the doctor in Red Lodge had recommended he stop in. "Go behind the curtain and remove your shirt and long john top."

The office smelled of antiseptic. Amos went behind the curtain and saw the narrow bed and a stool. He stripped to the waist, placed his shirt onto the bed and took a seat on the stool. He heard the doctor walking toward him. The white-haired doc stopped just inside. "That's my chair, please sit on the bed."

The prospector was holding the folder that the Red Lodge doc had given him. "I was to give you this," he said, handing it to Doc Morgan.

The old doctor read the contents and then said, "Hmm." He continued to look at the notes in the folder. He then removed his wire-rimmed glasses and cleaned them on his coat. He asked, "Have you been getting tired or short of breath for a long time?"

"Nothing I wouldn't expect at my age," Amos replied.

Doc Morgan began to listen to the prospector's chest and back. Finishing, he sat back on the stool. "I can hear something that's not right with your heart and the liquid in the lungs. You are in the early stages of heart issues."

"Are you saying I am dying?" Amos asked.

Doctor Morgan looked at the old prospector sitting in front of him. Amos carried extra weight while remaining fairly muscular for his age. He liked to chew and drink. Amos smoked on occasion and his diet was not the best. The prospector was active and often worked hard for hours at a time. The doctor knew that described most of the men who lived and traveled the frontier.

"You are not going to die from your heart anytime soon. What will happen is you will find things you did in the past will become more and more difficult. When you work hard you might feel palpitations. Your legs will get weaker and a time will come when getting up and using the bathroom will be exhausting." He saw the concern on Amos's face. "I would not worry. I am talking years from now."

"What you are saying though is I will have more problems with strength each of the coming years," Amos asked.

"Pretty much, that's what I am saying," the doc confirmed.

"Is there anything you can give me for this?"

The doctor went to a cupboard and took out a small bottle of powder. "This is Trinitrin. If you ever have severe pain in your chest take a pinch of this powder and put it into your mouth. It will help relieve it."

"Trinitrin?" Amos asked.

"It is Nitroglycerin. Being a prospector or miner, you should be familiar with it," the doctor answered.

"Why, hell, yes I am!" the prospector exclaimed. "If I click my teeth it could blow my head off."

Doctor Morgan laughed at the reaction. "That you don't have to worry about. It is called Trinitrin so folks won't worry about its other uses in explosives. This little bottle is safe. I would warn you, just a pinch at a time, no more. You could end up with one hell of a headache."

Amos pulled the long john top back on and slipped his shirt on, "I can't say you gave me any more comfort that the young doctor in Red Lodge, but at least I understand this a bit better."

"When will you be leaving Casper?" the doc asked.

"Our business is finished here," Amos said. "Hoss and I will be catching the train north in a couple days."

"You have a partner then, that is good," Doctor Morgan told him. "I wouldn't recommend that you ramble around the mountains by yourself."

"I ain't a baby, doc," the prospector replied, a little upset. "I don't need someone to watch over me."

"Trust me, Amos," the doc said, cautioning him, "If you run into trouble and are alone, the end could be slow and painful, plus unnecessary."

Amos touched the Colt on his hip. "I wouldn't suffer long."

"I can only recommend, Amos," the doctor said gently. "But I stress, your death might not be necessary and you would be cheating yourself from future pleasures."

Amos left the doctor's office with the little bottle in his pocket. Again, he was muttering to himself, "I hate when someone makes so much sense."

The prospector was not worried. Hoss would be traveling with him. Without any more leads on the source of the gold, he planned to go back to the canyon and build a cabin to live his final days. He could spend time making short trips to see if he could find some gold, enough to keep him in tobacco and rye.

Amos and Hoss enjoyed a ham supper with yams and vegetables from Angie's kitchen garden. Bert was slicing the meat when he asked his guests, "When will you be leaving? Pop was by and said you brought the horses back to the livery."

Accepting a thick slice of ham, Amos looked at his friend. "Maybe the day after tomorrow. Do you agree, Hoss?"

Smiling, Hoss replied, "If Angie keeps making these fine meals, we might never want to leave. He then asked the prospector, "Do you want to talk about the visit to Doc Morgan?"

All three of the diners stopped and looked at Amos. The prospector had had enough time to digest what the doctor had said and was ready to talk about it. "He told me that I wouldn't live forever, which I kind of knew before, and told me I'd need a friend like Hoss here to travel the world with."

"Well, Hoss. It looks like you have your future planned," Bert said, kidding as he passed the yams.

Everyone seemed satisfied with the prospector's explanation and dug into their meals. The brief strain on Hoss' face wasn't noticed by the others. Angie had baked apples for dessert. The next day the two men spent picking up items to take back to Red Lodge and saying their goodbyes to the many people they had become acquainted with in Casper.

They sat in Shirley's Café enjoying fresh pie and coffee. Hoss suddenly got a serious look on his face. "I am getting married when we get back to Red Lodge."

Amos' face broke into a smile. "You are? That is wonderful news."

"She's a town gal and wouldn't take to living in the country, not even the canyon," Hoss said, worry in his eyes.

"Don't fret," the prospector said. "You'll get used to living in town."

Frustrated, trying to make his point, Hoss said, "The doc wants you to have someone with you, and it can't be me."

"Well, I'll just have to find someone else that is looking for somebody to travel with," Amos said. "Maybe it will be a fine woman like Goldie."

"I know someone that might be good," Hoss replied. "He knows mining and is a good worker. Right now, he is available."

"Is he in Red Lodge?" Amos asked.

Hoss hesitated for a moment. "He is here in Casper . . . He is in Winslow's jail."

"You're not talking about the fellow that went after Pop?" the prospector asked.

"He is normally easygoing," his friend said, defending the man. "I talked with him this morning and he took to the idea of looking for gold."

"How long have you known him?"

"We met four years ago working in Red Lodge," Hoss replied. "He had planned to stand with me at the wedding."

"Will he be traveling with us?" Amos asked. "If he is going to be on the train with us, I'll have a chance to get to know him."

"He will if we pay his fine and ticket," his friend replied.

Smiling, Amos said, "We'll pay his fine and ticket to Red Lodge. We don't want you to end up standing at the wedding by yourself."

Bert met them at the train the next morning. He had a package with sandwiches for the trip. "Angie worried you would get some bad food at one of the stations."

"Thank your lovely wife for me." Amos looked around. "Hoss is supposed to bring a friend. Did you see him when you came through town?"

"The train doesn't leave for a half-hour. I'm sure he'll be in time," Bert assured him.

Bert was about to leave when Hoss came in with a dark-eyed man with black hair and a drooping moustache. He had penetrating eyes and was supporting a good-sized bump on his forehead.

Amos reached out a hand. "My name's Amos Mudd. This is Bert who owns the store."

The man looked at the hand as though he was unsure if he should shake it. Then he took the hand and gripped it firmly. "You can call me Jay."

"Good grip you have there," the prospector said. He held up the package. "We got some sandwiches for the trip."

The men climbed into the passenger car and stowed their gear. Amos noticed that this Jay had only a few items tied in a dirty shirt. Knowing Hoss liked the man, he decided that he would try and get off at a good start.

"You got a last name, Jay?" the prospector asked. "Maybe an Indian name?"

The man stared out the window as the train started to move. "Smith. Jay Smith."

Amos dug into the carpet back beside him for a tobacco plug. Cutting off a chew, he held it out to Jay. "Would you like a chew?"

"I don't use it," the new man replied.

The three men rode in silence for several miles. Amos spat into the spittoon every once in a while. Hoss had his hat tilted forward, appearing to be dozing. The prospector was bound and determined to learn more about the man who might end up riding the mountains with him.

"Have you done mining in the past?" he asked.

"Some," the dark-eyed man replied. Then after a short pause he added, "Mostly coal."

The new man got up and headed toward the bathroom in the back of the car. Amos poked Hoss. "Your friend seems a bit hard up and is awful angry."

Hoss looked back in the direction the man had gone. "Remember, he just come out of Winslow's jail and had his head rattled by the sheriff. He's got a room and some gear in Red Lodge. Once his head stops hurting, he'll be fine."

Unsure that his friend was right about the man coming around, Amos decided that, if needed, he would go to the canyon alone and, taking his time, build a cabin. After that he would find a woman to take care of him and bring her back to the cabin. She would be a lot better on cold nights that a grouchy man whom he'd met this morning.

"Your friend is part Indian," Amos said. "Do you know what tribe?"

"I'm not sure. Arapahoe, I believe," Hoss replied. "I know he's spent time at Fort Washakie."

"Probably in the stockade," the prospector mumbled as he watched the man come back to his seat.

Getting to know Jay Smith was not an easy task. Few words were exchanged between them on the three-day trip to Red Lodge. His mood seemed to mellow a bit and, when talking to Hoss about the wedding, he even seemed excited.

The coal smoke from the dwellings could be seen before the train arrived in Red Lodge. Freshly washed laundry hanging on some of the lines showed the black dust that drifted when the wind blew. When they reached the platform, Jay waved goodbye to Hoss and headed for town. Hoss gave Amos the address of his future wife and invited the prospector to join them for supper that evening.

"Will Jay be there?" the prospector asked.

"He had some things to do to get ready for the wedding and said he'd see me in two days at the church," his friend told him.

Amos asked, "So you'll be getting married on Sunday?"

Hoss smiled. "Yes. Right after the service while folks are still there."

The prospector envied his friend, who had a plan to marry and settle down. "I look forward to meeting the future Mrs. Horst Weber."

Shaking his hand, Hoss replied, "That sounded really good."

The prospector watched his friend walk toward town. Behind him, Amos heard the brakeman setting down items they'd purchased in Casper. It consisted of things needed to build his cabin. Bert gave him better prices than he could have gotten from the places in Red Lodge. There were woodworking tools, rope, harnesses, chain for skidding logs, a window, some hinges, material to caulk logs, spikes and nails, and a few other small items. He had made arrangements with the agent to store the stuff at the depot until he left for the canyon.

As Amos left the station, a string of freight wagons was pulling up, creating a cloud of dust. They would be loading supplies headed for the mines and local tradesmen. Leaving the noise of the station behind, Amos walked rapidly toward Goldie's Saloon, carrying the carpet bag. Stopping just short of the saloon, he leaned against a porch pole and caught his breath. His heart was pounding and he could swear that he felt the palpitations. "Damn doctors get into your head," he muttered.

Goldie was excited to see Amos back. "Come, let's sit and have a drink to your return."

They moved to her back table and she sat close to him while they warmed the cognac in their hands. "Are you back to stay in Red Lodge?" she asked.

"Only for a few days," he replied. "My friend Hoss is getting married and after that I got to buy a horse and buckboard to haul stuff to a canyon I found in the hills."

"It will be snowing soon," she said, objecting. "Why don't you plan on wintering here in Red Lodge?"

"I thought about moving to a town from time to time," Amos admitted. "It wouldn't be right for me. I need the fresh air and open spaces."

Goldie cooed in his ear, "You could move into my room. I'd make you forget about the mountains."

For just a moment he was tempted to take her up on the offer. It would solve the being alone problem. Finally, he gave her a hug. "You would tire of me being under foot in a hurry, and too much comfort makes a man soft. I appreciate the offer and if a time comes when I want to move into town, I'll talk to you first."

She pretended to pout. "Is it another woman in the mountains?"

"No. Not another woman," he told her, "just the mountains."

Once the saloon started to get busy, Goldie had to start working. Amos was feeling the warm glow of the cognac. Suddenly, he realized he was hungry. He left the bag in the cage with Goldie and headed for the café.

A hunter had sold them some bear meat and it was the feature. Lucy had a downcast look when she brought his coffee to the table. Pointing to the chalkboard, Amos said, "I'll have the roast bear plate."

"Saw your friend earlier," she said. "He come in with a young woman. They was mighty cozy."

"I believe they plan to marry," Amos informed her.

All of a sudden, tears ran down her cheeks. "She's lucky. They hung my man. He didn't do nothing to deserve hanging." Brushing away the tears from her face, she took a deep breath and told him, "I'll get your order."

The prospector sat with his coffee. It was still damned weak. While he felt sorry for the way she felt, he knew that she was lucky that Billy Bob was out of her life. Amos wished he could tell her just what kind of man the kid had been, but in her grief Lucy would not believe him.

The roast bear was served with buttered carrots and plenty of gravy. Two slabs of a coarse bread came with the meal. It was late afternoon when he left the café, happy to get away from the unhappy waitress. He headed for the livery to check on his mule.

Kelly was sitting on a bench alongside the open doors. He spat into the dust and then looked up at Amos. "Ya come to get your mule?"

"Not yet, Kelly," the prospector replied. "Just come to catch up on what I owe."

Getting up from the bench, the hostler began to cough as he headed toward a crude table that was used for his office. Kelly opened a cigar box and took out a slip of paper. Amos paid him for what was owed and included the days through Sunday.

"I'm looking for a wagon and a couple horses to pull it," the prospector told the skinny hostler.

"Will you need collars and stuff?" Kelly asked.

"I got the harnesses," Amos replied.

"Hold on a minute," the hostler told him. "Maybe I can help you with the horses."

The prospector went to see his mule. "Looks like you been fed well, Jenny." He patted the animal's shoulder. "I hope you're ready to go back to work." Happy with the presence of his owner, the mule shook its head as if in response.

Hacking and coughing, the hostler returned and took Amos to some stalls in the back of the livery. In the dim light, Amos thought he was looking at a couple of medium-sized blacks. Kelly pushed the back doors open, shedding some light on the animals.

They were two dark, or liver, chestnuts. The two animals had the build of horses that would be used for pulling a light wagon, or riding. "Have they ever pulled a wagon?" the prospector asked.

"They come into town pulling a broken-down wagon and were in poor shape," Kelly replied. "I poured some feed into them and they filled out some."

Amos could see the marks of a whip on the animals' rumps and backs. There were also scars from poorly fitted harnesses. "The animals still look rough."

"I put saddles on them a while back and rented them out to a couple of hunters," the hostler said. "They had no complaints about how they handled."

Running his hand along the horse's back, it shuddered and moved away. "They been beat and might be skittish, and could be hard to stop if they were scared."

For about an hour the pros and cons of the two animals were exchanged by Kelly and Amos. Finally, the hostler offered them at a price that would leave a little from Amos' share of the reward that the prospector had gotten.

Amos shook his head and started out of the livery, hoping to drive the price down just a bit more. The frustrated Kelly called after him, "You said you needed a wagon. The one that came with the cayuses needs a bit of work, and I'll throw it in."

"You feed them and keep them for me until Monday and we got a deal," Amos countered.

"Damn!" the hostler growled, causing a coughing fit. Finally, the man stopped and mopped him mouth with a soiled hanky. Wheezing, he added, "Come back. I'll show you the wagon."

A bit of work was an understatement. Two of the wheels had damaged spokes, with one of them needing a new rim. The axles appeared to be okay and there were broken boards on the floor and sides.

There was a blacksmith shop just outside town. The wheels could be fixed there. Amos could do the rest. Reaching into his threadbare coat, Amos took out the money from an inside pocket. He paid off the hostler, who was now showing his chipped teeth through his smile.

"I'll be here in the morning to move the wagon to the smithy and see how the animals I just bought take to the harness," Amos told the hostler as he took his leave and headed for Goldie's. He noticed Jay sitting on the edge of the porch in front of the mercantile, eating a can of peaches.

He walked over and saw that the dark-eyed man was looking up at him from under his flat-brimmed hat. "I bought a couple horses that I want to try out in the morning," Amos said. "I could use a little help with them."

The man finished drinking the juice from the tin can and tossed it aside. Standing up, Jay wiped his mouth. "What time?"

"Between eight and nine," Amos replied.

Nodding, Jay walked away. The prospector noticed he was wearing a Remington Model 1875, .44 caliber in a well-worn holster. While the man's attitude bothered Amos, he did like the way he carried himself. Any way he looked at it, the prospector would have some help come tomorrow.

It was just getting dark and Goldie was still in her cage when Amos entered the saloon. She smiled and waved at him. Two of Goldie's women were on the stage, dancing and singing to the tune played on the piano. Ted brought a bottle of cognac and two glasses to the table near the cage. "Bring me a beer also," Amos requested.

The Faro table and roulette wheel were busy relieving hard-working miners of their wages. Goldie's ladies were working the men for what they could get. Amos wasn't bothered, because they all knew he was Goldie's man. It made him feel special, but he did miss being chased by the ladies of the evening and anticipating their charms.

The sounds of cards shuffling and chips clicking came to a stop as three women dressed in revealing French costumes and two men in tails and top hats took the stage, drawing the attention of the men in the saloon. Goldie came out of the cage and joined the prospector. "Things will be quiet in the cage until the troupe is finished," she told him. "They are pretty good and I got them for a good price."

While Amos was aware of the soft, pretty smelling woman beside him, he couldn't help being drawn to the entertainment. He agreed, they were good. "I have to admit something," Goldie said, leaning close.

"Uh huh," the prospector acknowledged, his eyes on one of the precocious ladies on the stage.

"I looked in your bag."

Suddenly, Amos' attention was on the woman beside him, "You looked in the bag?"

She nodded, frowning. "It's just a few clothes and a piece of old, rolled up leather. Why have you been having me guard it like it was full of money?"

A grin spread over Amos' face. "The leather has a message from a long dead Spaniard. I hope to sell it to an antique collector someday. I think of it as my retirement money."

"Would it be worth that much?" Goldie asked.

"Look at me," the prospector said. "I'm old and have been told by the young doctor that I have a problem with my ticker. I don't think I'll need a heck of a lot for it."

The normally smiling face of Goldie suddenly paled. "You're sick?"

Seeing her concern, he wished he'd avoided talking about his health. "Don't be concerned. I was assured that I still have several good years left."

The people on the stage were forgotten. Goldie replied, "I will buy it from you. I'll pay more than a collector," she promised. "I will take care of you."

Suddenly, Amos felt smothered. He knew that the woman beside him meant well. She now looked at him as someone in need rather than a man of strength. "My sweet," he said, as carefully as he could, "I am not without means and will be luckier than . . .," he waved his arm across the room, "than most of the men in this room."

The entertainment ended with a chorus of shouts and applause, the patrons of the saloon throwing coins and chips onto the stage. Several men hurried toward the cage to cash in or get more chips. Her face still showing concern, Goldie excused herself and went to take care of her customers.

The beer in front of Amos now tasted flat. He looked at the cognac and shook his head. He was in the mood for rye. The prospector moved from the table to the end of the bar. The two bartenders were busy with thirsty customers. Finally, Ted came over. "Another beer, Amos?"

"A bottle of rye, Ted"

"Is something wrong with the cognac?" the bartender asked.

"It is fine, but I have a taste for rye," Amos assured the man as he placed a coin onto the bar.

Back at the table, the prospector filled his glass and took a healthy drink. "Ahh, that's good," he sighed.

He began to refill the glass and then stopped in mid-pour. At the far end of the bar he recognized Jay. The man had a shot and beer in front of him. The prospector had no desire to invite the difficult man to join him and shifted his eyes to the other goings-on in the room.

That evening Amos did his best to let the generous Goldie know that he was in no hurry to sell the leather scroll. She did offer to keep it in her safe which he accepted. He also gave her an overview of what the letter said, downplaying the part about the gold.

Amos arrived at the livery an hour after daylight. Jay crouched next to the open doors with several cigarette butts stubbed out in front of him. "I see you start work late," the dark-eyed man pointed out. "Did you stay up too late with the blond woman?"

In no mood to take guff from the man, the prospector replied curtly, "It ain't none of your business what I do or where I do it. If you have somewhere else to be, I can take care of business here."

Holding his hands up to show he was backing down, Jay said, "I am here to work."

Amos got the two chestnuts from their stalls. Each of the men led a horse as they went over to the train depot. The prospector retrieved the harnesses from his gear, promising the manager that he'd be back for the rest of the gear in the next couple of days.

Taking their time, the harnesses were put onto the skittish horses. Jay ran a gentle hand over the back of one of the horses. "Who did Kelly say sold him these horses?"

"He didn't say," Amos replied.

"If I meet the man, I'll give him some of what he gave his horses," the man said, anger clear in his eyes.

"We got a chance to make up for the treatment," the prospector said. "Whoever comes with me to the canyon will be responsible for these animals."

As they brought the animals back to get the wagon, Jay's horse held its head high and pushed against him, trying to show its dominance. The dark-eyed man stopped and slowly pulled the horse's head down. Standing close to its head, he spoke softly for several minutes while preventing the horse from raising its head. Amos stood nearby with the other horse, watching.

They continued toward the livery. Jay had a tight grip on the reins holding the animal's head down and continued to talk in a voice too low for Amos to hear. The horse watched the man as they walked.

They tied the horses to a front wheel, and the two men walked around the wagon. "What did this cost you?" Jay asked, skepticism in his voice.

"Kelly threw it in with the horses," Amos replied, satisfaction in his voice.

Shaking his head, the dark-eyed man replied, "You paid too much."

Amos chuckled, "Maybe so."

As they hitched the team to the wagon, the horses snorted and rolled their eyes. There was no doubt this process had been painful for the animals in the past. Once hitched, the prospector hurried into the livery and returned with two feedbags. Setting them into the wagon, he and Jay led the team with the creaking wagon toward the smithy.

Once the wagon was in front of the smithy, they unhitched the team and led them to a shady area. The feedbags with a good portion of oats were hung on the horses' heads and the two men went back to help the blacksmith, Jorge, remove the damaged wheels.

"I can have them ready on Monday," Jorge told them.

"We're going to repair the rest of the wagon," Amos said. "Mind if we borrow a few tools?"

With the sound of the blacksmith striking metal with his heavy hammer, the two began repairs on the wagon bed. It was evident that Jay had experience working with wood. Soon all four wheels were off the wagon and the two not requiring repair were lubricated and put back into place.

At midday they took the animals to a stream for water. Jorge had some hay and let them feed the horses. All this time the chestnuts remained harnessed as a team. By the end of the day the wagon box was fixed, including a new tailgate. The remaining two axle spindles were lubricated, awaiting the repaired wheels.

While Jay walked in front of the horses and Amos drove them with the reins from the rear, they went back to the livery. The two men spent extra time removing the harnesses and brushing the animals. Amos also gave the mule a good rubdown. Hay and additional grain were given to the animals before the men left.

"You'll make 'em soft if you feed them too much," Kelly warn them. "The animals need a good workout."

"I'll take them for a run in the morning," Jay offered.

"You got a wedding to attend," Amos reminded him.

"I'll do it early. Mind if I ride the mule?"

"Go ahead, ride the mule," Amos answered. "I will see you at the church."

CHAPTER TEN

The wedding left Amos with mixed feelings. In his sixty plus years, he had been to very few weddings. He watched the glow on the couple's faces. They looked like they'd just found the mother lode. Tomorrow they would wake up as the same two people, yet they would be different. The preacher had said, "As one."

Jay stood beside Hoss in new, store-bought shirt and pants. He had even polished his riding boots. Two much younger girls stood up with the bride. There was a lot of singing and the elderly black preacher took full advantage to deliver a sermon before the vows.

Amos noticed a black man with snow-white hair and a closely cropped moustache and beard sitting in a front pew. The man was of slight build and wore a dark suit that was buttoned up in spite of the warm temperature. Two ladies sat next to him. The prospector guessed that these were Hoss' family.

That was confirmed before the meal in the yard next to the church. Hoss called Amos over, "This is my father, Elijah Weber, and my sisters Wenona and Nituna."

Amos was impressed with his family. There was pride and a closeness he had missed in his life. "I am pleased to meet you," the prospector replied. "I understand you were a mountain man as well as a Flathead warrior."

Smiling, Elijah replied, "Those days are long gone. Now I sit and enjoy watching my family grow."

"No doubt earned by doing things that were right," Amos acknowledged.

Amos learned that Wenona's husband had died defending their village during a raid by another tribe. Nituna's husband was an army scout and was away with his command. He also learned that Hoss was an uncle to several of the young children running in the church yard.

The bride, Sara, came over to the group. She was a picture of beauty in the modest white dress. Amos had met her before the wedding started and she had immediately claimed him as part of the family. "It is time to eat," she said, "and save room for the cake."

As they walked toward the tables, Amos noticed that Jay was missing. "Isn't your friend going to eat?"

"Sara made him a little something to go," Hoss explained. "He told me he had something to do that couldn't wait."

An autumn breeze made the afternoon comfortable as everyone enjoyed the food. After Amos ate his fill along with some cake, he excused himself and headed for the smithy. To his surprise, the wagon was gone. He saw Jorge putting away some tools.

"I come to finish up on the wagon and its gone," Amos told him.

"Your man come earlier with the team," Jorge explained. "He helped me put the wheels on and it was ready to go, so he brung it back to the livery. Said you'd settle up with me."

"Was the linkage on the front wheels tightened up?" Amos asked.

"Sure was. The wagon is as good as new," the blacksmith assured him.

Amos settled with Jorge and then went to find Jay. The wagon was in front of the livery and Kelly was slowly walking around it. "Is this the one I give you?" he asked.

The prospector snorted, "You didn't give me nothing. I overpaid you for the horses."

"Your darn lucky I didn't get a better look at them two chestnuts," the hostler replied. "The price you paid was the same as stealing them."

The two men were still exchanging barbs when Amos heard some running animals behind the livery. Around the side came Jay on the mule, leading the horses. He stopped in a cloud of dust and swung out of the saddle.

"Don't be running the meat off them animals before we head for the canyon," Amos warned him.

"Don't worry, old man," Jay said, his eyes flashing. "I am making sure that they're limber before pulling the wagon, so they don't go lame on us."

Amos felt a little hot under the collar seeing the attitude of the dark-eyed man, but figured that he'd proven his worth so far and decided to let it go.

Speaking a little carefully, the prospector said, "We best get them rubbed down and fed. I'd like to load the wagon at first light."

Jay led the animals into the livery while Amos headed uptown to Goldie's. Kelly watched the two go their ways and shook his head. "They'll kill each other up in them mountains."

Goldie smiled and waved to Amos as he came through the door. She motioned to Ted, who brought a bottle of cognac and rye to the table. "Ted said you preferred whiskey to cognac."

Amos stroked his beard, his eyes twinkling. "I do take a preference to good rye."

"Well, this is your last night and you get whatever you want," she said, winking.

"It was a fine wedding," he told Goldie.

"I understand Hoss has taken a job in one of the mines," Goldie said.

"That he has," the prospector replied. "Won't be long he'll be hacking like old Kelly."

"How has the man Hoss recommended worked out?" she asked.

"It's too early to say," the prospector replied. "The man knows how to do everything and ain't afraid of work. But . . . he is carrying a whole lot of anger and it just might get one of us hurt."

"Then I would recommend you work him hard and don't step on his toes," Goldie suggested.

"Now," Amos said, "let's talk about anything I want."

* * *

The sun was just coming up over the rolling plains when Amos arrived at the livery, carrying his carpet bag, saddle bags, and Winchester. The team was already hitched to the wagon and his mule was tied to the back.

Amos had awoken with a touch of sadness that morning. He would have liked to spend more time with Hoss and his new wife before leaving Red Lodge. Amos had reminded Hoss that they were still partners, should he find the Spanish mine. He had gotten the leather scroll from Goldie's safe and stowed it in the carpet bag.

Jay was drinking coffee with the old hostler. Seeing the prospector coming, he took the final drink and tossed the dregs out before handing the cup back to Kelly. "We riding or leading the mule?" he called to Amos.

"We'll be climbing a long grade today, so you best ride the mule," Amos replied. "Have you got a saddle?"

"Yes, I do," Jay replied. "I'll check out the fit and if it's good, I'll use it."

The prospector climbed onto the wagon and took up the reins. He saw the chestnuts tense. The prior owner probably used a whip or the end of the reins to start the team. Releasing the brake from the wheel, he gave the reins an easy flip and said, "Let's go you cayuses."

The horses lurched forward and then fell into a slow walk as they pulled the wagon toward the depot. Jay walked in front of them, singing softly. Amos had noticed the saddle and two bags in the wagon when he had climbed on. He wondered how much other gear the man would have.

The lumber for the door and trim was loaded first. Two kegs of nails, the rope, a nine-plate stove for cooking and heating, stove pipe, hinges and other items including flour, salt, and other staples were loaded. Bert had also sent him with cold flour, jerky and a container of hardtack for leaner times. Amos planned to stop in Absarokee to make arrangements for other items he would need.

With the wagon ready and Jay's saddle on the mule, they pulled out. There was a bag of oats on the wagon for the animals to keep their strength up. It would be three days to the canyon. Amos planned an overnight at the Williams place. The trip could be made in two days by horseback with a stop at the Williams farm. Amos liked the family and planned to stop and see them most every trip.

The team was able to handle the wagon, requiring a breather every hour. Jay ranged ahead looking for the best crossings at the rivers and creeks. They chose to spend the first night on the Rosebud Creek. It had a stand of cottonwood trees providing some protection from the elements and wood for their fire. Once the animals were taken care of, Jay went down to the creek and rigged up a fishing pole. Amos mixed up a batch of sourdough biscuits and put them into the Dutch oven to bake.

It was the end of September and the evening breeze was cool. The smell of the biscuits mixed with the wood smoke was something Amos had enjoyed more times than he could remember while living in the wilds. He heard Jay coming back from the creek.

"We got some trout to go with your biscuits," the dark-eyed man said, dropping them next to the fire.

"Sounds good," the prospector replied. "You best get them cleaned. The biscuits are about done."

Tossing the pole next to a cottonwood, the sullen Jay picked up the fish and went down to the stream to clean them. Amos had grease from some side meat sizzling in the blackened frying pan when the man came back. Soon the trout were snapping and popping in the pan.

"Got some coffee ready," Amos called to his traveling companion.

There was little conversation as the two men ate. The pink sweet flesh of the trout was most satisfying. Amos wiped his biscuit in the hot frying pan grease. They planned to keep the extra biscuits for their breakfast.

A light, cold rain was falling when the men awoke in the morning. The golden leaves of the cottonwood kept most of the moisture off the men while a few heavy with moisture fell, covering their blankets and camping area.

After a quick meal of biscuits and coffee, they got the team hitched and the mule saddled. "I'll start off riding the mule," Amos said.

"You're the boss," Jay said as he climbed onto the wagon.

"I'm glad we understand each other," the prospector replied as the mule led the way out of the grove of trees.

A misty rain continued through the morning. Both men had donned slickers and rode with their hats tilted toward the breeze. They chewed jerky and drank water while giving the team a breather. "We're about three hours from the Williams place," Amos told the dark-eyed man. "She and her kids are nice folks. Her man was killed in Red Lodge and they're continuing the potato farm he started."

"Potato farming is hard work," Jay said. "I take it you don't much care for hard work."

A bit irritated, Amos replied, "I don't much care for uninteresting work. I have never avoided hard work."

The rain had stopped, while the sky remained overcast. They watered the animals at a shallow stream before continuing toward the Williams cabin. They turned off the trail into the clearing. Lucia and Chip had their team and wagon in the field and were digging potatoes. Elly was sitting on one of the horses. When the young lad noticed the wagon, he shouted a hello and ran across the field to meet them.

Lucia stood up from her work and wiped the back of the gloved hand across her forehead. She broke into a smile. "Amos, welcome back," she called.

Riding the mule toward Lucia, the prospector waved. Chip ran along behind him. Swinging off Jenny, Amos tipped his hat. "Mrs. Williams. It is a pleasure to see you again."

Jay sat on the wagon, back near the trail, witnessing the reunion. He looked over the clearing and noticed that about half of the potatoes had been dug. The cabin and barn were well-taken care of. There was a large wood table near a stream that ran behind the barn, and there were washed potatoes spread across it, drying. He also noticed a wooded area to the right that was being cleared.

Chip took the reins of the mule. Lucia took Elly off the horse while Amos led the team and potato wagon toward the cabin. "You have some nice potatoes here," the prospector acknowledged.

"It has been a good year," the woman said. "We could do without the rain during harvest. It makes more washing for us."

After watching for a moment, Jay drove their wagon, stopping near the cabin. He climbed down and waited for the others. Once in front of the cabin, Amos made the introductions to the dark-eyed man.

"What happened to Hoss?" Lucia asked, putting Elly down.

"He got himself married," Amos replied. "Jay here is a friend of his and come with me this trip."

Jay removed his hat and smiled. "It is a pleasure to meet you, Mrs. Williams."

"I'll finish cleaning these potatoes and then make some supper," Lucia said.

"Please, Mrs. Williams," Jay said. "Let me take care of the potatoes with your son."

"Okay then," she said, smiling. "I'll start supper now. Mr. Mudd, would you like to join me?"

"I should take care of the animals first," Amos replied.

"Come on inside," she said. "Chip would be glad to take care of the animals. You talked of being a fair cook when you were here last. Elly and I'd like to see what you can do."

The young man talked a mile a minute as he and Jay headed for the washing table. The cool air and water numbed their hands as the two of them dipped from the stream and removed the loam from the tubers. They had put the dried potatoes into burlap bags to be stored in the lean-to on the barn.

"Ma and me are going to build a sorting shed next year," Chip informed Jay. "Then we don't have to worry about rainy days."

Once they finished with the potatoes, all the animals were put into the corral and given hay. Jay admired Chip's burro. "They're not a big animal, but sure can do a lot of work for you."

Beaming at the compliment, Chip said, "I got to milk the cows before supper. You go to the house and I'll be right along."

"It's been a while, but I was once a fair hand at milking," Jay told the young man.

While the two of them headed into the barn, they heard the laughter of Amos and Lucia in the house. "It sounds good," Chip said. "Ma doesn't laugh enough since pa died."

It was just getting dark when they all sat down to supper. Chip had shot some pigeons in the barn earlier in the day and the meal was pigeon pie loaded with potatoes and carrots, covered with a flaky, light-brown crust.

"You still have enough shells for the shotgun?" Amos asked the young man.

"I shot about half of them keeping pigeons out of the barn and hunting meat for the table," he replied.

"We'll be re-roofing the barn if he keeps putting holes in it," his mother told them.

They all laughed at the blushing young man. After the meal, Amos stepped outside to have a chew and drink his coffee. He could hear Jay talking to Lucia about her potato crop. He also heard him offer to come by next summer and help build the sorting shed.

Amos thought about helping his own father with the potato shed in Maine. It had been long ago, but the memories seemed like yesterday. In fact, he realized that he'd been thinking about life in Maine a lot lately. He wondered if it was because of what the doctors had told him. Or maybe it came with age.

Before they left the next morning, Amos gave Lucia a few items he had brought for her from Red Lodge. To Chip he gave some shells for the shotgun and both kids got a big peppermint stick. Then, to the boy he said, "I don't want to be responsible for damage to the roof. Make sure you knock the pigeons down outside the barn," he advised.

Amos was driving the wagon and Jay was on the mule. They were saying their goodbyes when Mrs. Williams suddenly asked, "Did you ever catch up with the two men you were looking for last time?"

Thinking for a bit, he answered, "Justice caught up with them."

"I guess that's good," she replied.

"It was," Amos replied. He then smiled and waved goodbye. The weather was cool despite the bright sun. The prospector was looking forward to getting back to the canyon. Amos stopped at the small town of Absarokee and made arrangements with a freighter to bring a load of lumber and shingles to arrive in a week.

CHAPTER ELEVEN

The leaves were a blaze of color when the two arrived at the trail into the canyon. Amos had not done any improvement to the trail in order to make the opening less obvious. Now the prospector knew that there was no reason to hide the canyon. There was little of value other than water and good grass to protect.

They set up camp just outside the opening and spent most of the next day cutting trees and moving rocks and windfalls. Amos looked for any new tracks on the original trail and found none. The opening into the canyon had a couple of turns, which obscured it even with the cleared road.

Jay rode the mule into the canyon while Amos drove the wagon. They set up camp under the cut where he'd stowed his gear. Everything remained as he'd left it. The two men lifted the stove under the rock overhang. "We might as well use it for cooking until the cabin is built," Amos said.

Smoke rolled out of the cast iron stove as the men huddled close for warmth. "You're going to freeze this winter in that old worn coat you have on," Jay said, rubbing his hands together.

"I have a wolf skin coat in my packs," the prospector informed him. "Once winter sets in, I'll get it out."

They had another couple of hours before dark, so Amos saddled the mule and shoved an axe in place of the Winchester. "I'm going to look for some timber to use for the cabin," he told Jay. "You might want to rig up some walls to cut the wind." Without waiting for an answer, he rode further into the canyon, looking for good building trees.

The canyon wound back to a hillside covered with a stand of pine. Patting the mule on the shoulder, he said, "Perfect for the cabin."

Using the axe that he'd carried in the scabbard, Amos walked up to one of the trees. Spitting on his hands, he gripped the axe. Making effortless swings, he cut a notch. He then chopped into the far side, felling the pine. Using the length of the axe to measure along the log, he made a notch. Amos then limbed the tree. He didn't have a bucking saw, so he used the axe to cut off the top.

Standing back, he admired his work for a moment before getting the mule. Rigging a rope to the saddle horn, he led the mule back to the camp with his prize. As he came up the canyon, Amos noticed that Jay had cut and woven some brush to fashion walls to cut the wind.

The dark-eyed man watched the prospector approach. "That'll be a damn big log for this here stove, old man."

Ignoring the remark, Amos replied, "This here is the first log of our winter home. There's a nice stand of pine a half-mile into the canyon."

Jay had taken to calling him "old man" and Amos was sure it was not a compliment, but he had decided to ignore it because, after all, he was an old man. If it made his disgruntled, dark-eyed companion feel better, it was a small price to pay.

While Amos unhooked the mule, Jay walked up to the log and gave it a push with his foot. "It looks to be 15 feet long, maybe a bit more."

"It is six axe handles long," Amos explained. "That measures 15 feet. The other walls will be eight handles long, or 20 feet. I have built several cabins and they were all 15 by 20."

The dark-eyed man headed back toward the rock cut. "Beans and side meat okay for supper?"

"Sounds good," Amos said. He felt invigorated. He loved making things and wanted to get right at it. There was a windfall near their camp that they had been cutting for firewood. The prospector took his axe and cut two three-foot pieces from the trunk. He then flattened one side and chopped a wide notch in the other. He set them near the pine log and lifted each end into the notch.

Amos went back to his cache of packs and dug out some line and a box of chalk powder. He also got a broad axe. He then measured the small end of the log. Using the measurement, he marked the larger end. Shaking the line in the box of powder, he carefully removed it and strung it along one side of the log. He snapped it and the put the line back into the box.

Taking his felling axe, Amos walked along the log chopping notches, staying shy of the chalk line. He then removed the excess wood, roughly flattening one side of the log. Then, taking rhythmic swings with the broad axe, he finished the side to the chalk line.

Taking up a whetstone to touch up the axe edge, the prospector continued marking and cutting the other three sides, squaring the log. Stepping back, he surveyed his work. Amos was sweating and breathing hard from the effort. He could feel his heart pounding in his chest.

"It may kill me," Amos called to Jay, "but I'll need a couple dozen of each length for the cabin."

"The beans are about done and I'm about to put on the side meat." Jay replied. "You best stop admiring your work and take care of that mule."

Setting the axes against the log, the prospector snorted, "Damn upstart," as he went to take care of the patient animal.

The night was more comfortable, so the two men sat on the log and ate their supper. Amos got a bottle of rye out of his packs and added a little to their coffee. The smell of the fresh pine chips always brought him back 40 years, when he'd worked at a logging camp for a winter during his trip west.

The moon was bright and Amos was feeling right at home in the canyon. He hadn't given up finding the source of the Spanish gold, but that would have to be put off until next spring. The horses and mule were picketed on the tall brown grass in the canyon. Amos had brought a scythe with plans of stacking some hay for the winter.

The next morning found Amos up with the sun. He had a chew in his cheek and his eyes on the ground. Finding the best location for the cabin was the next order of business. The spring-fed pond made him believe that a well could be dug in most locations in the canyon. Amos looked around for a place that would offer the most advantage. Closer to the pines would save distance for dragging the logs, but snow drifting was likely in the canyon and come winter it could be a long, difficult trip in and out.

Finally, he settled on a flat rise near the stream. It should be safe during spring flooding. There was enough room for a small barn in the future as well as a corral. Amos had a handful of short poplar sapling stakes and his axe. He saw Jay walking from the camp toward him.

"Come and give me a hand," he called over.

Jay trotted to the site. "Is this where you're going to build the cabin?"

"It is," Amos told him. He drove one of the stakes into the grass-covered sod and then handed the axe to Jay. "Measure down six lengths of the axe and pound in another stake."

The prospector had Jay move a little toward the canyon wall. After Jay pounded in the second stake, Amos then had the dark-eyed man measure out eight axe handle lengths. The fourth stake was located six lengths up to the final corner. The prospector took out a length of string from his pocket and then handed one end to Jay.

Stretching it out diagonally across the corners, they marked the length on the string. They then checked the opposite corners. They continued adjusting the stakes until the distance of the diagonal corners were the same. Amos then double checked the length of the walls. They measured exactly the length they wanted and the rectangular cabin had square corners.

"What are you going to make the floor with?" Jay asked.

"I figure we'll start with packed dirt," the prospector replied.

"We got some rock near the opening that can be split and we can fit them to make the floor," the dark-eyed man said.

Nodding his head, Amos agreed. "We build the cabin first and then if we ain't up to our butts in snow, we'll fit the floor."

In the past the prospector had built cabins for short-term use, maybe two or three years. The extra work of putting in a floor had made no sense. Here in the canyon he planned to live out his days, and with luck that would be some time yet.

They quickly fell into a routine. Jay would fell the trees and cut them to length, then drag the logs with the horses to the cabin site. By then Amos would have the previous one squared. The two of them would move the finished log to the side of its future wall and then lift the new log onto the hewing blocks.

At Jay's recommendation, pieces of split rock were placed onto the ground to support the first log of the wall. When he got ahead on logs, he'd go the opening and Amos could hear him splitting the stones with a chisel and hammer. Some evenings Jay would work until well after dark. Each morning more of the walls were lined with rock, awaiting laying of the first log.

The hard work had tempered Jay's attitude. He seemed to enjoy staying busy and it seemed to take his mind off whatever was bothering him. One afternoon Amos had just finished squaring a log before Jay came back with the next. The dark-eyed man was standing on the log, riding it behind the horses. A half-smile came to the prospector's face as he remembered when he and a friend used to do that. His face changed as he recalled the friend being killed under a runaway log sledge.

Jay looked at Amos. "How about letting me square some of the logs while you go bring them in?"

Amos' heart was pounding in his chest and his arms felt like rubber. "You know how to square logs?"

"I've done it before," Jay replied coldly. "If you ain't happy with my work, old man, we will only waste one log."

The prospector was too tired to debate with his fellow worker. Fetching the logs would offer him periods of rest. "I got coffee on and some cold biscuits. Let's eat and then we'll switch."

Jay did a good job squaring the logs and by the end of the week they had all they needed for the walls. Amos showed him how he wanted the corners notched and they started fitting the logs onto the walls. There were spikes in one of the kegs for nailing the ends. In the past Amos had used an auger and made pegs to secure the logs, or depended on the interlocking notches to hold them. There was a buck saw in the packs for cutting the logs for the window and the door. The rough-cut boards brought from Red Lodge were used to frame them in.

Amos was standing on a crude platform next to the eaves while Jay worked at the ridge of the cabin roof. They had cut spruce poles for the rafters. One side was complete and they were working on the other. The sound of horses coming into the opening of the canyon caught their attention. The prospector hoped that it was the lumber and shingles he'd ordered. He did not hear the sound of a wagon.

Climbing down from the platform, Amos fetched his Colt from the holster hanging on a spike driven into the log wall. Jay swung down from the rafters and dropped inside the cabin. Sticking his Colt into his waistband, Amos stepped away from the building and watched three riders coming toward him.

The leader was riding a roan and wore a leather deerskin vest and a tan, broad-brimmed hat. He had a short, white beard. He also carried matching revolvers on his hips. The two men behind him wore clothing typical of miners, calf-high work boots and caps with the front brim turned up. The two men both carried scarred army rifles across their saddles.

The three men pulled up short of the cabin. The bearded man called out, "It's a fine-looking cabin you're building."

"It'll do for winter," Amos replied.

"Do you mind if I step down?" the man asked the prospector.

"You're welcome to," Amos said. "I'd offer you some coffee, but it is a bit early in the day for taking a break."

It was evident that the man was used to being in charge and he carried himself with a certain amount of authority. "I come across an interesting bit of information a short time back."

"What would that be?" the prospector asked.

"Well, it was a map to this canyon. I was told that there was a second one with directions to a Spanish gold mine," the leader replied.

"Would this map have come from a thief named Billy Bob?" the prospector asked. "Whatever you might have paid him, you made a deal with a liar."

Casual-like, the white-bearded man moved away from his horse. "A dying man seldom lies."

"I hate to disappoint you, but there is no map to a Spanish mine," Amos said in a controlled voice. "I think you and your ruffians best ride back out of this canyon."

Determined to keep control of the discussion, the leader said, "No need to get your hackles up. I am prepared to pay you good money for the map." Looking at Amos and glancing around, he continued, "By the looks of things, you could use it."

"I have been most patient with you mister," the prospector said with an edge in his voice. "You best get on your horse and go back to where the hell you came from."

One of the ruffians started to shift his rifle when there was the sound of a revolver cocking behind Amos. The prospector knew that it would be Jay with his .44 leveled at the three men. Amos continued, "I have no control over the fellow behind me and he carries a hair-trigger revolver, so you best hurry out of here."

The leader's face turned red and he got back onto his roan. "I will have that map," he threatened.

"The next time you come back into this canyon, you will not live to leave it," Amos warned the man. "Whatever Billy Bob told you, he took you for a fool. Don't make a second mistake."

The leader jerked the roan around and rode out of the canyon, followed by his henchmen. One of the ruffians looked back and spat as he rode away.

Amos heard Jay walking up behind him. The two men watched the riders disappear beyond the opening. "You think they'll turn and come back shooting?" the dark-eyed companion asked.

"I believe I saw a shadow of doubt in the man's eyes," Amos replied. "It's unlikely he'll come back again without being sure of the outcome."

Jay slid the .44 back into his holster. After a moment he said, "Is there something you need to tell me about?"

Amos turned back toward the cabin. "Ain't nothing to tell. We got work to do before the snow."

"If I'm going to end up shot at, it would be nice to know why," Jay said as he headed back up to the ridgepole.

The freight wagon came in the next day. A cold wind blew from the north, telling of snow soon. Both man now worked wearing their revolvers and the Winchester leaned against the wood pile near their cook fire. The mule skinner climbed down from the wagon and joined the two men at the fire, rubbing his hands for warmth. Amos offered him some coffee and beans with biscuits.

The freighter looked at the two men. "Kind of looks like an armed camp here."

"We've had a little trouble," Amos replied.

"I imagine about the Spanish gold mine," the man said. "I heard about it, but don't believe a word. People been chasing rumors out here as long as I can remember."

Ignoring the comment, the prospector said, "As soon as we eat, we'll get you unloaded."

Sitting near the temporary fire pit, the men ate their midday meal. "Mind if I have a second biscuit?" the freighter asked. "They is mighty tasty."

Once the boards and shingles were unloaded, the muleskinner declined Amos' offer for him to spend the night and he headed out of the canyon. Jay sat staring at Amos.

The prospector looked at him and said, "We got work to do."

"What we have is some talking to do," Jay replied. "I took this on to help you build a cabin and spend the winter. I need to know what else I might be in for."

While the cold October wind tore at their clothes, Amos told Jay about the Spanish gold. That night he got out the leather scroll made by the Spaniard and the translation of the letter. The two men sat under the rock cut as the dark-eyed man looked at the scroll. He opened it enough to see a few lines.

To Amos' surprise Jay read aloud what he could see. "You read Spanish?"

"I get by in Spanish," the man said. "I also know some French."

"They teach you that on the reservation?" Amos asked.

Giving the prospector a cold look, Jay replied, "I learned from my grandfather and mother."

Affronted, the prospector said, "You don't have to get that way about it. I was just asking."

"If I was you," Jay advised, "I would just nail this thing to a post near the opening and if anyone comes in asking, just point to it and let them see there ain't nothing."

"I suppose I could do that," Amos said, "but I was given a map that led me to this roll of leather and reading this man's words might be the closest I ever come to the mother lode."

"You're a crazy old man," Jay said as he went to his blankets.

The cabin was finished before the first snow fell. The two men worked together splitting the stones for the floor. Once a seam was located, just a few taps with the chisel and hammer split off a slab. It took two days to fit the stone on the floor. Jay spent several days cutting the brown grass while Amos worked on a lean-to against the back wall of the cabin and a corral for the horses. The last thing they built as snow fell from the sky was an outhouse. There had been an abundance of lodge pole pine and spruce to use for building material.

Amos had built two bunks against one of the walls and filled ticks with hay for the mattress. The stove was put in the middle of the cabin for cooking and heat. A small plank table with two stools were used for eating. A plank sideboard was along another wall for food prep and washing dishes. The stone floor worked well and prevented much of the mud caused by a dirt floor.

The door looked toward the graves and cave while the window looked down the canyon. There was a narrow loft to store the gear from the rock cut. Amos had also cut one of the logs in the loft wall so it could be pulled out to help heat escape in the summer. It could also be opened to give them a view of the canyon opening. The stream ran along the back of the cabin and across the stream was scattering of trees and the canyon wall.

Jay had commented after the building was finished that the cabin had defenses from three sides and was protected from the back by the canyon wall. The days just before heavier snow came were spent cutting wood for the winter. A stack of dry windfalls was piled alongside the cabin to be cut as needed while a good-sized pile of wood was split and piled against the cabin wall, ready for easy access. Chips from squaring the logs were used to start their fires.

The two men had a visitor named Rosco, who stayed with them during a week-long snow storm. The man was heading to Cody for the winter and had been trapping in the Crazy Woman Mountains. He and Amos talked for hours about trapping in the past and hunting grizzly or buffalo while Jay listened.

Amos had a good supply of rye and the trapper helped himself to the whiskey while a guest. Both men were glad when the storm ended and the man rode out of the canyon leading his pack horse. "That man liked to eat us out of house and home," Amos said. "Another week and he'd have drunk all my rye."

"Rosco kept looking over our stuff like he was shopping," Jay pointed out.

"That will happen after a man's been in the mountains too long," Amos admitted. "I remember coming out and meeting up with men that had more than me and a chew or coffee looked like treasure."

The day-to-day winter monotony soon set in: Tending the stock, fetching water for cooking, cutting and bringing in wood and, if the weather was fair, riding down the canyon looking for game. Amos carried books in his packs that were read and re-read. Their crude furnishings were improved by Amos.

He had built a shave horse and used a draw knife to form legs and spindles. The wood shavings made starting the morning fire much easier. Jay spent a fair amount of time with the leather scroll and the translation. He found a few words that he didn't agree with, but they made little difference in the final message.

Most conversations between the two men were civil, but Jay could be quick to anger and it did wear on Amos. He had decided that, come spring, he'd go back to Red Lodge with the man and cut him loose. Jay's knowledge of the Spanish gold would do Amos no harm. By all appearances the location of the mine was lost in time.

In February, a man leading a scrubby mustang hitched to a sledge loaded with packs came from down the valley, toward the cabin. Jay was getting an armload of wood for the stove. Hurrying to the cabin, he dropped the wood next to the stove and grabbed his .44 from the peg on the wall.

Looking up from the chair he was making, Amos asked, "What is it?"

"Someone coming from the west," Jay said before heading out the door.

The canyon ended in a pond fed by the stream behind the cabin. In a few places the edge of the canyon had sloping, tree-covered areas. It was from such an area that they had cut the pines for the cabin. Beyond the canyon was a mountainous area for hundreds of miles.

Amos joined Jay in front of the cabin. He had the Colt in his waistband. The snow was over the man's knees and his progress was slow. While Jay continued to watch the man, Amos went back into the cabin and put coffee water on to heat. If the man was friendly, he could offer him something to warm his insides.

When he went back outside, the visitor was about a 100 paces from the cabin and staring as though surprised. "Come on in," Jay called.

"You best put the revolver in your belt," Amos advised. "A man don't like to come forward looking into one of those things."

It turned out that the man had made the trip through the valley every year for some time. He followed an old Indian trail and the route cut several miles off his trip from the Yellowstone. Seeing the cabin in the canyon had almost made him think he'd taken a wrong turn. He had a sledge full of dried fish and was headed for Absarokee to trade with one of the tribes near there. For the fish he would get leather goods to sell elsewhere.

The man wore buckskins and a coonskin hat right down to the tail. He said they called him Fishin' Jon. He had always made the trip in February because it was about starving season and he got the best trade for his fish. The two men enjoyed the company and encouraged the man to stay longer, but Fishin' Jon was on a mission and needed to keep on trudging.

They did swap a knife and hatchet for some dried fish. After the man had left, Amos made a pot of fish soup using the last of the potatoes they'd gotten at the Williams farm. Both men were fair cooks, but Jay often chose to take care of the animals while Amos started the meals.

In early April, the two men got into a heated discussion, no doubt heightened by the cabin fever after the long winter. Amos woke up feeling poorly and it was his turn to buck some firewood. He had asked Jay to bring in the day's wood. It went from there to about who worked harder and such other foolishness. Finally, Jay stomped out shouting, "You pay my fines and buy me a ticket to Red Lodge! How the hell much do I have to do to settle up with you?"

It was over an hour before Jay returned to the cabin with the wood. He had a sullen look on his face and a don't-talk-to-me attitude. It was okay with Amos. He had some overcooked porridge ready for the man's meal. Putting on the wolf skin coat, the prospector went out to take care of the animals. He found that that had already been done and extra wood had been cut and stacked for the next day.

Amos sat near the lean-to on a split-log bench and chewed tobacco. He spat into the dirty snow as he tried to think about more pleasant times. His thoughts kept coming to the angry man in the cabin. The prospector realized that he hadn't paid him for the work he'd done. Unlike Hoss, who had a stake in the Spanish gold if it were ever found, he had promised Jay nothing.

As Amos sat there brooding about the mornings conflict, the wind picked up. It had the feel and smell of a change in the weather. The first telltale signs of spring. "It can't come soon enough," he muttered.

The smell of spring in the air must have been just the elixir the two men needed. The anger of the morning was forgotten and they started making plans for the trip to Red Lodge. While it was not cheerful, at least the rage was gone.

In the next week more of the temperate days continued and the snow began to melt, first dripping from the eaves. Soon a bare spot or two appeared. One afternoon Jay pointed at the pond. "Amos," he called. "Look at the water in the pond."

Water was welling up in the center and the stream leading from it had rushing water. The following day a waterfall began to cascade over the canyon wall a quarter-mile down from the cabin. It was evidence of the melting snow in the mountains and Amos figured it would be of short duration. Both men enjoyed the sight and sound of the falling water.

The hay was gone and the men had been cutting aspen branches for the animals to chew on. Jay took the horses and mule out and picketed them on bare spots to graze on last year's grass. Amos climbed into the loft and started going through his packs, looking for items that might need to be replaced or things he needed to take to Red Lodge.

Amos loved working with wood and had spent much of the winter hours improving the interior of the cabin. When the prospector wasn't using it, Jay would take the draw plane and make extra handles on the shave horse.

He sat on the edge of the loft and looked down at the cabin. He now had four sturdy chairs around a square, four-legged table, which had been planed smooth. There were cupboards above the sideboard and shelves underneath it. There were two comfortable benches for extra guests or for doing projects on. The window had shutters and a proper door swung on the iron hinges.

The prospector noticed that some of the morning light coming from between the logs toward the east. Climbing down from the loft, he took a wooden wedge and his mallet. Amos went outside to the area and tapped the caulking back between the logs. He watched the horses and mule grazing. It was a good day. Spring was here.

Jay came around the end of the cabin, carrying the Winchester. "I saw some deer feeding back a way in the canyon. I'll see if I can get close enough for a shot."

"Take one of the chestnuts. I'll move the others to another spot in a little bit," Amos said.

The prospector watched him ride away. "He is a damn good man to have with you, but mighty hard to live with," he muttered.

He hoped that Jay could knock a deer down. They'd be thin this time of year, but other than a little jerky, all their meat was gone. In a week their diet would become cold flour for every meal. Amos moved the horse and mule to another bare patch further down the canyon, and used the mallet to pound in the picket stakes.

He was walking back to the cabin when six riders came charging through the opening of the canyon. Clods of mud and snow flew from the horses' hooves as they charged ahead, led by the white-bearded man on the roan! They began shooting as soon as they spotted Amos. Their guns shattered the morning calm.

The prospector had left the cabin unarmed. Dropping the mallet, he ran toward the door. Bullets sprayed him with slivers of wood as he ducked into the cabin. He felt burning across one butt cheek. Amos grabbed his Colt and a box of shells. Jay's .44 was in the holster on its peg. This he stuffed into his waistband. His heart was pounding and he felt short of breath.

Amos dropped to the floor as he heard the riders coming. He would empty the Colt at them as they went by. The men or their horses were his objective. He had to inflict damage on the attackers. He fired as fast as he could as they went by. The attackers were firing high, expecting him to be standing. As the last rider went by he saw the man slump to the side as he clung to the saddle horn.

The snow just beyond the cabin door was spattered with blood. The prospector moved to the window while holding the .44 in his hand. The rush of the attackers had been slowed by his return fire. They were dismounting and scattering toward the back of the cabin, seeking cover. One man sat on his horse, too injured to dismount. Amos listened to the men moving as he reloaded his Colt.

He reached for the door to push it shut. A bullet struck the jamb just as it slammed closed. He pulled in the latch string. Bullets shattered the window glass, spraying shards across the stone floor. The stove pipe rattled as a bullet went through it. The shutters had a firing port in them, but it was little help because they had been open to let in the sunshine.

Amos climbed up to the loft. Pushing his gear aside, he gripped the cut log in the wall. He moved it out and had a good view toward the canyon opening. From behind the cabin came three of the men, running low. They were circling between the outhouse and the stream, planning to take positions toward the front. Their mistake was believing it was a blind side of the cabin. As the men dodged between the little house and trees, the prospector opened fire, knocking two down and forcing the third to hunker down in the icy stream.

The two men Amos had hit crawled for cover, leaving streaks of blood on the remaining snow. It would have been simple to put another bullet into them, but the prospector had no desire to kill any of these men. As far as the leader, he would not hesitate to empty his gun into that man.

Then Amos heard shooting from down in the valley. Was Jay firing at the other men or were they ambushing him? Amos nearly fell off the ladder as he hurried down from the loft. He moved to the window and carefully looked out, shielding himself as much as possible. There stood Jay with the rifle level. One of the men was standing with his hands up. Another, and the leader, lay bleeding on the ground.

Rushing to the door, Amos pushed it open and shouted, "There are three more on the other side of the cabin!"

"I see 'em," Jay called back. "It looks like they had enough."

Amos circled around to make sure that the three he had shot at were no longer a danger. The men were sitting up with their hands in the air. "We're done, mister. Don't shoot no more," one of the men begged.

None of the two had life-threatening wounds, while the third was soaked and blue with cold. The wounded men would probably be laid up for a while. Amos herded the men toward Jay. The prospector saw the first man he had shot was now lying in the slushy snow. Slight movement told Amos that he wasn't dead, at least yet.

The leader had a bad wound. He was gut-shot. Amos went over to check on the one he had shot riding by. The man had died. Two of the horses lay dying on the grass. Two others stood bleeding from their wounds. They had been hit in the hind quarters and had a good chance of survival.

The prospector went back into the cabin and came out with the leather scroll. He ripped it open in front of the dying leader. "I thought you should see what you thought was worth being killed for. It is just words of a lone surviving Spaniard named Salvador Ximenez. It was left with some gold that has been long gone. There is no map or mine."

The white-bearded man's jaw was shaking and his eyes were filled with pain. Amos wondered how many more like this would come to find the Spanish gold. He threw the leather to the ground next to the leader. It remained open, the brittle leather cracked in the center.

Then, in a flat, emotionless voice, Amos said, "Jay, would you please collect their guns and get the wagon hitched? I'll get what we need from the cabin. We'll take them back to Absarokee. They got some kind of sawbones there."

While Amos gathered the things they'd want to take with them, he heard rifle fire outside. Jay was killing the horses that wouldn't survive. When the prospector came out carrying two bags to take with him, Jay was helping the wounded into the wagon. They had already loaded the dead man and the gut-shot leader.

Walking near the side of the wagon, Amos searched the wounded leader and found a leather wallet. Opening it, he saw the folded map given to the man by Billy Bob. The prospector removed it and tossed the wallet back into the wagon. He then threw in the bags and a couple of old shirts for them to tear into strips for bandages.

It bothered him when one of the men put a bag under the leader's head, to try and make him more comfortable, but he chose not to say anything. The saddles were stripped from the dead horses and put into the wagon along with blanket rolls and saddle bags.

"If you have any weapons in the bags, boys, don't touch them. We'll kill you and leave you to the coyotes," Amos warned them.

The prospector was mad. Having to kill good horses went against his principles. He also figured that killing men should be avoided. He had had no choice but to do what he had done to stop the attack. The fine-looking roan was one of the horses that had to be put down.

The cabin was closed up and Jay drove the wagon through the opening of the canyon. Four of the horses were tied to the back of the wagon, the two wounded ones limping as they walked. Amos knew that soon the snow would melt and the spring rains would wash away sign of the fight. Coyotes and wolves would take care of the dead horses.

It was late morning and they would be in Absarokee sometime after midnight. The prospector told Jay that they would be traveling straight through. They gave the men in the wagon canteens of water and let them take care of each other.

A cold rain began to fall after dark. Amos and Jay put on slickers and the men in the wagon huddled under blankets. Moans were heard every time the wagon lurched. The prospector wished the town was closer. While the men probably deserved the abuse of the trip, he wanted to be rid of them as soon as he could.

As they neared Absarokee they could see the lights of the saloon. It was the only building that showed any life. Amos' memory flashed back to the Spaniard's leather letter lying in the mud and snow near the cabin. It was just as well. He had decided that it was cursed. All it had brought him was bad luck.

Amos sat on the mule, his bottom stinging, while Jay jumped off the wagon and went into the saloon to get directions to the doc's. He came out with a portly man in a black coat and baggy pants. "This here's the doctor," Jay told the prospector. They followed the doc a short distance down the street to his office.

The men in the wagon were shivering with the cold as they carried their leader into the doctor's. The man had lost consciousness or was dead. Amos didn't know which and did not care. It was obvious the doctor had had more than a little to drink, as he waved his arms and staggered while herding the men into his office.

Amos followed them in while Jay stayed with the horses. The doc took a look at the leader, shook his head and crossed himself. "He is beyond help. I'll check him last."

Two of the men were just suffering from the cold. The doctor expertly took care of the other two wounded men, despite his condition. The door opened and a rough-looking man with a badge came in. "I'm Sheriff Packer. Can someone tell me what happened here?"

Amos replied, "I can, sheriff." He commenced to relate the facts of the attack while the lawman listened with a furrowed brow.

When the prospector finished, the lawman turned to the others. "Is that how it happened?"

The other exhausted men nodded their agreement. One added that they had been paid by the gut-shot man to help him drive those living in the cabin out of the canyon.

Sheriff Packer glanced at the leader. "It looks like justice has been served. The bad guy is dying." He looked at the other men and said, "You'll have until noon tomorrow to be out of Absarokee." He then looked at Amos. "That is, unless you would like to press charges."

"Nope," the prospector said. "I agree, justice has been served."

Amos headed for the door and the lawman stopped him. "Write up a little something on this and drop it at my office just in case anyone should be asking questions." Then he asked, "Did you know you got blood all down your ass?"

"No, no I didn't," Amos replied.

The doctor brought him to the back of the office. "I think you been shot. Drop your pants."

Amos winced when the doctor swabbed his butt cheek with carbolic. "Damn, that hurts."

"The wound ain't too bad, but you're going to be riding light for a while."

Once the bandage was on, the prospector asked one more favor. "There are two horses out there that was shot. Would you see if there's anything you can do for them?"

The doctor hesitated and Amos placed a gold eagle on his table. "Will this cover it?"

Nodding, the doc said, "I'll see what I can do."

Amos left the office and saw that Jay had the ruffians' horses tied to the rail. He asked Amos, "What did the lawman and doc have to say?"

"They said I got shot in the ass," Amos replied. "Let's find a bottle and a place to sleep."

CHAPTER TWELVE

The two men spent the next day in Absarokee. Amos had several things he wanted to do, including dropping off the note to the lawman, while Jay hung around the livery visiting with the hostler. The weather had cleared overnight and the men who had attacked them were gone. The leader was close to death, plus there was the man Amos had killed. The lawman had taken one of the ruffians' horses to pay for the two burials.

The two men had taken rooms in the back of the saloon. While the prospector and Jay were having supper at the saloon, Amos took to talking with one of the ladies working there. Once she found out he'd been shot in the butt, she brought him a pillow to sit on. He slipped a coin into her bosom as a thank you.

Jay watched Amos and finally said, "Don't you ever get tired of chasing these saloon whores? You seem to have an endless supply of money while I ain't seen a penny."

Amos had had enough to drink to ease the pain in his buttocks and was feeling philosophical. He looked at the dark-eyed man and replied, "I hope to never stop chasing these beautiful woman, and when it comes to money, I share what I have with those that need it, and I hope to die broke."

Jay snorted and pushed his glass away. "I've had enough of your deep thinking. I am going to bed."

The prospector sat in the saloon, enjoying the glow of the rye. The pillow-supplying woman came back and shared a drink with him. "I see your friend has given up for the night."

"Yes," Amos told her. "He's had a couple of tough days."

"Were your days rough?" she whispered.

"I was there. I got shot, remember," the prospector answered.

Leaning a little closer, she nuzzled his ear and said, "Spend the night with me and you will forget all about the rough days, and even your wounded bottom."

* * *

The sun was bright in the brisk spring sky when Amos walked out of the saloon. He headed toward the livery and found Jay brushing the chestnuts. "Did you sleep well?" he asked the man.

"Not much," Jay said, his eyes on his work.

"I figure we'll leave for Red Lodge first thing tomorrow," Amos informed Jay.

"I won't be going with you," the dark-eyed man said.

"You won't?" Amos replied, surprised by the remark. "What are you going to do?"

"It shouldn't matter to you," Jay snapped, looking at the prospector.

"Take it easy now," Amos cautioned. "I was just asking. You're free to do as you please."

"I killed a man for you," he said, staring at the horse. "Staying with you won't help *that* memory, and how many other men will come after you that will need killing?"

"I didn't mean for that to happen," Amos said. "I didn't need you to come with me for protection. That just happened and I had no control of the situation. I have a heart problem and the doc in Casper wanted me to have someone with me in the mountains."

Dead silence followed the last statement. Jay stood holding the currycomb, staring at Amos. Realizing what the prospector had told him, Jay finally shouted, "I spent the winter in that God-forsaken canyon building a cabin for you and now you tell me your dying!" Turning back to the horse, he hissed, "What a waste."

"I am sorry you feel that way," Amos said, controlling his tone. "I ain't dying tomorrow and expect to live in the cabin for some years. I . . . I appreciate the help you gave me."

Without waiting for a response, Amos walked away, afraid that the discussion could quickly go south. The prospector walked back to the saloon and asked the sleepy bartender for some paper and a pencil. He jotted down a few words and went to put it into his pocket. He felt the folded map. Taking it out, he ripped it into small pieces and threw it into the spittoon.

He looked again at what he'd written and then put the paper into his pocket. Satisfied, he nodded and headed back outside. His heart was pounding and he felt a bit lightheaded. Grabbing the hitching rail, he waited for things to calm down. "Take it easy, old man. You don't want to die today," he murmured.

Feeling more settled, Amos continued back to the livery. Jay was coming out from putting the horse away. Reaching into his pocket, the prospector fished out the paper. He handed it to the dark-eyed man.

"What's this?" Jay asked.

"It is ownership papers for the team and wagon," Amos replied. "I feel I owe you that much, maybe more." He then reached in his pocket and took out a double eagle. This he placed into the man's hand.

Staring at the paper and coin, Jay asked, "You think this makes us even?"

"I wish it was more," the prospector said. "But that's all I got right now. If you don't want the team and wagon, sell them. The money, you can use. I think you can make a good living hauling supplies to the mines."

Feeling his heart starting to pound again, Amos turned and walked into the livery and started saddling the mule. It was time to leave and find places with happier people. When he led the mule back into the sunshine, Jay was gone. Amos tied the mule in front of the saloon and went to his room. He looked at the gear he had brought from the canyon. Little of it seemed important now. He stuffed a few things into his saddlebag and walked back into the saloon carrying them, his rifle, and his bedroll.

"I'll be on my way," the prospector said, tossing a few coins onto the bar. "I left some stuff in the room. Could you move it to Jay Smith's?"

There. He was done with the dark-eyed man. Shortly, Amos was riding out of town looking forward to a stop at the Williams farm. He would have gotten her and the kids something, but he was getting short of money. On this stop, his smile would have to do. Once he got to Red Lodge, his first stop would be the bank.

* * *

After a visit with Lucia and the kids, he had a long ride to Red Lodge and Amos was feeling much more relaxed. He looked forward to seeing Goldie and Hoss. He also wanted to visit the doctor. Amos felt that he was getting tired too easily and was a little concerned.

As he walked into Goldie's Saloon the blond owner's eyes lit up and she hurried to meet him. "It's been months since you left. I was worried you'd never come back."

"Nothing could keep me from coming back," Amos assured her.

Ted place a bottle of rye and cognac at the table. Goldie poured a glass of each and toasted his return. "You want me to put the leather thing in my safe?"

"That's not necessary," he told her. "It's lying somewhere in the mountains rotting right now. It had brought me nothing but bad luck."

"Well, you stay here and I'll bring you good luck," she replied with a mischievous grin. "That is, except for at the Faro table. That is where I draw the line."

It was two days before Amos had a chance to look Hoss up. His friend invited him to stay for supper. The prospector noticed that his wife was showing. "Has Sara been eating too good or are you going to be a father?"

Without giving Hoss a chance to answer, Sara proudly said, "The baby is due this fall."

After supper the evening was filled with laughter and music. It turned out that Hoss' wife played the piano and regaled them with several songs. It was dark when Hoss and Amos stepped outside to have a chew. The houses in the neighborhood were rather close, and they could hear several conversations and one rather loud discussion.

"How are things in the mine?" the prospector asked.

"It's killing me," Hoss replied.

"I wish the gold mine had worked out," Amos said.

"You never found any gold? Not even in the stream that runs through the canyon?" his friend inquired.

"You know, I never even dipped a pan in the stream. Things kept me too busy or distracted." Amos replied. He then told Hoss about his winter, the difficulty he'd had with Jay and about the attack on the cabin. The furthest thing from his mind had been looking for gold.

"Jay is a good man," Hoss said. "He is just a little confused. Bad things happened years ago and he never talks of them."

"Lucia Williams asked about you," Amos told him.

They continued to make small talk for the next couple of hours and finally Amos headed back to the saloon. Hoss told him that he had a day off coming soon and wanted to spend more time catching up.

The evening was cool and the stoves were keeping the homes warm. The smell of the burning coal was strong as Amos weaved his way through the streets on his way back to Goldie's.

Amos realized that he longed to be back in the canyon. Just himself and the mountains. There were miles of streams he could pan in. With luck he could find enough color to pay for next winter's groceries. As he walked, he started making plans for the return trip. He wouldn't tell Goldie until just before he left. He feared that her wily ways would convince him not to go.

The next morning Amos went to Doc Jennings. The man seemed pleased to see the prospector, maybe he'd never expected to see him again. Amos told him about the pounding he was getting in his chest.

"Those are the palpitations I told you about," the young doctor reminded him. "When you overstress your body you can expect that."

The doc poked and prodded Amos. He listened to his heart and breathing. He commented on the healing wound on his buttocks. Overall, the doctor did not think that much had changed. The lungs even sounded a bit better. Most likely it was just that Amos was aware of the condition.

"Are you saying it's in my head?" the prospector asked.

"No, it is in your heart, but your head can affect the heart," Doc Jennings explained.

Once the prospector was dressed, Amos said, "I got a nice, quiet cabin in a canyon up in the mountains. I plan to move there."

"Alone?" the doc asked.

"I would like to take a lady friend along, but I don't think that will happen," Amos told him. "More than likely I will be alone."

"How far to the nearest town?" the young doctor asked.

"Maybe eight hours," Amos replied.

The doctor put a few things away before he spoke. "I would only ask that if you start feeling weak or if normal movements become difficult, please ride into town and get help."

Smiling at the concerned Doc Jennings, Amos assured him, "In that case, I will ride to town."

As Amos was brushing his mule at the livery and the hostler, Kelly was still complaining about being taken advantage of in the chestnut horse's sale. Spurring the man's frustration, the smiling prospector asked, "Did I tell you how well the wagon worked out?".

"Damn bad deal," the hostler said, and then went into a coughing fit.

Amos heard someone walk up behind him. Turning, he looked into the smiling face of his friend. "What brings you here today, partner? Aren't you supposed to be working?" the prospector asked.

"I quit the mine," Hoss said.

"Does Sara know this?" he asked.

"I'd thought I should wait until supper to tell her," his friend told him.

Amos kept brushing the mule. "Damn hard to get all this winter hair off the animal."

Hoss picked up a currycomb and started working on the other side. The two men brushed for a half-hour without saying another word. Finally, they were done and stepped back to admire their work. The mule stood surrounded by clumps of hair on the hay-covered, wooden floor.

"Do you want to go to the café for some coffee?" Amos asked.

"Can't do that," Hoss confided. "My wife is apt to stop by there herself."

"Hey Kelly," Amos called out. "Put on a pot of coffee. We got company."

The two men hid out in the livery all afternoon, enjoying each other's company. Kelly even joined in on some of the conversation. Talk of the chestnut horses was avoided. The shift change whistle went off and Hoss stood up. "It's time for me to head home. Sara will be expecting me."

"You can put off telling her until payday if you come here each day," Amos suggested.

"I am a married man, and don't intend to be a dead married man," Hoss replied.

His friend started out of the livery and then turned back. "I would like to make a trip to the canyon with you. Maybe stay two months. Sara can go to her cousin's."

"I don't want to cause trouble between you and your wife, taking you away like that," Amos cautioned him.

"It wouldn't be no trouble. She likes you and I'd tell her about your health," Hoss said. "It wouldn't be no lie."

"I hadn't decided when I was leaving, but it could be anytime," Amos told him.

"I will be ready when you are, partner," Hoss replied, a smile creasing his cheeks.

Sitting on a feed sack, Amos watched Hoss walk away. It wasn't like a man who was about to face an angry wife, but rather a man who was anxious to share news with his bride. Suddenly, Amos thought about his own situation. He had to tell Goldie.

Walking back to the saloon, Amos made his decision. They would leave on the coming Monday. That would give Hoss a chance to take his wife to church and Amos could join them. He had enjoyed the preacher's sermon at the wedding and looked forward to another.

While Hoss hadn't expected too much trouble with Sara, it was a different story for Amos with Goldie. She had taken quite the shine to the prospector and had hoped she would have the summer to convince him to move to Red Lodge.

Smashing a glass on the table when he told her was unexpected. Normally the blond owner was much more in control. Goldie left him sitting among the glass shards while she stomped off to her room. Amos carefully cleared the glass pieces away with the edge of his hand. Satisfied, he poured himself another shot of rye.

Ted came over to clean up the table. "I haven't seen her that mad since the Faro dealer she fell for took a job in Virginia City."

Unsure if he should remain, Amos asked Ted, "How long does the anger last? I got things in her room. Maybe I should just forget them."

"Just give her a little while and enjoy your rye," Ted said. "If you see your stuff landing on the street, you know it's time to leave. Otherwise, she'll be back after a cry and a bit to fix her makeup."

It was an hour before Goldie came back to the table, "I want to apologize for making such a scene. I admit I was taken off guard by your leaving so soon."

"I should have probably found a better way to tell you. Maybe a note from far away."

Goldie shoved him, "You are . . . you are something else."

Sunday's sermon was everything Amos had hoped for. It had him shouting amen with the rest of the congregation. Sara made a special meal after church and had the preacher join them. It turned out the man had been a mountain man in his youth and he and Amos had much to talk about. The preacher had gotten religion facing down a grizzly.

"I told the lord that if he got me out of that fix I would spend the rest of my life doing his work."

Later the two men stepped outside. Amos offered him a chew. The preacher thanked the prospector and shoved it into his cheek. "Some folk don't abide chewing, but I figure the lord will overlook an occasional chaw."

Amos had the mule ready to ride at sunrise. A sleepy Goldie stood outside the saloon and grumbled, "I don't know why you men have to leave so early. I would look much better after a few more hours sleep. Maybe I could even change your mind."

"Nothing is as pretty as you in the morning," he complimented her.

"Except those damn mountains," she said, pouting.

Hoss rode up on his bay. His eyes were bright with anticipation of the coming trip. Goldie gave Amos one more hug before heading back into the saloon and her bed. Hoss watched as Amos climbed stiffly onto the mule.

Noticing his friend watching, Amos told him, "Gunshot wound in the butt got me moving slow."

"Ya, it's the wound. Let's go!" Hoss said eagerly, as they trotted the animals out of Red Lodge.

Once they were out of sight of the town Hoss said, "I got to thank you."

"Why is that?" Amos asked.

"The work in the mine would have killed me. Seeing you gave me the nerve to quit. Sara didn't seem to mind too much. She had seen me coughing up the black dust more than once," he confided in his friend.

"You may not be as thankful when we get there," Amos told his partner. "Billy Bob made sure folks in Virginia City knew about the Spanish mine, so we can't be sure someone won't come and try and take it. Even though we know there isn't any map showing its location."

"At least I will be able to defend myself in the mountains. Under them, there's no defense. Coal dust will kill you for sure." Hoss said.

CHAPTER THIRTEEN

The sky was blue with puffy clouds, and grass was getting green on the rolling hills, making travel a pleasure. Deer and antelope were plentiful and even a few buffalo were seen. It was dusk when they reached Rosebud Creek. The two men stumbled around setting up their camp. "It's almost like someone added more rocks," Amos said, laughing.

They decided to make a meal from some of the cornbread Hoss' wife had sent with him. The prospector added a little rye to the coffee to give it a bite. Amos banked the fire and the two men turned in early. They were both tired from the time spent saying goodbye to their ladies the night before.

The clear sky gave the promise of another nice day as they crawled out of their blankets. Amos went into the trees to relieve himself. Hoss had the fire started by the time he got back. "My turn next," he said. "You put on the coffee."

After finishing off the corn bread, Hoss washed the coffee pot in the stream. Amos was getting the bay and mule saddled. "Did you realize that this stream has trout in it?" Hoss asked.

"I sure did," Amos informed him. "Jay caught us a meal on the last trip."

"Why didn't you tell me?" Hoss complained. "Fresh-caught trout and cornbread would have been a meal from heaven."

With the animals ready, the two men continued on, with the Williams farm as their next destination. Suddenly Amos held up his hand, motioning to stop. Two black-tailed jack rabbits were nibbling on the new grass about 50 feet away. The men pulled their revolvers and at Amos' signal they fired.

The two rabbits kicked briefly and were still. The prospector slid off the mule and hurried to get the game. "They'll make a fine meal at Lucia's," the prospector replied, holding the rabbits high to admire.

"Not so fast, Amos," Hoss said. "Let me see them." After a quick inspection he told the prospector, "Mine's a head shot, you hit the neck. You'll be doing the cleaning."

"How do you know I wasn't shooting at the neck?" Amos replied, defending his accuracy. Then the bearded prospector laughed, "Your right, I'll clean them."

The men were laughing and kidding each other as they weaved through the trees, approaching the Williams farm. Amos pulled up. The four-acre field was plowed and planted. He also saw that the additional two acres had been cleared and was ready to plow.

Then he noticed Jay's wagon near the cabin. He could hear hammering from beyond the barn. "I think your friend is here," he told Hoss.

They rode across the new field, stopping at the barn. Tying the animals to the corral, the two men walked around the building. Lucia and Chip were holding a wall up as Jay nailed the corners, joining the two walls. Elly was busy building a stick house for her rag doll.

Chip saw them first. He yelled a welcome as he continued to do his share to keep the wall standing. Jay looked up and waved. Swinging down, he took a pole and used it to support the far end of the new wall.

The three of them pulled off their work gloves and headed toward Amos and Hoss, led by Mrs. Williams. Something was different. Then Amos noticed what it was. Jay had shaved his moustache.

"I didn't expect to see you until fall," she said to Amos.

"I got to thinking about the cabin in the canyon and had a hankering to get back," Amos told her.

Jay was happy to see Hoss and took him over to the new building to show him what they'd completed. Chip shadowed the two men, wanting to be one of the guys.

"I see you've got some help," Amos told her.

"Help?" she said, smiling. "Jay has been more than help. He's been a godsend. We had fallen behind getting things done and I felt about to give up. Like a miracle, he showed up one morning with his wagon and pitched in, getting us out of trouble."

"Was the moustache your idea?" he inquired.

She glanced back at Jay. The lines next to her eyes crinkled as she smiled. "It had just a bit of gray in it, and I mentioned he'd look younger without the moustache. The next morning it was gone. Neither of us have spoken of it since."

"The two acres looks ready to plant," Amos told her.

"I didn't have enough seed potatoes to plant the new field," Lucia explained, "so I'll leave it lay fallow this year. With a good crop, it'll be in potatoes next year."

The two of them walked toward the cabin with Elly holding her hand. Amos took the rabbits hanging on his saddle horn. "We come with something to put on the table," he said.

"That will work out well," she said. "We've been busy and I was wondering what to do for supper. I will make a nice rabbit pie."

"If it is as good as your pigeon pie, it will be something to look forward to." Then Amos changed the subject. "How has Jay been?" he asked. "I mean, he showed a lot of anger over the winter. Have you seen that in him?"

"He talked of the winter in the cabin, but didn't have anything bad to say," she told him with surprise on her face. "He has been very happy working on the farm. It has been for just a short time, but each day he wakes up with a smile and ready to go."

"I am glad to hear that," Amos said. "Maybe it was living in the small cabin all winter that made little things seem bigger to me."

Satisfied with his explanation, she smiled and said, "Get those rabbits cleaned and I'll put on some coffee and get some crust going."

Amos and Hoss stayed a week at the farm, helping with the spring work. The prospector helped Mrs. Williams finish putting a vegetable garden into the corner of the new field. They also dug some parsnips and horseradish from the prior year. "I don't believe I've had a parsnip since leaving Maine," Amos recalled.

Jay spent most of his time with Hoss. Chip was always in tow with them, even when watching his sister. Lucia and Amos took charge of the meals and stepped in to help finish the sorting shed when necessary. After supper Amos would sit alone on the porch, watching the sun go down and listen to the goings-on around him. Mrs. Williams sure made a fine home.

Jay and Amos took the two wagons to Absarokee for lumber to finish the roof of the shed. The two men stopped in the saloon for a drink and some lunch. For reasons Amos couldn't explain, Jay was a different man than he'd been over the winter, and it was more than just the lack of a moustache. The prospector was pleased with the change and could only attribute it to the influence of Lucia and his mentoring Chip.

Leaning on the bar, Amos watched as the bartender poured his rye. He raised a glass to Jay and suddenly his eyes widened. Amos saw Jay draw his revolver and fire. The prospector threw himself clear, the bullet barely missing him. Stumbling, Amos landed sitting on the floor, staring up in wonder.

Then what had happened became clear. When he and Jay had come into the saloon, they hadn't noticed the men playing cards. Ace now stood near a table, stunned as he stared at his shattered hand, blood spraying from severed blood vessels. "The son-of-a-bitch tried to back shoot you," Jay said as he holstered his revolver and helped the prospector up.

"I . . . I thought you were shooting at me." Amos said, obviously shaken.

"He was behind you and all I saw was the derringer in his hand," Jay replied.

"Well then, that was damn good shooting," Amos replied as he watched the bartender wrap a towel around the card shark's hand, who sat wide-eyed in a chair.

There was a bang on the batwing doors and Sheriff Packer burst in, his guns drawn. "Who the hell is shooting in here?" he demanded.

The bartender spoke up, "Ace here tried to back shoot the old man. His friend here did the shooting and foiled his plan."

Amos wanted to ask, *Who's the old man your talking about?* but instead said, "That's how it happened. I'd been deader than hell if it weren't for Jay's quick action."

With the familiar furrowed brow, the lawman said, "Seems you two bring trouble to this town every time you visit." Then, to Ace, he said, "Shooting men is illegal and especially if it's in the back. Come with me to the doc's, then you'll sit in jail until the circuit judge comes in two weeks."

Ace's face was pale and he seemed unable to comprehend what had happened. Sheriff Packer pulled him to his feet and pushed him along through the batwings. The lawman called back as he left. "Stop by the office. I'll need your statements unless you want to hang around for the trial."

The bartender came back around the bar and poured another rye, including a drink for himself, "I guess Ace's days of dealing from the bottom are over," he said, raising his glass, adding, "Let him be damned."

The bartender went out back to get the men some sliced meat and bread. Amos picked up the bottle and noticed that his hand was shaking. The two of them sat at a table that was spared from the spraying blood. "Damn glad you didn't decide to let the bastard shoot me."

Jay smiled, but the smile left some question in Amos' mind. "I couldn't let him shoot you," the dark-eyed man explained. "I got something to tell you."

After a moment of silence, Amos asked, "And that something is what?"

"You threw the leather scroll on the ground and didn't appear to be going back after it. I tossed it under the wagon seat before we left the cabin," Jay said.

"And that is what you had to tell me?" Amos asked, confused.

"No, there is more," Jay continued. "When you ripped it open, you broke the leather in a couple places. Some of the writing that couldn't be read before can now be seen."

Lowering his voice, Amos said, "I suppose you're going to tell me it gave directions to the mine."

Shaking his head, Jay replied, "No, it didn't do that, but it does give . . . maybe a clue."

"Where is this scroll now?" Amos asked.

"With my stuff back in the barn."

The prospector nodded. "Okay. When we get back, I'll get my translated copy and you tell me what should be added to it. We'll see if it makes any sense."

The bartender placed two plates onto the table with cold lamb and bread. There was a gob of soft butter next to the bread. Amos handed him some coins to cover the meal and the bottle. He invited the bartender to sit and have another drink with them.

During the ride back with the wagons loaded with lumber, Amos' mind was racing. He wished he'd have asked Jay to tell him what else was written on the leather. He cautioned himself not to get his hopes up too high. It could just be another dead end, and as Jay had said, it was just another clue.

Everyone helped unload the wagons while Jay told about the shooting in the saloon. "You drew and shot the gun out of his hand?" Chip asked.

"I drew and shot at the only target I had," Jay explained. "It was just good fortune I hit what I was aiming at."

"I see you have powder burns on your coat," Hoss observed.

Looking down, Amos exclaimed, "Really!" Then he looked up at the smiling Jay.

They plan was to work on the shed roof the next day. It would be higher in the middle to allow a wagon through. Each side had a wing for sorting and storing the potatoes before taking them to market. Lucia had a large root cellar under the cabin to keep next year's seed potatoes and those for personal use.

That evening, after supper, the three men went outside to smoke and chew. Chip was told that he could not join them and that he was to stay and help his mother and Elly clean up after the meal. They stopped near a stump on the newly cleared land. It had two logs next to it and had been used for resting and eating midday meals.

Hoss set a lantern onto the stump and the men sat huddled around the light.

Jay set down the leather scroll that now laid open. His face was expressionless in the glow of his cigarette as he fished a piece of paper out of his pocket.

He pointed to an area where the leather had collapsed during its long storage in the cave. "This is the area that couldn't be seen before. It was only a couple lines of writing," Jay explained.

Holding the lantern closer to the leather, Amos looked at the Spanish writing. He folded it together and then opened it. "With the leather in a tube Jose wouldn't have been able to make out those lines, Hoss." Then he looked at Jay. "You were able to read them and know what they say?"

"I had to guess at a word or two but, right after 'The ground shook and the mine flooded', I was able to read:

"The men working had no chance. Two days later their bodies were floating on the new pond. The falls that we got water from stopped flowing. The water coming from the mine is good."

Jay continued, "Then it read: '3 men drowned leaving only 4 of us to bring back the gold', which you already knew."

Hoss shook his head, "It doesn't mean anything more to me. We knew the mine flooded, but we don't know where it is or if it is still flooded. Remember, it was 100 years ago that this was written."

Amos was filled with excitement and was having a hard time sitting still. "We . . . we saw the falls this spring!"

"That's what I was thinking," Jay said. "There must be some kind of river above the canyon wall. It could have started flowing into the mine when the earth shook. Our pond isn't spring-fed. It's the one the Spaniard is talking about. When the snow melts, there is too much water to flow through the mine and it takes the original route to the falls."

"I am still confused," Hoss responded. "You say there was a water falls?"

Amos told him about the thaw, the water welling in the pond and their seeing the falls over the canyon wall. "Most of the others in the expedition died away from the canyon and were lost, or would have been buried where they were killed. Three are buried in the canyon. They must have been the ones that drowned."

"If it could only be that easy," Hoss said. Then he shook his head. "If the mine is under the pond, it is beyond our reach."

"We'll go to Virginia City and buy a steam driven pump to empty the pond," Amos replied.

"I know where there's a wagon we could use," Jay said, chuckling.

"And what do we use to buy this pump?" Hoss reminded the two men.

The three men sat in silence. Amos knew that he had enough in the Cheyenne bank, but that was not to be touched. He also had money in Red Lodge. For years he had saved any extra for harder times in the future. The cost of a pump was more than he had in that account. But the prospector had another thought.

"That pond we believe covered the mine has been flooding each spring for 100 years," Amos pointed out. "I am willing to bet there's a good amount of gold in the sands along the stream."

The two men's eyes grew large. "You're right," Hoss said, "and if the gold is in the sand, it will also prove that the mine is under the pond."

"There is one other thing," Amos said, addressing Hoss. "You and I are partners. I feel it's only fair if we take Jay in for an equal share of whatever we find."

His friend looked at him, his mouth half-open. "I . . . I thought we already had."

"That's good enough for me," the prospector said. "Jay, you are now an official partner in the lost Spanish mine search."

A confused look came on Jay's face. "I figured I already was because I helped find the mine. But, I am glad to hear it is official."

"And," Hoss pointed out, "the vote was undisputed."

Jay and Hoss said their good nights to Lucia before heading for the barn. Amos sat in the dark near the stump with a chew. There was the sound of something digging nearby and the prospector spat in that direction. The digging continued.

He was excited, finally being so close to a big strike. He had spent his life in search of the mother lode and had only made enough to keep him in rye and groceries, with a little to spare. He wondered what he would do differently if they actually found the mine. One other thought came to him. The Spanish mine could be nearly played out. He looked at the star-studded sky. The Lord wouldn't do that to him.

The shed was completed, and the crop was in, so the Williams family was in good shape for the summer. Now, success depended on the weather. Lucia and Chip were in the fields early the day the three men were leaving. They were busy with the hoes, getting after the weeds. Elly ran along the rows singing and pulling an occasional weed.

Mrs. Williams stopped for a moment when the men pulled up. "I would like to thank you for your hospitality," Amos told her.

"I should thank you for the help," she said. "Especially you, Jay. I hope you come back this way."

They waved to the family and Jay led with the wagon as the men rode north. Amos figured that her last words were meant mostly for Jay. They would make a nice couple, he thought. If the three of them should strike it rich, it is unlikely that the dark-eyed man would want to settle down to farming when he could afford to do whatever he wanted.

They stayed clear of Absarokee, not wanting to bring attention to their return trip to the canyon. Everywhere there were rumors about the lost Spanish mine. Amos would have liked to have gotten some additional mining equipment such as a cradle, more picks and shovels, extra pans, candles, some drill rod, fuse and blasting powder. Anyone purchasing these items would be followed to the ends of the earth.

Amos already had four pans, a pick and two shovels in the canyon. The 12-inch diameter pans stacked together and were easy to pack, while picks and shovels were not. The prospector could build a cradle, but that would take time. Three good men with pans could go through a lot of stream bottom and if the gold was found, a long board-sluice could be built. Amos figured that would be in the distant future.

If it was found and they had enough gold, it would pay for the steam engine and pump. Amos knew that they would not be able to empty the pond, but if they could just lower the level and proved it was the Spanish mine, then they could use blasting powder to collapse the mine and stop the flow. There should be rich, gold-bearing dirt on the bottom of the pond. The prospector also knew that it was seldom that only one spot contained gold. There should be other places in the canyon. It would take one step at a time.

As they rode into the canyon, Amos' faulty heart almost stopped. There was smoke coming from the cabin stove pipe! Someone had moved in!

"Looks like we got visitors," Hoss said.

Glaring at the cabin, Jay proclaimed, "We built that cabin. Ain't nobody going to force us out."

Hoss and Amos rode toward the occupied building. Jay jumped off the wagon with his .44 in his hand and ran toward the back of the cabin with intentions to work his way to the far front. Amos saw two horses in the corral. He had seen them somewhere before.

He thought back, trying to remember if they'd been ridden by the ruffians or someone he'd seen in Virginia City, Absarokee or even Red Lodge. Swinging off the mule, he moved to the front edge of the cabin. He could see Jay poised at the other end.

Suddenly, Amos had a flash of memory. "Rosco. Hey, Rosco. Are you in there?"

The door swung open. "Is that you Amos?"

The hungry trapper from last winter had returned. Putting their guns away, Amos and Jay followed him into the cabin. Several packages of their staples had been opened and left out. The blankets that had been left neatly folded on the bunks lay in a disheveled heap. He had even been in the loft and had gone through items left there.

"Did you find the rye?" Amos asked.

The trapper's face flushed. "You could tell I looked?"

Behind Jay, Hoss stepped in. "It looks like you've kind of moved right in."

"I got to be heading north tomorrow," Rosco replied. "I'm already late meeting my partner in the Crazys."

"You're welcome to stay in the lean-to tonight," Jay told him, setting some boundaries. "I got a bottle in the wagon that will help you get to sleep."

The three men were kept busy putting the cabin back together and unpacking the supplies from the wagon. Rosco watched while sitting at the table. His eyes followed every item being unpacked. Parts were also brought for a third bunk.

"I didn't see no bottle," the trapper complained.

"We left it in the lean-to for you," Hoss informed him.

Rosco sat fidgeting for a bit and then got up. "I got to check on my horses."

"Do you trust him out there with the rye?" Amos asked.

Smiling, Jay said, "It's just one bottle. The box of rye came in with the bunk parts."

While Amos started their supper, Jay and Hoss erected the bunk and hid the case out of sight under it. They had no hay to fill the ticks, so Jay went out to cut some evergreen boughs. They would give them some comfort and make the cabin smell fresh. The dark-eyed man saw Rosco sitting, nursing the bottle in the lean-to, his horses unattended.

The trapper was in no shape to join them for supper. The men watered his horses while taking care of their own animals. When they awoke the next morning, Rosco and his animals were gone. Hoss discovered this and told the others.

Amos replied, "It saved us some food and he may have stayed until we came up with some more rye."

CHAPTER FOURTEEN

While they ate the pancakes Amos had made, Hoss sat at the table looking around the small cabin. "You two did a fine job here. A proper stone floor, squared logs, sturdy furniture. It sure is mighty home-like."

"Jay was the stone cutter, we both squared logs and it was a long winter, so there was plenty of time to make chairs, the table and such," Amos told him.

"Fixing the place up kept us busy," Jay said. "Little did we know we were so close to a fortune in gold."

"I've never panned for gold," Hoss admitted. "Is there much to it?"

"It can be tough on the back and knees, but if the color is good, it helps you forget the pain," Amos said. "I'll show you how to pan today. It will take time before you stop washing your profits out with the sand and dirt. You needn't worry though. We'll get that back when we build the board sluice."

While his partners cleaned up the breakfast dishes, Amos climbed into the loft. The air was hot from the cookstove, so he pulled the log out to get a breeze. Rosco had been thorough in his search of the packs. The neatly packed items had been stuffed back in a haphazard way.

He handed the two shovels and a pick down to Jay. Amos then got out a pick that had no handle. He would make one for it later that night. Amos wished that he had some quicksilver to capture the smaller flakes and dust, but that could also come later when they went to get the pump.

Hoss returned from watering the animals and had made a discovery. "You know the fire pit and shelf near the pond? I believe the pit was where they smelted the gold. It has a groove on one side that could have been fitted with a bellows. The shelf was probably used for breaking down the rock to help get the high-grade out of it."

Like a puzzle that was scattered about, the pieces were coming together. Amos had to fight down the urge to shout to the heavens with joy. He had to remind himself of all the times he had thought he'd found the mother lode only to come away with barely enough for a good drunk. The difference of this find was that gold had been taken out. While heading for the outhouse, before starting work, he wondered, how much gold was left.

The men started panning just downstream from the pond. The pan had a small flat center and side tapered to the outer edge. The prospector squatted next to the water and scraped up some gravel and water from a ridge in the stream. He then showed the men how he swirled the contents, spilling some, allowing the water to take the lighter dirt partials out. Amos then picked out the larger pebbles, checking each and then dipped a little more water into the pan. Again, he swirled the water, allowing it to take out more of the sand and dirt.

This was repeated a couple more times before the prospector inspected what remained. His heart raced as he saw color in the pan. "You see them bits of gold?" he asked his partners.

"It seems like a lot of rinsing for a few bits of gold," Jay said. Hoss nodded in agreement.

"Panning is a slow process," Amos told them. "In a 10-hour day you can only expect to do 35 to 40 pans. Most of the time you'll just find a few particles which are of little value alone, but as these bits are collected with the occasional nugget, they do add up."

"Well, we got a whole lot of dirt to wash in this stream, so we may as well get started," Jay concluded.

"Look for any kind of riffle or ridge that could collect the heavier gold," Amos advised them. "If you find color, keep working the area until it stops. Try going a little deeper in the gravel before you move."

Soon the three men were intent on their panning. Jay went through several pans of gravel before he finally exclaimed that he'd had success. "Remember," Amos reminded them, "if you swirl too fast you'll wash the good out with the bad."

By midday the men had worked less than 30 feet of the long stream flowing down the valley. Between the three men, they had just under an ounce of gold, with Amos having the most success. The two men, new to panning, complained about their backs as they headed for the cabin. Amos, in turn, was beaming.

"At this rate we'll be working most of the summer to find enough gold to purchase the engine and pump," Jay complained.

"I don't know if it will be my back or my knees that give out first," Hoss said. "It almost makes digging coal look better."

"Have patience, my fellow prospectors," Amos told them. "We have had a good take so far today. If the yield keeps up, we'll have that pump in a month."

His comment was greeted with groans. "Maybe we should be working from the other end of the stream. Could be all the gold washed to the lower end of the canyon," Jay suggested.

Shaking his head, Amos told them, "Any gold we're going to find will be in the first half of the stream. Even before that, we may stop finding any color. The sandy areas we're working came from the quartz in the mine being broken down. Along with the quartz, gold is washed out. The gold settles behind a riffle or bend long before the sand. We need to keep working the stream closest to the pond. That's where the richest placer deposits will be found."

"I thought we had panned all the gold from that end already," Hoss replied.

"The water from the mine has only been flowing for a hundred years. The deposits in the Virginia City gorge were made over hundreds of thousands of years. There are three areas of placer deposits I think we'll find: Where we are panning now, below the falls area and eventually in the bottom of the pond," Amos explained. "With luck we will be able to go after the best gold in the mine once we have a pump."

"I just hope my back doesn't give out before we get that pump," Jay said.

"What I can do," Amos told his partners, "is make us a cradle or rocker. It will save our backs and put through a lot more gravel each day. I'll start working on one in the evenings."

"Heck with working on it in the evenings," Hoss exclaimed. "Me and Jay can keep panning while you get one of them cradles built."

"It sounds like a plan to me," Jay agreed.

"There is one other thing I need to do," Amos said. "I need to climb up above the canyon wall and find out what was feeding the mine. It might still be an underground spring."

He dreaded the sound of his own words. It had to be something else, he hoped. The falls had stopped and what fed it had also increased the flow from the pond.

Trying to sound confident, Amos continued. "I think it's a river, and maybe we can divert it and stop the water from flowing into the pond."

Stretching his back, Hoss suggested, "Why don't the three of us go and look? I know I'd like to see above the wall."

"Maybe we should," the prospector replied. "Of course, it is a damn shame. A half-day of working and we're looking for reasons to get away from the stream."

After fresh coffee and leftover hotcakes, the three men saddled two horses and the mule. As they started to leave the remaining chestnut began to run around the corral whinnying and complaining about being left alone. Jay rode back to the corral and opened it. "You may as well come to," he told the horse. "Then we'll all see what's above the wall."

As they rode past the spot where the two horses had been put down, there were only remnants of some hair and a skull. Wild animals had devoured or dragged any other evidence away. The three partners rode into the lower part of the canyon. The unmanned horse stayed close, making sudden runs and kicking up its heels like a young pony. It was enjoying the freedom from the corral.

They climbed the slope where the pines had been cut for the cabin. They viewed crevasses, ancient rivers and rock pinnacles eroded from weathering over thousands of years. They had barely entered the area when Jay pulled up and pointed to one such pinnacle. "What's that in the crack of that rock?" he wondered. Swinging off his horse, he walked to the reddish wall. Pulling at the item, he withdrew a helmet of some sort. It was some sort of a rusted steel cap with a pointy end.

Amos pointed to depressions below the pinnacle. "I think we have found the resting place of more of the Spaniards."

Jay put the helmet back in the crack and stepped back, "Looks like three, maybe four old graves. Could be the wood cutters or the hunters."

Climbing back onto the chestnut, Jay led them on. Amos followed after taking off his hat and saying a few words. It had been a hundred years since the attack that had killed these men. Their attackers had come from beyond this slope. He felt a stirring inside, or maybe it was just a palpitation.

The riders worked their way back above the canyon wall. They had to turn back several times and seek out another route. The terrain around them was rock cuts, pinnacles, and ledges. Finally, they hit a dry stream bed.

Pointing toward the canyon, Amos said, "This is probably where the water had run to the falls. Ahead we should find where the water flows into the mine."

The dried-up bed twisted through the rocks and became too narrow to continue following. Both sides were steep and eight to ten feet high. With difficulty the men were able to turn the horses and mule around after backing them up a way. The unmanned chestnut led them as they worked their way back, looking for a way to climb out of the stream bed.

Suddenly the horse turned right, into a narrow passage. "Damnit!" Jay cussed. "Now I'll have to go in there and bring the fool horse out."

Swinging off the chestnut he was riding, he handed the reins to Hoss. Jay disappeared, following the horse, talking softly, encouraging the horse to stop. The sun burned down in the dry waterway, reflecting from all sides. Amos and Hoss sat sweating as they waited.

"I sure as hell hope we don't have to go in there and find Jay," Hoss complained.

Amos took a drink of the warmish water from his canteen. The mule was stomping impatiently, wanting to move on. "One of us is going to have to go in there and find out what happened to the horse and Jay," the prospector suggested.

"And that would be me, right?" Hoss answered.

"You guessed it," Amos said. "I would recommend you leave your horse with me."

Hoss swung down from the bay and handed his reins and Jay's to Amos. "If we ain't back before dark, you can take the horses back to the cabin, Amos."

Before he could take a step into the narrow passage, Jay appeared on the rocks above them. "Did I hear some doubt that I'd be able to find my way back out?"

"There was a whole lot of doubt with us baking in the sun," Amos replied.

"I found the water, or should I say, the horse found it. I figure it could smell the water on the breeze coming through the passage," Jay informed them. "The passage is too narrow to ride, but lead the animals through and just trust that it will eventually get wider."

It was good advice. After hanging their stirrups onto the saddle horns, Amos and Hoss led the horses and mule through the passage. It got so narrow at one point that the big-bellied mule scraped both sides as it squeezed through. Finally, it began to widen and came out near the rapids of a river that flowed from the mountains beyond.

The majority of the water churned around a bend and flowed back west toward the mountain. A smaller portion flowed toward the canyon. It collected in a pool. Jay showed them a spot that he guessed was the other end of the dried stream bed.

After taking a long drink of the cool mountain water, Amos climbed onto the rocks to survey the area. It was plain to see that when the level of the pool rose, the water would flow into the dry bed and then spill over the falls. A hundred years ago the earthquake had breached the bottom of the pool, sending the water into the mine, thus keeping the level too low to flow over the falls. Only during the spring thaw was there enough water to raise it again.

Slowly he came up with a plan. There was a way to divert the water back to the original waterway using the narrow passage they had come through. It would take a fair amount of blasting and some difficult hauling of rock, to prevent the water from flowing into the pool. But it could be done.

A simpler plan would be to blast and drop rock into the area where the water split and keep all the water going back toward the mountains, but that would leave the canyon without water and make his future mining plans impossible.

Amos also saw a fair amount of quartz in the rocks around the pool. It was possible that there was more gold than he'd expected in these rocks. The Spaniards may have only followed one vein of gold-bearing quartz.

Standing under the blazing sun, Hoss called up to him, "What do you think, Amos? Can we stop the water in the mine?"

"I think we can," the prospector replied. "Now, let's get the hell out of this oven."

Getting back to the pine-covered slope turned out to be more of a challenge than they had expected. The men had wound back and forth in search of the source of water and hadn't worked out a clear route, making the return just as difficult. Finally, they came out near the slope. It was dusk when they rode back into the canyon.

"You feel like some fresh meat?" Hoss asked.

A quarter-mile up the canyon were several deer grazing. "I'll cook it if someone cleans it," Amos offered.

"If you can hit one from here in this light," Jay challenged, "I will clean and skin it."

Smiling, Hoss dismounted and pulled his Springfield Model 1884 from the saddle scabbard.

"You're going to lose this one, Jay," Amos chuckled.

* * *

The prospector sat at the table sketching out what he had seen while the venison sizzled in the pan on the stove. Jay was outside finishing the cutting up of the deer and Hoss was taking care of the horses. Today's discovery had been important. While they couldn't be positive that the water only came from the pool above, it appeared that it was the source.

The prospector thought about the two men outside. They had what it would take to divert the water to its original stream bed. But that work could take the rest of the summer. It would mean another winter at the earliest before they could pump out the mine.

Another option would be to blast rock into the pool and try and plug the fissure created by the earthquake that had allowed the water to flow into the mine. Amos knew that it must be a rather large gap to fill it so fast and drown the men who'd been working.

Amos also weighed different ways of closing off the water to the upper pool with some simple blasting. He just couldn't do that. They would not be able to allow the water back or it would again flood the mine. He was hopeful that there were several veins of quartz to mine. Water would be needed to process the ore containing the gold.

His two partners were in good spirits as they wolfed down the venison. Amos had some day-old biscuits to sop up the juice with. They put the gold they had found today into a glass jar so they could all look at it while they ate. The problem of the water seemed simple to Jay and Hoss. All that was needed was to shut it off and then haul out the gold.

The prospector laid awake for a long time that night, then finally went outside and sat on the split-log bench. He had a chew in his cheek, a half-cup of rye in his hand and a lot on his mind. What he had suddenly felt inside was the last thing he had ever expected. He was thinking about how the canyon would change once they started blasting to get at the gold.

Amos had spent a lifetime searching for the mother lode. Within an easy shot was a chance for more gold than any man could spend in a lifetime. To get at it, they would have to stop the water and then would come the drilling and blasting.

He thought about his life, about his health. How much time did he have left? The trip into the rocks had left him exhausted. He might not live to see another summer. While it would be nice to go out with a big strike, he wondered what the cost would be?

After hours of sitting on the bench Amos finally scolded himself. "These are stupid thoughts. There is nothing you can do about this tonight."

Spitting out his chew and drinking the rest of his rye, the prospector went back into the cabin and was soon fast asleep.

His partners were up early, and after a quick breakfast they took their pans and headed for the stream. They had instructed Amos to build the cradle to save their backs. He found himself back on the shave horse again. Amos no longer worried. He worked carving parts for the cradle using wood left over from their building. He made the hopper screen from leftover chimney tin.

Once he had shaped the handle and rockers using his draw knife, boards were cut to length with the bucksaw. He used canvas for the apron, and in the lower box he put the riffle bars. The anxiety he had felt the night before drained away as he shaved and formed the wood.

He had a pot of bean and venison soup for Jay and Hoss at midday. They chatted excitedly. Jay had found a nugget that might weigh a half-ounce. They complained that the black sand that settled in the bottom of the pan made picking out the small pieces of gold more difficult. It took no encouragement to get the two back in the stream after gulping down their meal.

The prospector did not tell them that what they had in the stream was as big of a strike that most men searching for gold ever found. It would be considered a good strike. Amos knew that the gold-yielding gravel wouldn't go too deep due to the short time it had been accumulating, but it would be more than enough to purchase the engine and pump.

He presented the men with the first cradle when they came in at the end of the day. Their mood had been dampened a little because they had expected to find more nuggets quickly. Seeing the finished cradle perked them back up. Amos told them that it could be operated by one man and he had started a second one.

The day's haul of gold was added to the jar. Once full it would be worth $300 to $400. It would take two to three jars to purchase the pump and other things they needed. Jay held the jar up. "It's not very much so far, but doesn't my nugget look good on top."

It did not take Amos long to build the second cradle because he had made the most difficult parts along with the first one. By the end of the week Jay and Hoss were experts with the cradles and were able to process much more gravel without ending the day with sore backs. Amos continued with the pan, working his way down the stream in search of deposits for his partners to wash.

It wasn't long before they were working on their second jar of gold. Amos had found good color below the dried-up waterfalls. It confirmed his belief that there was more gold in the area than just the mine. The now-dry stream above the canyon had cut through quartz veins for hundreds of years, washing the gold over the falls.

For a while now Amos had realized that the amount of gold in the canyon might be more than the three of them could ever protect. If word ever got out about the richness of the rocks, they could never hold the canyon against the hordes of gold seekers who would besiege the area. If Amos and his partners got in the way, they would be driven out or killed.

In the meantime, Amos was enjoying the prospect of a strike. He had the pleasure of knowing that he had found a rich strike, maybe a mother lode. After 48 years, he had found one. The gravel downstream from the falls area had provided what they needed to fill the jars. They now had enough gold to purchase what was needed.

They stored the mining equipment under the cut with the animal drawings. Normally, mining areas had piles of processed dirt or tailings from crushed rock. This type of evidence would alert anyone traveling through the canyon that someone had been panning for gold. The three men had made sure that the diggings had been spread or dumped back into the stream in areas that they felt had been depleted.

The next step was something to worry about. Amos had met lots of assayers who could help convert the gold to money, but he had never met one he trusted. He now had more gold than he'd ever had before to convert and there would be questions and much talk of the amount.

Jay and Amos were in the wagon with the mule tied to the back when they left the canyon. Hoss rode the bay, following them. Virginia City had seen better days and had a lot of used equipment that could be purchased at attractive prices. As they bounced along in the wagon, Jay suddenly asked. "Do you know how to operate a steam engine?"

"I have seen them at work," Amos replied. "Maybe I'll be able to get a manual with the engine."

"I worked on the Mississippi for a couple years," Jay told him. "I started as a stoker and worked my way up to running the gang. I had to learn operation and some maintenance of the engine."

"I think you will be in charge of the steam engine and pump," Amos declared.

They passed several men traveling between Virginia City and Red Lodge. One of the nights they camped with two brothers. The boys had come west from Chicago to work in the mines. They had been employed in the packing houses and had longed for the excitement of the mining towns.

Amos put on a pot of beans for the five of them. The boys provided side meat to add to the pot. "Why did you decide to leave Virginia City?" Amos asked them.

"People been talking about the lost Spanish mine and we hope to get more information in Red Lodge," the younger brother said.

"You figure the coal miners will be able to help you?" Hoss asked.

"Nah," the older brother said. "We plan to hit the saloons and keep our ears open. Men with a few drinks in them can't help but talk."

"At least you got a plan," Jay told them.

The two brothers were up early and heading for Red Lodge. Watching them go, Hoss commented. "I just hope they survive the saloons of Red Lodge."

A day out of Virginia City, Amos put packs onto the mule containing a pan, his pick, a shovel, and a few other items needed to prospect the mountains and streams. The gold had been put into well-worn leather bags. The plan was for Amos to go to an assayer with a plausible story of panning the gold. Hoss and Jay would come in after and be looking for work hauling for folks.

That morning, Amos took off at a brisk pace, leading the mule. For much of his adult life this had been his main mode of travel. Hoss and Jay had waited another hour before leaving and by mid-morning, they passed the old prospector. Amos waved as he trudged on. "A few years ago, you young'uns would have never caught me," he mumbled.

His legs were fatigued and Amos was sweating and breathing hard by the time he reached Virginia City. Hours ago, he had regretted camping so far from the town. He saw the wagon sitting in front of a saloon. "Hope you boys are enjoying your drinks," he grumbled.

Continuing by the saloon, Amos stopped at an assayer he had used in the past. The man was of slight build and wore a green eyeshade over his thinning gray hair. A scarred roll top sat in the back on one side of the room and a hobnail safe on the other side. A counter spanned the middle of the office and supported a scale. The far side of the counter had several drawers and pigeon holes containing items needed for the assayer's trade.

As Amos walked in the assayer recognized him. "I see you're back in town, Mr. Mudd."

"Yes, I am, Mr. Wilson," the prospector replied. "It's been three or four years since I crossed your threshold."

"Yes . . . yes. What can I do for you?" Mr. Wilson asked with a degree of impatience.

"I've been working the Yellowstone for a few years and have managed to pan a fair amount of placer gold," Amos told him.

"Let's see it," the man said, pointing to the counter. "Let's see what you got."

Amos was carrying the carpet bag and reached in, taking out two small leather bags containing the gold. He placed them near the scale and saw the look of surprise on the assayer's face. "If that's not full of gravel, you got yourself a good amount of gold."

Walking around the end of the counter, Mr. Wilson went to the door and slid the lock. He then placed a small sign saying he was at lunch in the window before lowering the shades on the street side.

He then returned to the back of the counter and withdrew a metal pan. He poured out the contents of the first bag. He placed his desk lamp on the counter. The assayer hemmed and hawed for a while as he stirred through the gold. Mr. Wilson mumbled, "Placer gold, hmm."

He then took out another pan and poured the second bag, slowly going through it. Amos looked at the gold dust that remained on the stirring stick as the assayer set it under the counter. *He could make a good living on what he leaves on the damn stick,* he thought.

Taking great care, Mr. Wilson weight out the gold, jotting down each measure on a piece of paper. "Two pounds, fourteen and one quarter ounces," he announced.

Amos had no way to dispute the weighing of the gold, so he agreed. "Let's see," the assayer said, figuring, "Gold is selling in the east at, $20.67 an ounce, and with transportation and further processing, . . . ah, let's see. I can give you $18.50 an ounce."

"$18.50?" Amos asked. "That's quite a discount from eastern prices."

"Yes, yes, it is," the assayer said, smiling. "Have you seen the sheriff since they hung Billy Bob?"

Bastard! Amos thought. "No, I haven't," the prospector answered. "I must do that."

Mr. Wilson scribbled on the paper in front of him and looked up smiling. "I can give you $850 for the gold. Would you like that in a bank draft, or cash money?"

I would like what it's worth, the prospector thought. "Cash money, please."

"I take it you'll be needing some tools before you leave town," Mr. Wilson said as he opened the hobnail safe. "I've got a brother that can get you some good prices."

"I won't be needing much, thank you," Amos told the man. "I plan to spend some time enjoying my hard work."

As the man slowly counted out the money, including several Double Eagle gold pieces, he said, "Say hello to Goldie for me."

Mr. Wilson gave the two leather bags a shake over a pan before handing them back to Amos. The prospector left the assayer's office with the money in his carpet bag. While he was aware that Wilson was a crook, he was the most honest assayer in Virginia City. He had the reputation of having an honest scale, unlike many of the local retailers. After that, all bets were off.

By the time he had gotten the mule and reached the planned camping sight, Amos was feeling pretty good. Over $850 for just a couple weeks of work. That would be considered a major strike by many. He had the fire going under the cottonwoods when he heard the wagon coming.

Amos put on water for coffee and then stood waiting for Hoss and Jay. The two men climbed down from the wagon and Hoss handed Amos a bottle of rye. "How did we do?"

"$850 for the gold," Amos told them.

"Damn, that's good," Hoss replied.

"I saw the shades come down after you went in," Jay said. "Why is that?"

"Like most crooks," Amos replied, "he don't want honest town folk to see him at work."

The prospector poured some rye into his tin cup and tasted it. "We'll buy the equipment and stuff we need and what's left we split equally."

Both of his partners were satisfied with the plan. After the coffee was done, Jay rolled a smoke and then sat back against a cottonwood to enjoy the hot brew and a cigarette. After a minute he said, "I may have a line on a portable steam engine."

"We'll have to carry whatever we get on the wagon," Amos said.

"The man said it has its own wheels. All we have to do is hitch a horse or mule to it and go," the dark-eyed man said.

"I saw the sheriff," Hoss said. "He said that Billy Bob had to carried up the scaffold. Messed himself and everything."

Shaking his head, Amos replied, "The boy did not like the thought of a rope."

"No, he didn't," Hoss chuckled. "But the sheriff seemed to have something else on his mind. He asked about you."

"Well we were together when they caught Billy Bob," Amos responded. "I'm afraid Billy Bob told everyone he saw about the map and the Spanish mine, hoping it would get him out of a hanging. It don't surprise me that he would ask."

"The assayer's office is right across the street from the sheriff's office. He had to see you walk in," his friend pointed out.

Ignoring the coffee, Amos poured another measure of rye into his cup. "We didn't fool anyone," he concluded. "We best get what we need and leave in the dark of night. Too many of the wrong folks know where the canyon is. We best get there to protect our claim."

Flicking his cigarette butt into the fire, Jay sat up. "I been meaning to mention that. We best get to the land office and register our claim."

"It's already been done in Absarokee," Amos told him.

"In who's name?" Jay asked.

"Mine," Amos informed him.

"Well," Jay said, throwing up his arms. "That won't do Hoss and me much good."

"Don't worry," the prospector said, feeling a bit of the edge that was there last winter. "I got your interest covered."

"If Amos says we're covered, it is good enough for me," Hoss told the upset partner.

The mood was quiet the rest of the night. They broke camp right after coffee in the morning and headed toward the man's holdings that had the steam engine. Jay rode ahead on the mule and met the man. There was a large pile of tailings near the defunct mine shaft. To one side sat the portable steam engine. The prominent flywheel was on one side and the stack was tilted down along the other.

As Amos pulled up he recognized the man in the rumpled cloth hat. He had hoped that it would be someone he didn't know. In the past, he had shared more than one bottle of rye with the seller. "How are you doing, Zeke?" the prospector inquired.

With recognition on his face, the man shook his head, setting his negotiating position. "Not worth a damn, Amos. As you can see, I'm trying to sell enough equipment to live on until I find another strike."

Hoss and Jay sat on their steeds looking at the two old friends. "Jay here says you got a pumper for sale."

"Well, he just talked of the engine, but I got pumps and belts. Probably most anything else, considering you probably got the need," Zeke replied, looking slyly at Amos.

"Lots of used equipment around," Amos said. "We're kind of buying tight."

"Heard someone saw you at that assayer's yesterday," the man countered.

"Just had a little panned gold to sell," the prospector said. "Barely enough to keep me and these two in whiskey and tobacco."

"Got any with you?" the man asked.

"Gold?" Amos asked.

"Hell no," Zeke snorted. "Whiskey!"

Jay got down from the mule and reached into the wagon, handing him a bottle.

As the morning waned away, the two men dickered. Jay and Hoss sat in the shade of the wagon and listened, seeing no end to the haggling.

The two men continued until the middle of the afternoon speaking of everything but price and drinking from the bottle. Each continue positioning themselves as being the hardest up and claiming nothing was worth what it used to be. Finally, Zeke asked, "So, do you plan to buy today? This damn bottle is about empty and I got to get something to eat."

To the amazement of the two partners, in a matter of minutes the deals were made on everything they needed. And to Jay and Hoss' surprise, Zeke was coming along to set up the steam engine. Amos led the mule near the portable engine and used the harness that the man had provided.

Zeke directed Jay to bring the wagon to one of his sheds. A pump, additional picks and shovels, sledge hammers, drill rod, metal stakes, dynamite, fuses, black powder, belting, hoses, and many other items that would be needed. Zeke had no animals, so he would be riding with Jay in the wagon.

The new man ran back to his shack to get the few personal items he had. Jay and Hoss cornered Amos. "What are you doing bringing him along" Jay demanded. "You don't think I can run the engine?"

"I want to know if we can trust him to keep his mouth shut," Hoss worried. "For all we know he'll kill us in our sleep and take everything."

Amos glanced in the direction Zeke went. "First off," he said, "our gold is no longer a secret. There ain't a man from Virginia City to Red Lodge that won't know about the mine by the end of tomorrow. Zeke sold us the equipment from a useless mine. It was left to him to cover back wages. We didn't pay as much as you might be thinking for this stuff."

"But you are taking him on as a partner and he ain't done nothing to deserve it." Jay objected.

"The man will only be an employee," Amos assured them. "We won't be telling him about our suspecting the mine to be under the pond. He'll figure the engine is needed to pump water in a sluice box or long tom. Maybe even nozzles to break down banks with water."

"The fact is we will need to take on employees. Zeke is good with explosives and knows steam engines and pumps inside and out. We will owe him money at the end of every month and he will be a man we can trust not to be trying to take over the mine. He was loyal right to the end to the man who had the place we bought the stuff, and he will be loyal to us."

"What did you pay him?" Hoss asked.

"We got the equipment for $300 and that included Zeke's first months' pay," Amos explained. "We'll pay him $50 a month plus meals. Rye is optional."

"Whose money does his pay come from?" Jay asked.

While Hoss didn't ask the question, he was also curious. "It comes from all of us. We will each take $150 from the gold and that will leave $100 for two more months of Zeke's pay. We can continue to look for placer gold to help pay other bills."

The two men's attitudes changed abruptly. The $150 sounded pretty good to them. It was as much as they would make in three months, working 48 hours a week with Sundays off. They quickly forgot about the money Zeke would require. The new man came back with a burlap bag carrying his stuff.

There was a crude seat at the front of the portable steam engine and Amos climbed up and tried to get comfortable. He flipped the reins and the mule pulled forward. The lack of suspension and iron wheels made the ride bone-jarring. Jay's heavily loaded wagon followed Amos while Hoss rode ahead, keeping an eye out for problems.

The men all had their rifles and revolvers at the ready. From now on they would be an armed camp, ready to defend their claim. The road was in decent shape well south and east of Virginia City, so the caravan continued plodding on well after dark.

Hoss appeared from the dark, trotting back toward them. "Clean water in the stream about a mile ahead. It'll be a good place to make camp."

He then grabbed a pack from the wagon and set it in front of him. "I'll go get coffee and some supper going." With that, Hoss rode away into the dark.

The next morning, at first light, the men were awake. Jay watched Amos limping around the camp. "Would you mind if I drove the steam engine today?" he offered.

The look on the prospector's face was pure relief. "I would appreciate that."

They were unable to travel very fast with the steam engine and it took most of a week to reach the mouth of the canyon. They had pushed through the last day until after dark and they saw several campfires out in the rolling hills. Without stopping the men rode into the canyon.

Amos and Jay were leading with the wagon. He pulled up just inside the canyon. There were no less than a half-dozen fires going just below the cabin. Each was surrounded by several men. Hoss rode up alongside the wagon. Zeke stayed behind with the steam engine. Amos pulled his Winchester from below the seat while Jay took the loop off his .44. Hoss already had his Springfield across his saddle.

The prospector spoke loud enough to be heard by his group. "I don't want anyone to do something foolish and get yourself killed, but somehow we got to move these men off our claim."

Zeke walked next to Jay, his cloth cap pushed back on his salt and pepper hair. He was holding a W. H. Greenfield double-barrel shotgun. "This here scatter gun can take down every man at any one of the fires you want me to shoot at."

"Hold your fire unless necessary, Zeke," Amos cautioned him.

A large-boned man was walking toward them. Fires in the background reflected off the two revolvers he was wearing. Amos whispered, "Be ready. This could go south in a hurry."

There was the sound of guns being cocked on all sides of the prospector. *Lord, give us guidance and wisdom at this dark hour,* he prayed. "You best stop where you are," he warned the large-boned man.

"We been waiting for you," the man said.

"Can you explain what you and all them others are doing on our land?" Amos asked, a hint of anger in his voice.

"I imagine you know what *them* behind me are here for," the man said. "I'm here trying to stop any bloodshed."

The man waved an arm behind him when Amos saw the firelight reflect off the badge. "You wouldn't be the lawman from Absarokee, would you?" Amos asked, hopefully.

"Yep, Sheriff Packer," he replied, "and you're the one that keeps bring trouble to Absarokee."

"That I did," Amos admitted, "and now it looks like I got trouble right here."

"You might say so," the lawman replied. "Word come into town and we had us a sort of gold rush. I managed to get here with the group and slowed them down a bit. I told them they had to wait until you returned to see where your claim is staked."

"They're not going to like what you tell them sheriff," Amos warned him. "My partners and I own a thousand acres. It's a half-mile on each side of the opening and a mile and a half back into the hills."

"That's a damn big claim!" the sheriff exclaimed. "I believe there are limits to the size allowed on mining claims."

"That may be," Amos told the man. "The land was bought for ranching. Mineral rights were included. You'll find everything recorded at the land office in Absarokee. Any gold found was just good fortune."

"You didn't happen to put any stakes in?" Sheriff Packer asked.

"You'll find iron pipes driven in the corners by surveyors located in Absarokee," Amos assured the lawman.

"Damn," the lawman worried. "Come tomorrow, all hell is going to break loose."

Sheriff Packer walked back toward the fires. Amos and his group rode to the cabin and were relieved to find no one had move in. While they carried in food and such they could hear shouting as the men in the canyon began to leave.

Amos and his group were eating fried side meat and hardtack when the sheriff came in, ducking under the head jamb. "That meat you're frying smells mighty good."

"You are welcome to join us," the prospector invited him. "I heard some commotion outside. Looked like the squatters were leaving."

"They have left, and they're clustered around your opening, waiting until morning," the sheriff said. "I let them know that all the land in the canyon was already claimed and in the morning, I would announce the boundaries. They all wanted to be ready to look for gold beyond your land and hope to stake their own claims."

After finishing the meal, the sheriff and Amos went outside and settled down on the split-log bench with a bottle of rye. "What does a sheriff in Absarokee make a month?" the prospector asked.

"You don't become a lawman for the money," Packer replied. "You do it to make sure the folks in your town are safe and try and keep things fair."

"And for this, they pay you what?" Amos asked, persisting.

For a couple minutes the two sat in silence. "I make $40 a month and there is a room in the back of the jail for me to sleep in," the sheriff finally answered.

"How would $50 with room and board sound?" Amos asked. "We'll be needing someone to protect our interest."

"I believe you'll be needing that and more, but I'm not your man," Packer said, declining the offer. "I been spending some time with a lady in Absarokee and hope to marry her. She'd want a man that comes home each night and isn't off guarding someone's claim miles from town."

"Just thought I would offer you the job," Amos replied. Desperate, he added, "Would a share in what we find help you change your mind?"

"Nope," the sheriff said. "I will talk to the claim jumpers outside of the canyon, but after I show them the stakes, I'll be heading back to town."

The next morning, while the partners ate breakfast, the sheriff met with the men outside the canyon. A few of them left, hurrying to the north and south to search out claims, but most remained camped outside of the canyon mouth. Packer came back to the cabin to let them know the results and then bid them good luck.

Amos had Hoss follow the sheriff to the mouth of the canyon. The lawman headed for home at a trot, not looking back. The prospector had Hoss take a position on a ridge near the opening. He was armed with the Springfield and lots of shells.

"If they start moving this way," Amos instructed him, "fire a warning shot and bust something near them. Maybe it will keep them back."

Then he had Jay take Zeke into the rocks above the canyon to look over the possibility of blasting the walls around the pool and shutting down the flow of water into the canyon pond. Amos knew that this wouldn't make much sense to the new man. Zeke would be expecting them to pump water from the pond to process the gold-bearing gravel. The prospector told him to tell Zeke that they might want to divert the water to the falls in the future.

With the others doing his bidding, Amos got a cradle and went along the stream, beyond the dried-up falls where they'd had a better yield. His mind was busy while he worked. Amos couldn't be sure of the amount of gold left in the mine. All he was sure of was that they'd get the remaining gold in the stream. While it would make each man a nice amount of money, it would not be the mother lode.

Billy Bob's blabbing about a map to a Spanish gold mine had spread to the outlying towns and this had changed Amos' plans. He had hoped to pan the stream to get money to work with. He'd hoped to tackle draining the pond later.

Amos stopped and looked back toward the pond. "I'm sure the mine shaft is under the water, but damned if I know if there'll be any more gold in it."

The prospector considered the future as he continued the monotonous rocking of the cradle. Soon they would need more employees. This would require pay each month. Quarters had to be built for them. One other problem was that the discovery of any amount of gold would drive prices in the area out of sight.

After returning from looking at the upper pool, Jay joined him to run the other cradle. "What did Zeke think?" Amos asked.

"He thinks we're crazy to do it, but it can be done, and once the upper pool level rises it will flow back over the falls," Jay told Amos. "We would need to blast from three sides. Zeke says at the very least, it would slow the flow into the canyon pond and divert the water."

Leaving Jay to work a cradle, Amos went back to the cabin to warm the morning coffee. He would need to make some decisions and make them fast. He saw that Zeke was working on the steam engine. It was positioned near the pond and the stack was up. It would need to be lubricated and the boiler filled with water. The prospector hoped that there were no major repairs needed. The next problem would be the wood to fuel it.

If they were closer to Red Lodge, coal could be purchased to fuel the engine, but it was two long days of travel each way. With everything running through his mind, Amos was feeling agitated. He needed some air. Gulping the stale coffee, the prospector grabbed his Winchester and went to the ridge to relieved Hoss.

When he had come there earlier with Hoss, there'd been around three dozen men scattered around the plain. That number had now doubled. "Any problems with the crowd?" Amos asked.

"Folks keep coming and there is a lot of pointing towards the canyon, but so far they are behaving," Hoss replied.

"Zeke's working on the steam engine and Jay's working a cradle," the prospector said. "Grab yourself something to eat and go work with Jay."

Amos watched the men out on the plain as Hoss headed back into the canyon. The prospector knew that it was only a matter of time and the men he was watching would become a mob and nothing would stop them. There was a battle coming and gold wasn't worth losing your life for. While Amos had seen this scenario before, he hadn't expected it to happen here.

He looked out onto the plain and muttered, "Damn you, Billy Bob. Damn you to hell!"

As Amos watched, the number of men on the plain continued to grow. They were coming from all directions. It was a tide he and the men with him couldn't stop.

He walked back toward the cabin in the evening twilight. Amos had made a decision. Once made, it seemed easy. A load of worry had been lifted from his shoulders. Amos had realized that it was not himself, but the safety of the others that weighed so heavily. Amos would recommend that they move back to the pines and prepare to follow the trail taken by the trapper Rosco.

The steam engine would be disabled by removing key components. With regret, he knew that the cabin would have to be burnt, leaving little for those who came into the valley to use it. With luck claim jumpers would pan the stream and do some unsuccessful digging elsewhere.

The property would remain in his name, and in a year, maybe two, Jay and Hoss could return to the canyon. Any placer gold would be gone but they could reclaim the land. If the claim jumpers didn't discover the mine under the pond, there was still the chance they could continue as planned.

The prospector was walking with a bounce in his step as the approached the cabin, anxious to let the others know what was to be done. The smell of biscuits baking and venison frying greeted him as he entered the cabin.

The four men sat around the table, enjoying their meal. Jay and Hoss talked about the gold they had found that afternoon. Several nuggets were included. The usual level of excitement was tempered by worry of what lay outside the canyon. Darkness had forced them to quit the rich ridge. Zeke announced that the steam engine and pump were ready to run and in the morning, he would fire it up.

Amos let the men talk, liking their enthusiasm for the work. He waited until they were sharing an after-supper bottle of rye before he spoke. "I hate to put a damper on this evening's conversation, but I am afraid the crowd outside the canyon cannot be stopped."

The three men around him were quiet. It was as if they couldn't digest what he had just said. Amos continued. "When they come, they'll come in firing. Once we are dead, they will scatter across the canyon, staking claims and fighting amongst themselves. What we have found here is not worth throwing our lives away."

Suddenly, Amos chuckled, "I guess I would be throwing away the least."

Jay stood up, his eyes angry. "It sounds to me like you're telling us to tuck tail and run!"

"I guess, in a way, I am," the prospector agreed, "but just for a while. The men will come in and scrape the surface gold and will probably leave. We will still own the land and can come back."

"*We*," the dark-eyed man snorted. "You mean you will still own the land."

"You are missing the point, Jay," Amos said, trying to reason with the man. "If we make a stand and get killed, what do you have? Nothing! If we leave and wait, we can come back and with luck have most of what we have been working toward."

"I hate to say it," Hoss pitched in, "but I am with Jay. I say we barricade the entrance and make a stand. I'd been in worse places in the army. For the claim jumpers to attack they have to come in to a narrow opening. Not many men are willing to face the kind of fire we can lay down."

Fighting to stay calm, Amos debated with the two men for the next half-hour. Meanwhile, Zeke stared into his cup and sipped his rye. Finally, he cleared his throat and stood up. "Before we jump into killing or being killed, I would like to go out and talk to the men out on the plain. Most are family men. I believe I know a good number of them. I would like to try and convince them to give this up. All there is to be gained is the gold in that there stream. Each man would be lucky to pan enough for winter groceries."

The others stared at Zeke, surprised at his offer. They all realized that he didn't know about the potential of the mine under the pond. If by chance he could disperse the crowd on the plain, it was worth a try.

"I appreciate your offer, Zeke," Amos replied. "I don't see it working, but it is worth a try."

Jay sat down and poured rye into his cup. He raised it to drink, but before doing so he said, "Just in case it don't, I am going to start building a barrier. I do thank you for trying, Zeke."

"I'll help you with the barrier," Hoss said.

CHAPTER FIFTEEN

Amos watched the three men empty their cups and leave the cabin. The prospector was filled with mixed emotions. He felt pride that Jay and Hoss were willing to take a stand. They were good men to have on his side. But he also felt dread that in the near future they could be killed. On the other hand, he would also be lying dead with them. Dying defending the claim he felt comfortable with.

The prospector poured himself a little more rye and then found some packaging paper. Taking a stub of a pencil, he wrote out a last request. "In the event that all three of us are killed, I leave my money in the Cheyenne bank and my interest in the canyon to be divided equally between Lucia Williams and Sara Weber." Satisfied with what he'd written, Amos signed it.

He planned to give this to Zeke when he got back from talking to the men on the plain. Amos would not let Zeke stay and fight. If a miracle happened and they survived, he would be welcomed back to work. Again, Amos felt at peace. What happened next would be in the hands of God. Stuffing the note into his pocket, Amos walked toward the opening to join Jay and Hoss. The July sky was clear and the stars bright.

He found the two men busy at the opening. They had brought the wagon and tipped it on its side. They were dragging brush and trees that had been cleared when making the road, and stacking them across the remaining opening. Jay looked up as he approached. "I see you decided to join us."

"I wouldn't have it any other way," Amos replied. "I'll go up on the ridge and watch until you two are done. Then I would recommend Hoss position himself on higher ground. If it's okay, Jay, you and I can defend from the low ground."

Without waiting for an answer, Amos climbed up the steep, rocky side. Once he gained the top, he sat on a log, breathing heavily. "I hope they let me catch my breath before the attack," he muttered under his breath.

The moon would be coming up soon, making any sneak attack difficult. Amos fingered the piece of paper in his pocket. He was satisfied with his decision. It would make the women's lives easier. He suddenly realized that Hoss might never see his child. Worse yet, the child would never know its father. Shaking his head, Amos again muttered, "Damn stupid thoughts."

The moon was shedding a pale light across the plain when Hoss climbed the rise. The night sounds of the wolves and owls were mixed with the shouts coming from the men around the fires on the plain. The pungent smells of the wildflowers came on a soft breeze.

"It's a perfect night," Hoss said, speaking quietly. "It's the kind of night one hates to go to sleep."

Pointing to the men on the plain, Amos replied, "Looks like some of the claim jumpers decided to go to sleep. Several of the fires are out."

"I hope Zeke had good success talking with them," his partner said.

All of a sudden, there was the sound of someone climbing near their position. Both Amos and Hoss moved silently to better cover with their rifles ready. There was a hiss. Then a whisper, "Hoss, it's me, Jay. Don't shoot."

The dark-eyed man came and joined his partners on the log. "I expected Zeke back by now," Jay said.

"You don't think he might have joined the claim jumpers?" Hoss wondered.

"That won't happen," Amos replied. "There is a chance they won't let him come back."

Jay checked the action on his rifle and settled back down. "I heard wagons tonight."

"More gold hunters coming in," Hoss guessed.

"It sounded more like they was going away," Jay replied.

"Let's hope Zeke convinced some of the men to leave." Amos whispered.

One at a time the fires out on the plain burned out and the sound of the claim jumpers went quiet. Jay offered to go and get Amos' mule to stand guard so the three of them could get some sleep. When he came back he had a blanket for each man.

Before long, the three partners were asleep. The sun was breaking the horizon when they woke.

The eastern clouds were a blaze of color, giving warning of bad times coming. The glare from off the plains made it impossible to see.

Amos knew that if an attack was coming it would be while the sun was in their eyes. The men were stiff from sleeping on the rocky ridge. Amos went into the brush and relieved himself. He came out rubbing his hands on his pants.

"Pee on your hands?" Jay kidded.

"Just part of getting old," Amos replied, grinning. "Why don't you two go down to the cabin and grab us something to eat? You best bring back the coffee pot. I'll watch until one of you come back."

Alone on the ridge, Amos watched a mist rise off the plain. It and the sun obscured many of the camps. He caught a movement to his right. The prospector picked up his Winchester and squinted, trying to catch sight of it again. Slowly, a man walking toward the opening appeared. A smile spread across Amos' face. It was Zeke.

Amos called out and waved. Zeke stopped and waited for the prospector to climb down. A rock came loose and Amos slid the last few feet to the bottom. Sitting on the dew-covered grass, he muttered, "Now they'll think I messed my pants."

Zeke came over and gave him a hand getting up. "Have any luck talking to them?" Amos asked.

"Didn't have to," Zeke replied.

"You didn't?"

"Word come in yesterday about the Klondike strike," the man explained. "A boat come back to Seattle filled with gold. The Yukon River is lined with the stuff."

Amos asked, "Where the hell is the Klondike?"

Zeke rubbed his chin. "In a place called Alaska. Every man-jack out there is headed back to buy supplies to head for the strike." Zeke removed the rumpled hat and clutched it to his chest. "I don't know how to tell you this, but I'll be leaving and joining with two men I prospected with. I'll give you back the month's pay."

Amos felt a flash go through him. It was the same feeling he'd always had when he heard of a new strike. The prospector had met a man who had traveled to Alaska some years back. He had described the difficulties of crossing the mountains in Canada. The prospector didn't envy what Zeke would be facing.

"I understand, Zeke. Keep the pay and just get your stuff at the cabin and go," Amos said. "You won't want to keep your friends waiting, and good luck."

"I ain't got nothing worth going to the cabin for," he said. "I'll be leaving from here."

With that Zeke clamped his hat on his head and turned, hurrying back out toward the camps. Amos cradled his rifle and, after collecting the mule, headed back toward the cabin thinking wistfully, *If I was only 10 years younger.* Jay and Hoss were coming back with breakfast when the prospector met them. Amos quickly brought them up-to-date. After a short discussion about the Canadian Rockies, they all agreed that it wasn't a trip they would want to make.

After a quick meal they got their horses and mule. The three partners went back to the opening. Riding out onto the plain, they looked at the abandoned camps. Little was left other than charred wood in the fire pits, discarded tin cans and packaging paper. Jay swung down from his chestnut and picked up a torn newspaper. It was the front page of a Seattle newspaper dated July 17, 1897. The headline of "Gold! Gold! Gold!" drew the reader's attention. The page was too damaged to sort much out, but Jay did make out $1,139,000 in gold brought in on two ships.

"Wow," Hoss breathed.

"That's a lot of gold," Amos agreed, a shine in his eyes.

The men stared at the tattered newspaper for a moment before Jay crumpled it up and tossed it into a cold firepit. "I got to get my wagon upright and back to the cabin," the dark-eyed man said as he climbed back onto the chestnut.

"I'll use it to haul wood for the engine," Amos replied, glancing back at the discarded newspaper regretfully before riding away.

For the next two days Jay and Hoss worked the cradles, finding several hundred dollars' worth of gold in the latest sandy ridge. Amos took the wagon down the canyon and cut firewood. He managed to bring three loads of split wood and stacked it near the steam engine. It felt good to do the manual labor. He bucked and split windfalls first, including those near the canyon opening, taking frequent breaks to smoke his pipe or have a chew.

On the third day it was time to test the engine and pump. Right after a breakfast of sweetened porridge, the men went to the pond. Jay went over the engine operation while Amos handed buckets of water to Hoss as he poured it into the reservoir above the boiler, filling both to the mark on the sight glass. The belt hung loose over the pully near the flywheel and was crossed as it went to the pump pulley.

Iron stakes held the engine and pump in place. Zeke had done a superb job of setting up the equipment. Jay rocked the flywheel back and forth to check that everything was free. The first load of wood was in the firebox and the damper was open to help it build up heat. Clouds of dark smoke drifted up from the stack.

With the boiler filled and the fire going, the men sat back watching the pressure gauge as it slowly moved beyond 100 psi. Jay pulled a chain that operated the whistle. At the low pressure it gave a feeble sound, but the men were pleased with any indication that the engine would soon be running. There were popping and cracking sounds as the metal in the boiler expanded from the heat.

Once the pressure reached 200 psi, Jay rocked the flywheel again, positioning the piston into the thrust position. He then reached up and pushed on the handle, cracking open the valve that sent steam to the piston. With a little assistance from Jay, the flywheel slowly began to turn as the piston moved in and out, working the crank arm. Jay gave it a little more steam and let the engine idle as the components warmed up.

Once again he pulled the chain, giving a blast from the whistle. They all laughed with excitement as the engine came to life. Amos looked at the leather outlet tube from the pump, which lay limp.

"The pump ain't working," he observed.

Hoss piped up, "We got to prime it." With that he filled the bucket and went to the pump. Taking a nearby wrench, he opened the plug on the top of the pump housing and poured water in. Hoss quickly replaced it and water started to cough out of the tube. As Jay increased the steam the engine ran faster. The belt between the pump and engine slapped together as it snaked between the pulleys, and a solid stream of water shot out of the pump.

Unable to contain himself, Amos danced up and down, saying, "Yes! Yes! We got us a pump!"

Soon the wood had burned down in the firebox and the steam pressure decreased. Jay pulled the handle closed, shutting down the engine. With the damper closed and the whistle chain pulled, the engine hissed to a stop.

Once they started pumping out the pond, someone would have to man the steam engine at all times. A governor would control the speed, but water from the preheated reservoir would have to be injected to the boiler using a series of valves. It would then have to be refilled along with keeping the firebox full.

Jay remained to shut down the steam engine while Amos and Hoss headed back to the cabin. "Tomorrow we will start working on blasting the walls into the pool," the prospector informed Hoss.

That night Amos made corn bread and beans for supper. The men talked and planned their next steps: First, slow down, or ideally, stop the water from the upper pool; then, pump out the pond and expose the mine. In their discussions it sounded simple. Amos knew that drilling and blasting the walls would be dangerous. Then there was no guarantee that the flow would be slowed. He figured that now was not the time to bring these things up. It was time to enjoy the moment.

* * *

The July sun was hot and the rocks above the walls reflected heat at the men as they drilled holes for the blasting powder. Footing was precarious and the rock unforgiving. Jay and Hoss traded on and off holding and turning the drill rod, or swinging the sledgehammer. Both had bruises on their arms from glancing blows.

Amos climbed around the rocks, marking locations to drill and taking his turn at the drilling to spell one of the partners. It took a week to drill five holes in each location. At the end of each hot day's work, the men would soak in the refreshing pool before heading down to the cabin. They had found a shorter route back to the cabin by going across the rock to the ridge along the opening. It saved a lot of winding back and forth through the dry stream beds.

The grueling work drilling the walls had blistered their work-hardened hands. No one offered to spend the waning hours of the daylight working the cradles to find more gold. Once the drilling was done it was decided that Jay and Hoss would go into Absarokee to re-stock, taking time to hunt on the way. Amos tossed an extra shirt to Hoss to keep the morning chill off and reminded them to thank the sheriff for his help with the claim jumpers.

The two partners rode out of the canyon on the wagon, looking forward to a night in town. "A meal in the café and a few drinks at the saloon will suit me just fine," Jay told his friend.

"I should have taken a couple more days and went to visit Sara," Hoss said. He noticed Jay had rolled a cigarette and was looking for a match. Hoss check the pockets of the shirt Amos had tossed to him and found only a piece of paper in the pocket. Taking it out, he looked at the writing.

"I'll be damned," Hoss exclaimed.

Noticing his partner looking at the paper, Jay asked, "What does it say?"

"It says Amos didn't think we'd survive the attack from the claim jumpers."

"He wrote that?" the dark-eyed man asked.

"Well, not exactly," Hoss replied. "This here says if the three of us die, his share of the canyon and his money is to be split between Sara and Lucia."

"Hell, that don't make any sense," Jay replied. "He hasn't shared the canyon. The damn thing is all in his name."

"Jay, you aren't listening," Hoss said exasperated. "Didn't you hear, he is leaving everything he has to Lucia and my wife."

"Sure, he'd leave it to the ladies and skip right over us," Jay complained.

Shaking his head, Hoss said, "In that case you should be happy to know we would have been dead also, so we wouldn't feel cheated. My friend, you have one hard head."

Amos was happy to be alone in the canyon. He sat with his pipe and some rye in his tin cup. The sun was high and the only sounds were animals grazing and chipmunks and birds searching for a meal. The prospector liked being alone and had spent many days looking for gold, trapping, or hunting in his sixty plus years, with no one to answer to but Mother Nature. After months alone, his next pleasure was going to a town and spending time with a sweet-smelling lady.

Next to the split-log bench he had two kegs of powder, a tamping stick, and some fuse. Once his pipe went cold, he set it aside and took out his clasp knife. Taking care not to create any sparks or static, Amos made three fuse harnesses with five leads. Each would be lit with a single fuse and carefully measured to be the same length. The fuse would burn about an inch a second. It would take just over 30 seconds to reach the powder. With care he placed each harness onto a piece of leather and then rolled the leather up and tied it with a piggin' string.

These he set aside to be carried on the mule. He looked at the sky toward the west. Yesterday he'd seen dry lightning. In the dry conditions there was a lot of static in the air, and he was working with blasting powder that could go off from a hard stare. Tamping the drilled holes would be nerve-racking. A little more humidity would have been welcome.

Walking out into the canyon, Amos pulled the picket ropes from the horse and mule. bringing them back to the lean-to. Tying the animals to the corral rail, he went to get his saddle. Putting it onto the mule, he then got a sawbuck pack saddle and put it onto the bay. Amos hung the two kegs of powder on the pack saddle. He planned to cover the filled drill holes with the leather to keep it dry.

Before leaving the cabin, Amos left a note letting Jay and Hoss know where he had gone, and then he poured some water over the bay's back and the powder kegs. He didn't know how he would explain things to Hoss if he blew up his horse. Then Amos laughed. "Hell, I won't have to explain. There won't be nothing left of me either."

A mile to the left of the opening, there was a narrow ledge that ran from the plain floor to the top of the ridge. From there he could cut across to the pool above the canyon. The only challenge was a short span of talus that had slid down across the ledge. Amos arrived at the base of the narrow ledge and dismounted. He loosely tied the lead rope from the bay to the mule's saddle. If he and the mule went off the ledge, a hard jerk would pull it loose.

Amos said a short prayer before starting up the ledge. The mule resisted moving forward and the prospector turned back and scolded it, "Not now, Jenny!" The narrow ledge had some steep inclines that made leading the animals a slow process. The prospector could hear the powder keg on the rock wall side bump occasionally. All Amos knew was that if the powder went off, he would not hear it bump the wall.

He stopped when they reached the 20-foot talus-covered part of the ledge. Amos could see the outline of the ledge under the loose rock. For several minutes he stood there. The climb had tired him and he wasn't in any hurry to walk across the slippery rock. Taking a deep breath, Amos continued. The talus crunched under his boots as it trickled from above, flowing over his boot and cascading over the lip of the ledge.

The mule and horse didn't hesitate and walked through the covered ledge. Whether they were confident that Amos wouldn't lead them into danger, or if they didn't realize the danger of crossing the talus-covered ledge, he didn't know. Amos was just happy they weren't balking. After the talus the ledge turned into a cut in the rock wall and the trail was steeper. Amos had liked the looks of this way up while they were drilling, but now decided that he would definitely take the horses back down through the dry stream beds.

Once Amos made the top with the two animals, he sat on a boulder and rested. His face was covered with sweat, as much from the difficulty of the climb as from the worry of going over the edge. Amos took the horse and mule to the river for a drink before tying them a safe distance from the pool. He removed their saddles and double-checked that they were tied with a loose knot.

Taking a keg, a fuse harness, and the tamping stick, he climbed to the first set of drilled holes. He tested the depth of the holes with the tamping stick. He then poured a measure of powder into each hole, tamping it lightly to make sure there weren't any air gaps. Using small rocks to keep them in place he laid out the fuse and then put the ends into the holes. Using some of the drilled rock, he put it into the holes and tamped it firm. He then coiled up the fuse and placed the piece of leather over it.

Sweat was running into his eyes and down his back as he finished the first set of holes. He dried his hands on his pants and then climbed down to get what was needed for the next drill set. Amos drank the cool pool water and had a chew before starting again. After reaching the second set, again he poured the powder into the holes, coming short on the last hole. Begrudgingly he climbed back down to get the other keg. He sat looking at the last set of drilled holes and debated whether he should take the fuse with him and work his way across, saving another trip up and down.

Deciding that it would make reaching the final area much more difficult having to scale along the wall rather than making the trip up and down, he headed back to the second set of holes with just the powder keg. With the charges set in the second set, Amos sat near the animals, chewing on a piece of corn bread and drinking from his canteen. He kept looking up at the final set of holes. They were on a steep wall, with few toe and hand holds for climbing.

The prospector took a length of rope and tied it around the keg. Then he fashioned a sling to go over his shoulder. Noticing that the horse and mule had their heads hanging in the heat of the day, he untied them and took the animals to the pool for a drink. *Damn you, old fart,* he scolded himself, *you're just delaying now. Get your ass moving and set the last charges.*

Bringing the animals back to an area that would give them a bit of shade from a scrubby oak, he looped the reins and lead rope over a low branch. With that done, he got what he needed and slung them to the center of his back and began the climb up the wall. The holes had been drilled in a fissure near the top of the wall. That area offered good footing, but the way up did not. Twice, Amos lost his toe hold and ended up hanging from his hands. The second time his hat went bouncing down the wall, splashing into the pool. Kicking and scraping along the rock, he was able to again gain a toe hold.

The prospector's legs were shaking by the time he gained the top. He lay gasping for breath, the keg and fuses hanging next to him. His heart was pounding as he forced himself into a sitting position. He sat, swearing under his breath. It was damned frustrating getting older. He looked down at the hat floating, then saw that the animals had come loose from the branch and were pulling at a patch of grass near the tree.

"Hey, you two," he called to them, "don't go too far. I don't need to be climbing all over the mountain chasing you."

The charging of the last holes was finished as the sun burned down on his bare head. Sweat dripped off his nose and ran down his neck and arms. His eyes stung and Amos attempted to wipe them with his shirt sleeve. There was powder left in the keg and he debated if he should leave it near the holes. Amos knew that he couldn't. The powder would be needed once they got into the mine.

It was another two hours before Amos got back to the cabin. After stripping the gear off the animals, he picketed them on some lush grass. "You two didn't wander away and you deserve good grazing," he told them. Once back in the cabin, he stripped down to his long johns and laid on his bunk. The old prospector was drained.

It was dark and a cool breeze was blowing in the open door when Amos awoke. His mouth was parched and his stomach burned with hunger. Swinging his legs from the bunk, he sat up. His body felt tight, and with any movement his muscles and joints hurt. Slowly, he stood up and limped across the room to the bucket of water. The liquid dripped off the dipper and down his beard as he drank in large gulps.

Amos remembered the horse and mule. Pulling his boots on, he headed to get them in his long johns. The night air felt cool and the moonlight made inky black shadows on the canyon floor. The bay whinnied a welcome as he approached the animals. As he led them to water, Amos felt comfort with their closeness. In years past when Amos had traveled the mountains alone, his mule and pack horse became companions, warning him of danger and giving him something to talk to.

Once the animals were taken care of, Amos sat for a moment on the split-log bench. The moon was shining off the pond and the steam engine looked like a mechanical monster in the night. If the blasting worked to slow the water, it shouldn't be long before the water was lowered and they would have the final answer whether the Spanish gold mine was under the water or not.

Slowly, Amos got up and went into the cabin. Still feeling tired, he went to the larder box and got the last of the cornbread, making a meal out of it. He didn't feel like getting a fire going, so he again drank water with the meal. He could have gone for a bit of rye, but they had drank the last of it the night before. Brushing the crumbs from his mouth and beard, Amos went back to his bunk and climbed under the blanket, drifting into peaceful sleep.

CHAPTER SIXTEEN

Amos awoke to a gray, drizzly day. A front had come through, bringing the rain and wind. The sun was up, but it was difficult to tell what time it was with the heavy clouds. The split-rock floor was cold as he walked around getting a fire started in the stove. There was only enough water in the bucket to make a half-pot of coffee. He then remembered the canteen and emptied the rest of its contents into the pot. While the water heated, he pulled his boots on and donned his threadbare coat and hurried to the outhouse.

Before making breakfast, Amos took care of the morning chores, watering and picketing the animals, filling the water bucket, and bringing in wood for the cook stove. His coat and long john bottoms were soaked from the constant precipitation as he ran back and forth outside. It was a cold July rain and the warmth of the stove while making porridge stopped his shivering.

Jay and Hoss arrived back just before dark. The rain had stopped, but heavy clouds still lingered.

They laughed and joked as they unloaded the wagon. Jay told Amos that the lady at the saloon had asked about him. Amos was still in his long johns as he watched his partners put the groceries away. He grabbed a bottle of rye as Hoss was putting it under the bunk.

"You don't get dressed these days?" Jay inquired.

"Damn weather got me in a twist," Amos complained. "Hotter than hell one day and damn near snowing the next. It raises hell with my old bones."

"A couple of snorts of the rye should straighten your old carcass out," Hoss said, laughing.

The partners didn't speak of the note they'd found in Amos' shirt pocket. Hoss began to slice side meat to fry potatoes for the evening meal.

"I got a surprise for you, Amos," his friend said.

The rye and prospect of potatoes had lifted Amos' spirits some. "Them taters are already a fine surprise."

Jay couldn't hold back and blurted out, "Hoss brung you some bear sign from the café."

"The hell you say!" Amos exclaimed.

"Of course, we had some fresh this morning, but these with coffee will be a great end to our supper," Hoss said proudly.

Amos set his cup onto the table and went over to his bunk to pull his pants on. He couldn't believe how good he felt to have the partners back from Absarokee. Just yesterday he had enjoyed the quiet after they'd left. Shaking his head, he thought, *Damn old man. You're thinking too much.*

After the meal was eaten and the bear sign enjoyed, Amos told his partners that he'd set the charges the day before. Jay looked at the loft. "I thought some of the powder was missing."

"You were climbing in them rocks alone at your age?" Hoss scolded. "That's what you got Jay and me for."

"I can still climb the rocks as well as either of you," Amos said, defending his actions. "I just can't always get dressed the next day."

After a brief pause, Jay and Hoss realized what their partner had said and burst out laughing. Amos joined in, enjoying the laughter in the cabin.

The clouds remained the next morning, but the wind had died down. Over breakfast the decision was made to blast the rock without delay. While saddling the mule and horses, Hoss called over to Amos. "You're lucky the powder didn't go off and blow your mule to pieces."

After tightening the cinch strap, the prospector said, "I wasn't worried about Jenny."

Jay piped up, "You probably had the powder on Hoss' bay."

Changing the subject, Amos climbed onto the mule and said, "Let's go light the fuses."

Jay led the way down the canyon and through the dry stream bed. Coming out, he continued across the river to the large oak. "The flying rock can land a long way from the blast. It would be best to keep the horses a good distance away."

Hoss stopped the bay near the oak. He saw the sign that the rain hadn't washed away. "Looks like there were two horses tied here at one time." He then looked up at Amos and shook his head. The prospector pretended not to hear and said, "We best leave the animals further back. We don't want the blast to scare them out of the territory."

After they found a secure place for the mule and horses, the three men walked back to the pool and looked up at the wall. It was layers of sedimentary rock, and they hoped it would crumble when cascading into the pool. Amos had had the partners purchase short cigars in Absarokee to light the fuse. Before they started climbing, they lit the smokes and got good glowing tips. Above the wall there was adequate space to move back away from the blast, including an outcrop for cover.

Taking a puff on his cigar, Amos said, "Well, we may as well get up there and start the show. Once we're all set, I'll give a signal to light the fuses and then we run for cover."

Jay took the toughest climb and Amos the easiest. The prospector also had the shortest distance to the outcrop. Once the top was reached, they removed the pieces of leather that had kept the rain off and then stretched out the fuses. They made a quick check of the lead fuse to the fingers to make sure that they had remained connected.

The three men drew on the cigars, and then touched them to the fuses on the prospector's signal. As the fuses sputtered the men took off like startled jack rabbits, running for safety. Amos slipped on some loose drill sediment and fell headlong. "Damn!" he shouted as he got back up and limped back toward the outcrop. Jay pulled him to safety a moment before the detonations began.

The ground shook under them as the three sets of charges exploded within seconds of each other.

Rock from the outcrop they had hidden behind broke loose and dropped around the men. Seconds later they were engulfed in a cloud of dust. The sound of rock sliding and splashing into the pool continued after the blast. Once the dust had blown past, the men stepped out and waited for any delayed blasts. It was a wise move because there was a final blast, sending additional rock into the pool and another cloud of dust.

Keeping wide of the blast zone, the three partners worked their way down. Debris from the explosions was scattered over a hundred feet from the wall. The pool was half the original size and what remained was covered with foam and dust. Amos stopped and looked at the results. "That should do it."

"We best get the hell away from here," Hoss recommended. "There may be another slow burn."

The clouds had broken and the sun was shining when they got back to the cabin. There was a fine layer of dust around the area from the blast. Other than that, nothing had changed. The stream was still flowing from the pond. Amos was a little disappointed. He had hoped that it would stop, like shutting off a valve.

The men dismounted at the corral. "I'll put your mule away," Jay offered. "You were gimping pretty good from the twisted ankle."

Amos thanked him and continued to favor the ankle as he headed into the cabin. He got the coffee on and got himself another "cowboy donut", or bear sign. Hoss came in and sat with Amos, helping himself to one of the fried treats. "Jay and I are going to work with the cradles for the rest of the afternoon. You should stay off the ankle."

"Hell," Amos scoffed. "I've climbed over mountains with a worse hurt than this."

"Maybe so," Hoss replied, "but you were younger then."

He got up to check on the coffee and did not see the prospector glare at him. They had just poured cups of the brew when an excited Jay came into the cabin.

"The water in the pond is cloudy!" he announced, "and it looks like the stream is slowing down."

After coffee and donuts, Hoss and Jay headed out to work the stream before the flow got too slow. Amos stood at the door, watching them go. "I never had any kids, but these two would have made fine sons."

By evening the stream had slowed significantly and there was no doubt that the blast had helped. Amos had made sourdough biscuits and a pot of honey-sweetened rice with dried fruit for supper. Jay informed him that the stream was hardly flowing.

"How about the falls?" Amos asked.

"Nothing yet," Hoss replied.

The next morning, Amos awoke early to the sound of birds busily feeding in the canyon. Suddenly, he sat up. There was another sound. Kicking the blankets off, he hurried to the door, muttering, "Damn. Damn." Each time he stepped on the tender ankle. Sure enough, the water was flowing over the falls.

"Hey, you sleepy heads!" he shouted. "Let's get up. We got a pond to pump!"

The three men sat outside the cabin, watching the water falls while eating cold biscuits and drinking strong coffee. "Ain't that a sight," Hoss said.

"It looks like what the Spaniards saw a hundred years ago," Amos answered.

"Hoss and I should go and get some more wood, once the engine is running," Jay suggested. "There's more watching than work tending it, and you can rest your ankle."

Amos agreed. "I can do that, but make sure all the oil cups and the water reservoir are filled."

By mid-morning the steam engine was running and water was being sucked out of the pond. Amos brought a chair out of the cabin and sat watching the pressure gauge after loading wood into the firebox. He controlled the pressure by opening or closing the damper. Jay had shown him the sequence of the valves to add water to the boiler. If he had any problems, three blasts on the whistle would bring the partners back on the run.

The first day lowered the pond two feet. The men decided to shut the engine down for the night. When they returned the next morning, the men were disappointed finding that the pond had come up most of the way. This confirmed that they would have to run the pump around the clock.

Two days later Amos went to help with the wood, his ankle feeling much better. He and Hoss had the wagon half-full when the heard the steam whistle blast three times. "Damn," Amos said. "Jay's got a problem."

Climbing into the wagon, Hoss drove the team up the canyon at a trot, Amos hanging on as the wheels bounced over the canyon floor. There was smoke coming from the engine stack and as they got closer they couldn't see any problems. Jay stood by the edge of the pond and was waving anxiously for them to come.

Hoss pulled the team to a stop near the pond and jumped out. Amos got out a little slower. "There it is! There it is!" Jays shouted, pointing at the opening that had appeared from under the water.

The rectangular opening was exposed almost a foot. There was no doubt that the men were looking at the opening of a man-made tunnel. "I'll be damned," Hoss said. "It sure do look like a mine."

Relief washed over Amos. While he hadn't voiced his concern much that this might not be the pond with the mine, there was always that doubt. Any concern was now gone.

The diameter of the pond had narrowed significantly. Another 12 hours of pumping should lower it and show the whole opening. As they stared at the slowly emerging mine, the steam engine began to slow.

"Damn," Jay said as he hurried back to the wood pile. "The fire's getting low."

By the next morning the water was too low and the pump sucked air, losing its prime. It became apparent that the Spaniards had had to dig out the pond area to get low enough to follow a vein of gold that went under the canyon wall. The engine was stopped, but a head of steam was kept up in case they had to start pumping again. Water continued to flow out of the mine, but it was slow and would take days to refill the pond.

Amos informed his partners that he would be the one to go into the mine first. "If the rock is unstable in the mine, I don't want all of us to be caught down there. Besides, I know what to look for."

Begrudgingly, the two partners agreed with him. Equipped with a lantern and small pick, Amos gripped the rope they'd tied to the engine wheel and descended the slope to the mine entrance. Jay joined him and was to wait outside the opening. Hoss was to keep an eye on the steam pressure and stand by with the team of horses.

Standing knee-deep in muck and water, Amos peered into the opening. Water seeped from cracks in the mine wall, and he saw evidence of rotted wood beams that had been used to support the roof. Looking back at Jay, he said, "Here's what we've been working for. Wish me luck."

With that, Amos ducked under the low roof and started into the mine. Rocks and rotting beams cluttered the floor, making going slow. Holding the lantern up, it appeared that the tunnel went back over 40 feet. About 20 feet in front of him, Amos saw water dripping heavily from the ceiling and was probably where the pond had been flowing in.

Amos' heart was pounding with excitement. This was it! The Spanish gold mine. He was determined to try and bring out some proof that the mine still had gold in it. The water soaked him as he passed the breach. The air was heavy and damp in the mine, and every move echoed in the confined space.

The roof continued to get lower as he worked his way deeper into the mine. "The Spaniards must have been damn short," he complained. Finally, he was forced to crawl over rock that had fallen from the walls and roof. He heard Jay calling to him. Amos responded that he was all right.

The tunnel was turning up and he was out of the water. The sandy floor was also easier to crawl on. He worked his way around a couple of large rocks and finally reached the end of the mine. Amos pulled the pick from his belt and scraped around the rock. In the lantern light he was able to see the quartz. Forcing the pick into the edge of the rotting quartz, Amos pried out a good-sized chunk.

He inspected the piece of quartz as it lay on the mine floor. He tapped it with the pick and his heart leaped. There was gold in the quartz! His head was buzzing with excitement as he struggled to turn around. Amos' leg caught between the dripping wall and a large piece of rock. He pulled and twisted, trying to free the leg. As it came free, he lifted it to clear the rock and a cramp hit the back of the leg above the knee.

"Damn," he groaned as he tried to relieve the pain by straightening the leg. The pick slipped from his grip and he abandoned it as he pulled himself between the wall and more rocks. Amos clutched the piece of quartz to his chest and fought to keep the lantern up in front of him as he moved forward on his elbows and knees. The lantern struck the wall and the glass broke as splashing water doused the flame, so it was also abandoned.

Amos had reached the breach in the roof and had water raining down on him. He was gasping for breath and staring at the outside opening, which seemed to be filling with water. All of a sudden severe pain spread across his chest and left arm! Amos fought the panic that filled him and tried to continue, the pain almost paralyzing him.

The prospector tried to call out for help, but he couldn't catch his breath enough to make much of a sound. Then the world began to spin. Things were hitting him! The mine was caving in! Then he was under water and there was no sound, just his body wracked with pain. All Amos knew was that it would be over soon and the pain would stop.

Then he was in daylight. His eyes were blurry, but he was sure that it was Jay over him. The pain in his chest and arm had also moved to his neck and jaw. He blinked to clear his eyes. Jay was shouting something to him.

"The bottle . . . the bottle near the shells," Amos gasped. "Get it . . . I need it."

"What?" Jay asked. "I don't understand."

"I do," Hoss yelled as he ran for the cabin.

Reality kept slipping in and out for Amos. In the agony, all he could think was, *If you are a loving God, take me now.*

Then Hoss was back. "He needs some of this," he told Jay. "Not much, only a little in his mouth."

Fingers were forced between his lips and a blinding ache went through Amos' head as he lost consciousness.

CHAPTER SEVENTEEN

Jay sat next to the old prospector, tears in his eyes. "There's nothing we can do for him," Hoss told his friend. "It's in God's hands. It was his heart."

"I never told him," Jay whispered. "I . . . hated that old man."

"No. You shouldn't," Hoss replied. "Amos was a good man. He'd give his last dollar to a man that needed it."

"Or any damn whore he met," Jay hissed. "But nothing . . . nothing…" His voice faded as he tried to clear his throat.

A half-smile came to Hoss' face. "He did like the women."

Jay leaned back against the wheel of the steam engine. "Did I ever tell you about my mother?"

"No, you didn't," Hoss said. "Does this situation bring it to mind?"

Jay coughed and wiped his nose on his sleeve. "She was beautiful. He left her for gold. She spent her life waiting for him to come back."

"What?" Hoss asked. "Amos knew your mother?"

"Had he stayed he would have known me also," Jay said with regret.

"Are you telling me Amos is your *father*?" his surprised friend asked.

"Yes. He could have been a father but chose to chase gold," he replied as his dark eyes filled with tears again. "I should have told him what I felt for so many years, but he wasn't the monster I had built in my mind. I had come west to find him. I figured if I followed the gold strikes he would show up, or someone would know of him, or that he was dead."

"Did your mother love him?" Hoss asked.

"Did she love him?" Jay scoffed. "All she talked of is what a wonderful man he was and that he would be back some day."

In a soft, rasping voice Amos said, "I have always loved her."

Surprised that Amos was awake, the two men looked at him. "I'm feeling better now," the old prospector told them.

Jay stood up, wiping his eyes and moved away. Hoss bent over Amos. "We thought you were a goner."

"I'd have agreed with you." Amos said not moving. "I think you gave me too much of that powder. Liked to blow my head up."

"We didn't have much time to do no measuring," Hoss retorted.

"It worked," the prospector told him. "My chest don't hurt no more."

"What are you clutching that rock for?" Hoss asked. "We tried to get it loose, but you had it in a death grip."

"It's gold, Hoss. It's gold," Amos replied.

Setting the piece of quartz onto the ground, Amos attempted to sit up. Hoss reached out a hand to help him. Jay came around the steam engine. "Is this the mother lode?"

"Yes, I think it is," Amos replied.

The two men helped Amos to his feet and back to the cabin, the prospector again holding the quartz. The pain in his chest and arm was gone, but a knot remained in the back of his leg from the cramp. Once they got him seated at the table, Hoss put on some water for coffee and then put the little bottle back on the shelf.

Sitting in his soaked clothes, Amos brushed the dirt off the piece of quartz, exposing veins of gold. He stared at it until Hoss joined them. The prospector then looked at Jay. "What did she name you?" he asked. "I'm sure it wasn't Jay Smith."

Jay's jaw was set and he gave Amos a stony stare. Not waiting for an answer, Amos continued. "It hasn't been often, but when you would smile, a chill would go through me. It was like I was looking into your mother's face. She smiles with her eyes also."

"Amos Jacques Mudd," Jay said flatly.

Now it was the prospector's turn to get misty. "After Jake, Jacques Larue." he said. "We were supposed to go west together. I buried him above the Mattawa."

"She called me A.J.," Jay told him. "She told me it was a bit of her two favorite people."

"Son, I didn't know she was with child when I left," Amos confessed. "Your mother never told me."

"I don't know that I like having you call me son," Jay growled. "If you had known, would it have stopped you from going to chase gold?"

"I won't lie to you, . . . Jay," Amos admitted. "I would like to think I would have stayed. I was young and had a dream of finding gold. I figured it would make everything better. I will never really know."

Jay got up, knocking his chair over, and stomped out of the cabin, Hoss watching wide-eyed at his friend's actions. "It will take time, Amos. He got years of hate crowding his thinking. I think he sees a good man that doesn't fit his thinking." Then, wanting to change the subject, Hoss got up. "I'll check on the coffee."

For the next several days Amos spent most of his time on the split-log bench, watching Jay and Hoss work. Whenever he walked he felt weak, tiring quickly. Jay wasn't talking to him, but when he laughed and kidded with Hoss it reminded Amos of his mother, Ona, so much it made his palpitating heart ache. It didn't help that the scolding that Jay had given him about leaving his mother had also brought back memories of leaving his father's potato farm. Amos realized that gold had been a curse and nothing else had mattered.

Each day the mine would leak enough water that it took a day to pump it back out. The only way to get at the quartz vein would be to dig another shaft and come at the gold from above. That would take most of a summer by hand. The reward would come once they reached the gold. One of the days, unknown to Amos, Jay had gone back into the mine and took out several chunks of quartz. He and Hoss had pounded them to dust on the rock ledge used by the Spaniards, then put it through the cradle. The yield was impressive. They spent most of the time processing the dirt on the bottom of the pond, which was also rich in gold.

One might say that Amos' spirit was broken. A lifetime of searching and now in front of him was the closest thing he'd ever seen to the mother lode, and it was giving him little joy. He would have been willing to trade all the gold here to have Jay call him father and if he could call him son. He realized that these were foolish thoughts, but he just couldn't shake them.

The prospector tried to do his share, taking care of the animals and having meals ready when Hoss and Jay quit for the day. One evening Hoss came from working the claim and said he was going to Absarokee for some oil and a few other things they were short of. Amos offered to go so he and Jay could keep working. To the prospector's surprise, Hoss agreed.

"You might want to spend a couple days and see the old saw-bones," Hoss suggested.

The team and wagon would be needed to haul wood for the steam engine, so Hoss let him take the bay to ride, or use as a pack animal. Before Amos left the next morning, he asked Jay if he needed anything.

"No, I don't," Jay said. "Nothing at all."

Amos rode out of the canyon leading Hoss' bay. The sun was shining and a breeze made the August day comfortable. The grass was mature and starting to get a golden tint to it. Dark clumps of sagebrush dotted the plain. Reddish buttes rose in the distance. Amos was glad to get away from the canyon. The place had lost its allure and he had the feeling that it was time to move on. He'd been thinking about the Klondike. With a good horse or mule he could get over the Chilkook pass. Or maybe he'd go to Seattle and take a steamer. He couldn't help but wonder if it was the search he enjoyed the most.

The sun was low in the western sky when Amos got to Absarokee. Sheriff Packer was standing in front of the jail and waved to him. The prospector pulled his mule over to the rail. "Did you marry the lady?" he asked.

"I did," the sheriff replied. "She keeps a good house and is a fine cook. She is also mighty nice to come home to."

Amos climbed down from the mule and tied his animals. The long ride to Absarokee had left his muscles stiff. Grabbing the post, he pulled himself onto the porch. "You're kind of showing your age," the sheriff commented. "You been feeling alright?"

"Nah," Amos sighed. "Had me an episode back in the canyon. My heart ain't what it used to be."

"Of course, it could be you're just getting old," the sheriff kidded.

The prospector smiled for the first time in days. "It could be. Age is something that catches up to all of us."

"Let me buy you a drink," Packer invited.

It was early evening and the dimly lit saloon was quiet. Amos sucked in the smells of the spilt rye, tobacco smoke and traces of the ladies' perfume. He recognized the portly doctor and suggested to the sheriff that they join him.

It was evident that the doc had been sitting at the table since his midday meal. A dirty bowl and a plate with the crust of bread still sat in front of him.

He also had a mostly finished bottle of rye. "Get a glass and have a drink on me," the doctor said with a slur. "Introduce me to your friend, sheriff."

"I see it's been a tough afternoon, Doc," Packer observed. "This here is Amos Mudd. You patched up his butt when he brung in a gang that attacked him."

Reaching across the table the portly man shook Amos' hand. "Good to see you again. I must have done a good job. I see you're sitting okay."

The prospector held up his glass of rye. "Here's to your good work."

The sheriff set his glass down and refilled it. "Amos here has been having trouble with his ticker."

"Well," the doctor replied, "stop by the office when we leave and I'll have a look-see."

"I'll do that," Amos said. "But let's make it tomorrow morning."

After another drink, the doctor bid them farewell and staggered out of the saloon. "Does the doc pretty much stay drunk?" Amos asked.

"I can't be sure," the sheriff said. "I ain't never seen him sober."

The bartender came over and cleaned up the dishes left by doc's meal. "I could use a shot and a beer," Amos said.

"Make it two," Packer replied.

Once the drinks were at the table, Amos tasted the beer. It was better than average. Looking up at the sheriff he said, "I want to thank you for the help with the claim jumpers."

"Just doing my job," Packer replied. "I figured it was only a matter of time and they would take over the valley, but at least you'd have time to get out or set up a defense. When I got back to town everyone was talking about the Klondike strike. I sent a man back on a fast horse to let the gold-hungry crowd know."

"It worked, sheriff. They was all gone in a matter of hours."

"You ever find the Spanish mine?" Packer asked.

Amos looked at the sheriff for a minute, debating what to say. Finally, he replied, "You should have come to work for us for a share."

"I'm glad for you," Sheriff Packer said, smiling. "Now you can stop traipsing all over Hell's Half-Acre looking for the next strike. No, I am happy with what I got here in Absarokee."

The sheriff left to make his rounds. Amos couldn't begrudge the happy man. He had found what he wanted without wandering all over, as he had said, "Hell's Half-Acre."

He smelled the perfume before he felt the warm breath in his ear. "I see you've come back to thank me for the pillow again."

* * *

The prospector spent four days enjoying the hospitality of Absarokee. It included a visit to the portly doctor, who gave him a good going-over. Once the the exam was over, the doc pulled out a bottle of rye and poured each a drink.

"What you experienced was angina. Overwork, stress, or fatigue can cause it. Your heart issues make this typical," the doc told him.

"So, you saying my time is almost up?" Amos asked.

"That's not what I'm saying," the doc assured him. "If you start having the chest pains when relaxing on the porch, then it's a different story. I'd like to tell you that you got lots and lots of years ahead of you, but it wouldn't be fair to you."

Frustration filled Amos. "Am I supposed to sit in a rocker on the porch the rest of my days?"

"That would be a mistake," the doc said. "Do what you normally would do. Your body will tell you when you overdo things. Keep your Trinitrin close and don't do foolish things. I would also recommend you start settling your affairs. Things you leave undone will more than likely be left undone."

Amos left the office with a great deal of respect for the drunken old saw-bones. The doc had seen a lot and pulled no punches. The prospector felt the bottle of Trinitrin the doc had sent him away with. Having it with him would have to become a way of life.

The prospector was deep in thought on the ride back to the canyon. He did feel a little regret that the Klondike couldn't even be considered in his condition. While he did not like it, he had to agree with the old saw-bones. His days of wandering the mountains was over. He had a good cabin in the canyon and could retire just fine in it. A spring and fall visit for supplies at Absarokee would be all he would need. Once the gold was depleted, he did not expect Jay . . . his son, or Hoss to stay. The gold would give them both a better life.

Smoke was belching out of the steam engine when Amos rode into the canyon. Hoss was tending to the fire and waved to him. The prospector tied the animals to the corral and began to unload bags from the pack saddle. Hoss came trotting over after finishing loading the firebox.

"I need the oil," he said. "A few of the cups are getting mighty low."

Amos dug into one of the bags, fetching the can of oil and tin of grease. "I got some bear sign to go with our supper," he told the partner.

"I do look forward the donuts," Hoss said. "We been shoring up the walls and roof of the mine. We also shoveled down some of the blasted dirt into the pool and slowed the water a bit more."

"The two of you best take it slow in that old mine," Amos cautioned him. "We know it claimed at least three lives."

Taking the oil and grease, Hoss started to turn and then stopped. "By the way, some man come to see you two days ago. We told him you'd be gone most of a week and he said he'd be back."

Before the prospector could ask more about the man, Hoss was gone. Amos watched him run back to the engine. He wondered where his . . . where Jay was. The chestnut team and the wagon were near the engine. With a shrug, he picked up the bags and headed into the cabin. Things were getting away from him. It didn't seem like the partners had missed him at all.

That night, at supper, Amos found out that they had finished shoring up half of the tunnel. Water dripping from the walls had almost stopped, and with the breach slowed down they only had to pump the pond water every other day. They had even considered doing another blast into the upper pool to try and stop it completely.

Amos listened to the excited talk of his partners. Hoss did say that he would be leaving in another two weeks to be with his pregnant wife. Jay's mood seemed to have improved, though still he didn't address the prospector directly, but pitched into plenty of the conversations with Hoss.

To Amos' surprise the two partners had a cache of gold worth several thousand dollars. They were not sure where to take it. Hoss and Jay feared another run on the claim. "That much gold is a good problem," Amos told them.

Then Jay looked straight at his father. "In another few days we'll have the mine shored the full length and we can start bringing out some of the high-grade. We'll need you to go in and make a recommendation on the best way to bring it out."

The prospector felt a swelling in his chest. "I'd be happy to do that."

The next day Amos joined them at the pond and insisted on taking the wagon to get another load of wood. Before going he climbed down into the pond and waded through knee-deep water to the mine opening. The two men were doing a fine job with the wall and roof supports. They had cleaned all the debris from the tunnel floor as they'd went. Hoss told him that most of the stuff they had brought out had gold in it.

Climbing back out, Amos drove the team to the slope. He looked at the stumps and tops lying around. Memories of logging in Canada with Jake flooded back. It had been a good winter. Remembering the portly doc's recommendations, Amos worked at a very comfortable pace. The wood he was cutting wouldn't be needed until tomorrow or the next day. It felt good swinging the axe and bucking the logs up.

He noticed a nice stand of pine had been spared for future building. Much of what he was cutting was aspen and a few maples. While it was green wood, in the steam engine firebox it burned hot. While taking a rest, Amos heard pounding in the distance beyond their claim. There were others looking for gold. Not all had gone to the Klondike. It was fine with him. There was plenty of land for others to prospect.

The prospector drove the wagon with wood toward the pond, feeling better than he had since the attack. He had done a fair amount of work without a problem and what he had hoped for in the Spanish mine was coming to be. He decided that he'd do some hunting tomorrow. While cutting wood, he'd seen some elk grazing down toward the end of the canyon. What couldn't be eaten fresh could be made into jerky.

The next few days were a blur of activity. The supporting of the mine was completed and Amos had crawled back in. With all the loose rocks and dirt cleaned out, his movement in the mine was simple. It was still a one or two-man mine, but there was elbow room. Boards had been put against the roof of the breach and what water that continued to come through was channeled to the side. Hoss suggested opening up the end of the tunnel a little to make working easier, and it was decided that that would be the next step.

The prospector emerged from underground and complimented his partners on their fine job shoring the mine. Jay and Hoss seemed to appreciate his praise. "Now I'm going to see about getting one of the elk."

* * *

Amos was sitting in front of the cabin drying the elk meat on racks when two men rode into the entrance of the canyon. The prospector had a fire going nearby and had meat broiling for his partners midday meal. The prospector moved the Winchester within easy reach and removed the loop from his revolver. The two men stopped and looked toward the steam engine for a moment, then continued toward the cabin.

"Are you Amos Mudd?" the larger of the two called to him.

"That I am," the prospector replied.

"Might we come up to the cabin?" the polite visitor asked.

Amos waved them in and kept placing the strips of elk meat onto the rack. He continued until the two men dismounted. He then wiped his hands on his pants and stood waiting for the two men to join him.

"I got meat on the fire and can put a few more pieces on if you'd like some," Amos told the men. "We also got coffee on the edge of the fire."

"That is very generous of you, Mr. Mudd," the taller man said. "My name is Theodor Becket. This is Richard Kruse, my partner."

"Well, you know my name and I believe you were here a week ago and talked to my partners Hoss Weber and . . . A.J. Mudd," the prospector replied. "Now that we all know each other, let's partake of these steaks."

Amos got tin plates, forks and knives for the visitors. He put more meat onto the fire, expecting Hoss and Jay to come in any time. They sat on blocks of wood and enjoyed the meat, washing it down with strong coffee.

"I must tell you, Mr. Mudd, this could be considered fine dining," Theodor commented. "You broil a good steak."

Just then Jay and Hoss came in and picked up a couple of pieces of broiled meat and started eating it right off the stick. Amos offered to put some more meat on to broil, but everyone said they had had enough. The visitors seemed anxious to get down to talking.

With the meal finished, Theodor cleared his throat and began. "It is our understanding that you own 1,000 acres and that there may be gold on the land."

Amos grabbed a rag and wiped his mouth and beard. "There is thousand acres and it may have some gold on it, but you are wrong about one thing."

"What is that, Mr. Mudd?" Richard asked.

"To start off, you can call me Amos," the prospector told them. "This here 1,000 acres is owned by A.J. Mudd and Horst Weber, so anything you have to discuss has to be with them. I just take care of the cabin and make wood for the fire."

"Should I be needed for council, I will be tending to the animals." With that, Amos left the meeting and his partners, whose mouths hung open.

Amos sat on the split-log bench and lit his pipe. His heart was pounding. The visitors were mining men. He had heard of them in his travels. They owned Kruse-Becket Mines and specialized in gold and silver.

The tobacco settled his palpitating heart. He wanted to listen to what was said in the worst way, but he had taken his own name off the partnership while in Absarokee and wanted A.J. and Hoss to make the decisions.

The prospector tried to keep out of sight as the two men walked around the claim with the mine company men. After a couple of hours, the men came back. Amos was again drying elk meat. Kruse and Becket nodded to Amos as they mounted their horses and rode out of the canyon. The prospector was bound and determined not to go looking for Jay and Hoss. Soon enough they would let him know what had been discussed.

Amos was getting mighty fidgety by the time the two finally joined him near the fire. "Did they make you an offer?" he asked.

"You knew they were come to talk about buying the mine?" Hoss asked.

"I know the company and was sure they wouldn't ride all the way out here just to partake in my fine elk steaks," the prospector said.

"They want to have their experts look over the claim before making an offer," Jay said. "They did say they'd seen enough to be interested."

"I want you both to know, you have my blessing to sell the mine," Amos said. "As part of the price, I would make them pay the going price for the gold you've already mined."

"You brought us in as partners, Amos," Hoss reminded him. "Anything done here will be split three ways. Hell, maybe their offer will be an insult and we will turn it down. It's got to be three votes."

"You don't understand," the prospector told them. "I have already voted. My vote gave my share to the two of you. All I ask is that that whatever you decide, do good with what you get."

That evening, while Amos was taking the dried elk meat off the rack, he saw Jay coming toward him. "You want to try a piece of this fresh jerky, Jay?"

Reaching his hand out, he took a piece and took a bite. "It's good."

Making small talk, Amos replied, "I been making jerky for years, Jay. I . . ."

The dark-eyed man interrupted him. "Call me A.J. or . . . or Amos. I think it's time for Jay to go away."

"Is it okay to call you 'son'?" the prospector asked, avoiding looking at the man.

Nodding, A.J. said, "If you want to."

Things were getting awkward for the two men, so A.J. turned to leave. "I got to help Hoss with the engine."

Amos sat staring at the pile of jerky for the longest time. What he felt inside he'd never experienced before. It was different and didn't hurt, but it was different. He slowly packed the jerky into canvas bags. The prospector was not sure what tomorrow would bring, but he knew that things had changed.

CHAPTER EIGHTEEN

Kruse and Becket were back in two days with four mining experts. Amos, A.J., and Hoss sat near the cabin and let them wander around, assessing what the potential of the strike would be. The two partners had decided to sell if the offer was acceptable. What that might be they weren't sure about.

"You know they will do hydraulic mining," Amos told them. "Once they come in with the big equipment, this place will never be the same."

"That's what Mr. Becket told us on the last visit," A.J. said. "He is also in a hurry because right now there is a shortage of gold to support the dollar and the price will stay high until the gold from the Klondike gets to market."

Hoss chewed on a piece of hay and sat on the corral rail. After a bit he said, "I'm going to buy a ranch somewhere in Montana and raise horses. I'll move my wife and the whole family there."

"I'd send some back to my mother, but I think she has died," A.J. said. After a minute he continued.

"After I left, I would let her know where I was and we'd write. I stopped getting letters when I was at Fort Washakie. I heard there was a fever in Michigan."

A sadness went through Amos. He had never considered that Ona might be dead. He left the two partners to dream of how they'd spend the money. Amos stopped near the three graves and sat on a rock. The bank rose behind them and to the front was the cave that had held the gold. "I think I should warn you," he whispered. "There will be mining in this canyon and they won't leave a rock unturned. The bank behind you will be gone and with it your resting place. I didn't want it to come as a surprise. I hope you'll forgive the part we had in this happening."

It was after dark when Amos came back to the cabin. The mining people had left. A.J. and Hoss were drinking coffee at the small table. Warmth swept through him as he saw Ona's smiling eyes on A.J.'s face. This was an exciting time.

"How much should we ask for?" Hoss asked him.

"They will make an offer and that will be based on what they think they can buy the mine for and not what it might be worth," Amos told him. "It will seem like more money that you ever dreamed of, but it won't be enough."

A.J. set his cup down. "Would you be willing to do the haggling for us? I would appreciate it . . . father."

There was no arguing with them at that point. "Yes. Yes, I will, son."

Kruse and Becket came back confident of the offer they were going to propose. They weren't really happy when they found out that they had to negotiate with the old prospector. Amos had three blocks of wood set up near the drained pond, choosing that location for the talks. Theodor handed him a piece of paper. Amos put it into his shirt pocket. "I am not going to look at your offer so we can get off on the right foot."

And that's where it began. For the next two hours they sat discussing the mine. Twice the piece of paper came out of Amos' pocket and another replaced it. Finally, the two mining men went to the far side of the pond and turned their backs to the prospector. The discussion seemed to be heated, with lots of arm waving. Kruse finally appeared to get the upper hand and he and Becket returned to their blocks.

They handed Amos another piece of paper and took the one from his pocket. The prospector said "I'll see what the partners think." and then walked to meet with A.J. and Hoss. Handing it to them to look at, Amos whispered, "Do not show any emotion. After you look, talk to each other and then tell me something. It is not important what you say, but don't smile."

The two partners opened the piece of paper and Hoss whispered, "Oh my God." After a bit of talking, fighting to keep their emotions inside, Amos walked back toward Kruse and Becket. He smiled and nodded at them. Taking a seat, he told them, "I did not look at what you wrote on the paper. I had expected them to be more excited. I told them that I didn't think you'd go higher. They do have some gold cached and if you buy that at market price, I think we have a deal. Only one other thing, there are three graves on the far side of the canyon of the original

Spanish miners. If at all possible, they would like them to be left undisturbed."

Suddenly, Becket smiled. "We heard about a map or letter from one of the Spaniards. If we get that, we have a deal."

Out of curiosity, Kruse asked, "Do you want to know what our first offer was?"

"Nope," Amos replied. "All that is important is the last offer."

"Our attorney is in Absarokee and we'll be back in a couple days with papers to sign," Becket said. "I take it they have the ownership papers here?"

Kruse and Becket met with the partners before leaving to get the name of the banks the money was to be deposited in. They would also be coming back with men to take over guarding their investment. A.J. asked if they would be keeping the steam engine. He was told it could be dragged out of the canyon if he wanted. It was far too small for what they would need.

That night supper was exciting. Hoss asked Amos if he knew what they'd offered. He told them that he did not know and did not want to know. Both of the men tried to get Amos to take some of the gold cache, but again he refused. He assured them that he had enough money.

* * *

In less time than the three men expected, they were sitting with their worldly goods outside the entrance of the canyon. A.J. had the mule hitched to the steam engine. The pump and items from the cabin were in the wagon driven by Amos. Hoss, on the bay, was riding straight through to Red Lodge while Amos and A.J. planned to stop at the Williams farm. Amos cautioned both men about talking too much about the sale of the mine. It would bring the worst kind of people coming after them.

They had been paid cash for the gold they had in the cache. After additional urging, Amos finally relented to taking one third of this money. Each man's share was just under $3,000. The prospector figured it would be enough to keep him comfortable for a few winters with some to spare.

As the pump and wagon approached the farm, Amos saw Lucia and Chip hoeing the potatoes. Elly was playing in front of their cabin. The two men got a grand welcome as they pulled into the farm yard. A.J. was excited to show Lucia the engine and pump he had brought to be used for washing potatoes or irrigating the fields. Chip was thrilled with the elk jerky Amos brought them. "Wow!" he exclaimed. "Real jerky, just like the cowboys ate."

A.J. and Chip went to do the chores while Amos and Lucia made supper. To the prospector's delight, it included new potatoes from the field. Elly sat on the floor, asking Amos every question she could think of, and no matter what he answered she would ask, "Why?"

That evening, A.J. and Lucia took a long walk in the fields while the two children entertained Amos. They asked him if he would be their grandpa, and he told them he would be honored. Their house was everything Amos had always felt a home should be. The prospector planned to leave for Red Lodge in the morning and wanted to take in as much of the home life as he could while he was here.

He and A.J. took their blankets and headed for the barn to sleep. They spread them on fresh hay and lay listening to the cows chewing their cuds and the babbling brook flowing behind the barn. Amos felt that it had been a good day.

All of a sudden, A.J. spoke. "I asked Lucia to marry me."

"And she said?" Amos asked

"She said yes."

"What did she think about the money from selling the mine?" the prospector asked.

"I haven't told her yet."

Now Amos felt that it had been a perfect day.

The next morning Chip ran to a nearby neighbor and asked him to take care of the stock for a couple of days. By mid-morning the family was in the wagon with A.J. while Amos was riding the mule. There was going to be a wedding. Amos suggested the old preacher who had married Hoss and Sara. As they went, the prospector sat on the mule, enjoying the excited chatter from the wagon.

The wedding was a grand affair put together by Hoss and Sara. A.J. had asked everyone not to tell Lucia about the money. He wanted to save that for the honeymoon. The wedding included a sermon, which Amos enjoyed. Sara's cousins put the meal together and made a cake.

Hoss' wife was large with child but insisted on a dance with Amos, who was wearing a dark double-breasted frock coat with matching waistcoat and trousers. Hoss was also decked out in a new store-bought suit. He and Amos went and got glasses of lemonade. "I'm glad you and A.J. made up."

"He sure was carrying a whole lot of anger," Amos admitted.

"When you left for Absarokee, you were the saddest man I'd ever seen," Hoss told the prospector. "Well, I talked A.J.'s ear off about it. I told him he was mad at you for something you knew nothing about. I was about ready to pound some sense into his thick skull when he finally began to understand. If you'll excuse my saying, I told him you were an old man and he missed all the years with his father before now and it would be a damn shame to miss the rest of them."

Amos looked at the tall black man with admiration. "I thank you for that, Hoss."

The celebration went on until early evening. Finally, Amos was able to say goodbye to everyone and made promises to keep in touch. He then excused himself and headed for Goldie's. He left with one additional promise, that he would return in the morning for breakfast at the Carbon Café to wish his son and daughter-in-law on their way.

The prospector walked up the street in his new suit and a bowler hat. He was thinking that maybe it was time for him to marry. Life with Goldie sounded like a very good idea. He thought of how angry she had been when he'd left the last time. Now he could tell her that he was back for good. As the weathered clapboard building came into view, Amos fought the urge to run. *It wouldn't do much good to have my heart give out on her porch,* he thought.

Amos went into the saloon. He closed his eyes and breathed in the atmosphere. He liked the smell of his new home. Combing his beard with his fingers, he glanced at the cage. One of the Faro dealers was in it.

Walking up to the bar, he called to Ted, "I'll have a rye, and would you let Goldie know I'm here?"

The bartender gave him a blank stare. Amos suddenly realized that he was wearing clothing that was altogether different from what Ted had seen before. "It me, Ted. Amos Mudd to see Goldie."

The bartender grabbed a bottle and glass, quickly pouring a drink for the prospector. "She's not here, Amos."

"When will she be back?" Amos asked, smiling and tossing down the rye.

"She married and moved to San Francisco, Amos. She sold the saloon to the man in the cage. He probably paid for it with money he stole at the tables."

"San Francisco?" he asked, stunned.

"An old acquaintance came through town and asked her to come with him," Ted told him.

"San Francisco," Amos said again.

Ted led Amos to a table and placed the bottle and a glass for him. "Will you need a room?"

"Yes. Yes, I guess I will," the prospector said as the full reality of the news sunk in. It was going to be a cold, lonely winter. Suddenly, the pain in his chest was back. It felt so tight that he could hardly breathe. Fumbling in his pocket, he took out the small bottle and put a pinch into his mouth. Again, his head ached, but not nearly as hard as at the mine.

The bartender noticed that Amos was pale and holding his chest. He rushed over to the table. "Are you okay, Amos?"

The pain had already started to subside in the prospector's chest. "Yes. Just give me a minute, Ted."

The next morning at the Carbon Café, A.J. looked at his father. "You look down. Is it because you're going to miss me?"

Forcing a smile, Amos said, "More than you know. I'll be leaving Red Lodge soon, but I'll try and get to the farm before I go."

"Where will you be going to, father?" A.J. asked.

That question brought a genuine smile to the prospector's face. "Casper, I think."

* * *

There was a hint of color in the trees when Amos arrived in Casper. He had sent a telegram beforehand to Bert Hartwick. The merchant met him at the train station. Amos carried his worldly possessions in the carpet bag and his saddlebags. His mule was in the cattle car.

"Angie's got a fine meal waiting for you," Bert said. "Will you be staying in Casper for a while?"

"I'll be around for the winter months," the prospector said. "We'll see come next spring what the next move will be. The way my ticker has been working, this could be my last stop."

Concern spread over Bert's face. "The heart still giving you problems?"

"Not so much, Bert," Amos told him. "It just likes to remind me once in a while."

"Angie and I want you to stay the winter with us," the merchant said.

"I appreciate the offer, but I can't do that," Amos said.

"We got the extra room," Bert insisted.

"Thanks anyway," the prospector replied. "I am an old, crusty mountain man and would make a poor house guest. I will accept a home-cooked meal now and then."

After a few days in a room at the saloon, Amos rented a small cabin on the edge of Casper. It had two rooms and a lean-to for the mule. The prospector enjoyed making repairs to the place during the next month. Evenings found him at the Casper Saloon or dining with Bert and Angie.

In late October Dan and Mary August made a trip into Casper and Amos spent many hours with the rancher, telling him all about finding the mine. He told him about his son A.J. and about how his son and Hoss split the money from the sale of the mine.

Dan was happy to hear that things had worked out. "I read about someone finding a lost Spanish mine in Montana. It talked about the Kruse-Becket Mining Company but didn't say much about who found it."

"I hope your grandfather Oli doesn't turn over in his grave," Amos said. "Once they're finished with the hydraulic mining, there won't be much left of the canyon."

"The newspaper said that they were going to sink shafts to get the gold out, Dan said. "While there is a good amount of gold, it was concentrated in one area."

Thinking of the three Spanish graves, the prospector smiled. "That's good. There will be a good-sized pile of tailings, but the canyon should remain after that mining is done."

Amos stood on the mercantile porch as the August family left to return to their ranch. It would be spring before they made another trip to Casper. He wished that they had had more time to visit. Maybe he would make a trip to the valley once the snow started melting.

It was early December when Sheriff Winslow came up the street and called to the prospector, "Join me for a drink at the saloon, Amos?"

"Always happy to share a bottle," the prospector said, the crusty snow crunching under his boots.

The two men entered the dimly lit saloon. Lem the bartender waved them over. "Did they talk to you yet?" he asked the sheriff.

"About what?" Winslow asked.

"The Kelsey family had a boarder," Lem said. "He musta got some bad liquor or something. He shot old man Kelsey and took their daughter."

"He kill him?" the sheriff asked.

"No," the bartender said. "His missus took him to the doc's and then come here looking for you. She was all upset, bawling and everything."

"Damn," the sheriff said. "I just come in from checking on some missing cows. Do you know where she is now?"

"Her sister was with her and she probably went there," Lem replied.

"You want to come with me, Amos?" the sheriff asked as he turned to leave.

Amos hesitated. He'd come in for a drink, and didn't even have his gun on. *Damn,* he thought. "I'm right behind you, sheriff."

The prospector followed the sheriff, his coat covering his nose and mouth to prevent his chest from starting to hurt. The cold north wind tore at their clothing as they approached the sister's house. There was crying in the weathered home. When the sheriff knocked, the door was jerked open and the two ladies talked at the same time, trying to tell him what had happened.

The prospector stood alone in the street as Winslow got the information about the shooting and kidnapping. Amos moved around the corner of the building to get out of the wind. After a few minutes the sheriff came out of the house. "You still here, Amos?" he called.

The two men headed back toward the jail. The sheriff's jaw was tight. "You let a questionable man into your house and then are surprised when trouble happens."

The stove was out in the jail and offered no relief from the cold. "I got to go after the man with the girl," the sheriff told Amos. "I could use someone that knows the area and ain't afraid of a little snow. I could use you."

Amos thought about his ticker and what the strain of a manhunt could do. Then, he figured, the man had taken the girl. Getting her back would be doing good. "I'll help you," he said.

An hour later, the two men rode out of Casper. The boarder's name was Cat Biggins. He had just been fired from one of the mines for fighting. It turned out that he'd been making eyes at the 14-year-old daughter and old man Kelsey was putting him out when the fight began. Cat had stolen two of the neighbor's horses and rode out onto the plain with the girl.

Amos had his wolf skin coat on and heavy wool britches. A rabbit skin hat covered his head and ears. There was a neckerchief over his nose and mouth. His Winchester 73 was in the scabbard and the Colt .45 was on his hip. The mule was well-rested and ready for the rigors of the coming chase. The sheriff was riding a long-legged black and sat higher than Amos on the mule.

The tracks were plain in the December snow. One nagging worry that the sheriff had shared with Amos was that it was uncertain if she'd gone with Cat voluntarily or had been forced. They were four hours behind the two. As long as more snow held off, following them would be easy.

"One of our benefits," the sheriff had said, "was there was no planning on this. It will be hard to disappear."

"They are heading west along the North Platte," Amos said. "He might be hoping to lose anyone following him in the Wind River area."

"They have no supplies and I am not sure how well they're dressed for the weather," the sheriff replied.

"They will have to find a line shack or a small town to get what they need," Amos said. "I doubt he has any money, so he would have to steal from the small towns."

"How about the small ranches?" Winslow reminded the prospector.

"Let's pray they don't bring tragedy to an unsuspecting ranch family." Amos had come across more than one burned-out cabin or ranch house that had been the victim of thieves or raiders.

At dusk it began snowing. The sheriff swore, realizing that they would soon lose the tracks in the snow. The two men stopped for the night in a clump of cottonwoods. Cat had kept to the trail along the

Platte, which made Amos believe he had a destination in mind.

Lying under his blanket near the fire, Amos searched his memory of the area ahead of them. Suddenly, he thought about a summer lodge that was used for fishing. It would be closed for the winter but would have some staples and a place to get out of the weather. He and the sheriff wouldn't be able to travel until daylight tomorrow, and if the snow got heavier it might make travel impossible.

It was still dark when the two men awoke and got their fire going. Their blankets had been covered with three inches of snow. The wind remained light enough to prevent windblown snow. The two men shared a pot of coffee and stale biscuits. Amos told the sheriff about the lodge.

"It's off the Platte along one of the streams," the sheriff said.

"It is and could easily be missed once the tracks are covered," Amos replied. "The stream is about two hours ahead of us. I'm guessing that this Cat guy knows of the lodge and hoped to use it as a hideout until things settle down."

"You think they might be there?" Winslow asked.

"It would be another day's ride before they find anything else," Amos reasoned. "Without food and on tired horses, I can't see them continuing."

"How about an isolated line shack?" the sheriff asked. "He could be heading for one of them."

"He was a miner, not a cowboy who might have used a line shack. I would check the lodge first," the prospector said.

The eastern sky was barely showing evidence of the sunrise and there was still a light snow falling when the two men left the grove of cottonwoods. Amos figured that they'd be able to keep their direction along the Platte, and when they hit the larger stream they'd know it as the one with the lodge. Plus, it would be full light.

Once visibility improved it was clear that they'd lost any sign of the tracks. There was a wooded area ahead that might show some protected imprints. Amos pulled his Winchester from the saddle scabbard and carried it across the saddle horn. He didn't expect trouble before the stream, but he wanted to be ready just in case.

As they worked their way through the trees, the two men searched for any tracks. Approaching the stream, they still hadn't found any. Sitting next to the stream on their animals, the sheriff looked in the direction of the lodge. The building was out of sight, a quarter-mile through the trees.

Amos sat, chewing on a plug of tobacco. "There are three trails to the lodge."

"Three?" the sheriff asked.

"That is, if you count weaving in through the trees along the stream. Just after we left the cottonwoods there was one. It would have been impossible to see without full daylight. The last one is further down the Platte." Amos spat into the snow. "I think they took the trail we passed and that's why we couldn't find any tracks in the trees."

Amos started the mule upstream. "Let's go find out if they're here."

Halfway from the trail to the lodge, they caught a whiff of smoke. The sheriff whispered, "Someone is up there."

Dismounting from their animals, the prospector and sheriff slowly moved through the trees towards the lodge. Amos hadn't told him that the building was more of a fort than a lodge. It had a good view from all sides and notches for firing from. When conflicts with the tribes were common, a trader had built it on high ground next to a small waterfall. Later, when a fisherman found that the stream had an abundance of fish, he'd turned the old fort into a lodge.

Suddenly a shot rang out, sending splinters of bark tearing into the sheriff's face. The two men hit the ground. "Damn near blew my head off!" the sheriff growled.

"I think he was warning us," Amos guessed. "We were wide open from his view and he could have shot either of us dead."

The sheriff yelled, "Cat! Throw out your rifle and come out with your hands up!"

"That was Ronnie shooting," Cat yelled. "She don't want to go back."

The prospector was under thicker cover than the sheriff. He kept slowly moving toward the lodge. The sheriff continued to try and reason with the couple. "The old man is only wounded and the most you'll get is a couple years. If you kill one of us, you will hang. You too, Ronnie."

"So, there are two of you?" Cat called back.

"Damn," the sheriff muttered. Then he hollered, "Six, not two! We're coming from three sides."

Amos had reached the corner of the lodge. A wide porch had been built that wrapped around the building. The prospector had spent time at the lodge fishing years ago. It had been in return for guiding some businessmen on a hunt in the Rockies. He remembered a root cellar around the side. The original builder had planned it as a way to escape if the fort had been fired.

There was another shot. It was on the far side of the lodge. Cat was shooting at shadows. Amos worked his way under the porch and toward the side with the root cellar. It opened via a trapdoor into the galley. The prospector just hoped nothing had been set on top of it.

The space near the cellar door was too tight to squeeze through, so Amos would have to crawl out, exposing himself briefly. He lay near the edge for several minutes. Finally, the sheriff continued to urge the two to give up. During the exchange Amos moved into the open and then next to the cellar door. It was secured with a rusty lock. Pulling his skinning knife from his belt, the prospector tried to pry the clasp loose.

There was a groan from a nail. Amos held his breath, hoping that it hadn't been heard. Once again, the sheriff started negotiating. The prospector quickly pried the lock loose. The doorway consisted of two doors. Amos tried to open the one on the left. The upper hinge pulled loose from the rotting frame. Carefully replacing the left door, he tried the right. Slowly, he opened it. The door did not want to stay open, so Amos backed into the cellar and let the door close behind him.

The old cellar was almost dark and filled with cobwebs. The only light came from gaps in the foundation. The cellar was small and shallow. Amos sat on the dirt floor and felt around for the trapdoor. Finding the opening edge, he pushed up slightly. It moved. He remembered that the wood box was next to the wall and the trapdoor opened against it.

Above him there were two people with rifles and they had established that they would shoot. Opening the trapdoor would make noise, and he had to assume they wouldn't hesitate. Suddenly there was sustained rifle fire. It was the sheriff shooting. Amos had his Colt out and pushed open the trapdoor. He was face-to-face with a wide-eyed Ronnie, who had taken cover in the galley.

Amos looked her right in the eyes as he put his finger to his lips. In plain sight of the girl was his Colt. The prospector climbed out of the cellar and crouched in front of the girl. "Please don't kill him," she whispered.

Again, there was sustained rifle fire, causing the girl to jump. Amos saw no guns near her, so he moved to the edge of the door going to the main room. Carefully, he stood up. Peering around the door jamb, he saw Cat crouched near a firing port.

The prospector brought the Colt up through the doorway. He was about to ask Cat to give up when Ronnie screamed to warn him. The man spun, shooting. Amos returned fire. Suddenly the girl was on his back, scratching him and screaming, "You killed him! You bastard, you killed him!"

He threw her off his back and yelled at her, "He ain't dead! Yet!" The prospector stepped into the room with the Colt leveled. Cat sat near the wall, blood flowing from the hole in his leg. She came at Amos again and he reached back and threw her into the main room. Seeing Cat, she ran to shield him from being shot again.

Amos yelled down to the sheriff to come on up. He then scooped up the rifle near the wounded man. "You best let me put something on that leg before your boy bleeds to death."

Winslow came in and helped keep the girl off Amos as he put a bandage on Cat's leg. The bullet was still in the leg and the doc in Casper would have to take it out. To be able to get back to Casper today, there wasn't time to put the lodge back in order. Regretting leaving the mess, Amos got the kid's horses from the stable beyond the lodge and the animals from downstream. It had stopped snowing, making the trip back to Casper easier.

During the ride back, Ronnie kept telling the sheriff how mean her father was and how he would beat her. Winslow knew that it wasn't against the law to beat your kids and the sheriff told her he could not help her on that account. The sheriff also knew that Cat wasn't such a bad young man, but he tended to have a short fuse and hadn't found his way yet. By the time he got out of prison, maybe he'd outgrow it.

Amos rode quietly back toward Casper, listening to all this. He didn't believe in beating kids, but then again, he had never had any around him. With the young man's temper, it might only be a matter of time before Ronnie would be less of a novelty and Cat might start hitting her.

It was dark when they reached Casper. They learned that old man Kelsey had died. Amos felt sorry for the sheriff. Now he would be holding Cat for a hanging. On the other hand, the old man wouldn't be beating the girl anymore. The prospector thought about all of the happiness he had seen with A.J. and Lucia, Hoss and Sara, and even Sheriff Packer. He remembered another girl whom he and Dan August had brought back home and how it had brought joy to the family. Life wasn't always fair.

The routine for the rest of the winter was coffee with Pop at the livery each morning, lunch at the Carbon Café, drinks at the saloon with the sheriff, and twice a week a meal with the Hartwicks. The sheriff was relieved that Cat was only convicted of manslaughter and the horse theft was dropped. He would only spend six years in prison. If Ronnie was willing to wait, maybe it would work out.

By the spring, Amos knew what he had to do. The words of the old doctor in Absarokee kept coming back to him. "I would also recommend you start settling your affairs. Things you leave undone will more than likely be left undone."

CHAPTER NINETEEN

Black smoke puffed from the train into the brisk morning air as it idled beside the Casper depot, taking on anxious passengers. With the help of Dan August, Amos got the mule, Jenny, into the cattle car of the train. "So, you're going back east."

"I spent the winter thinking about it, and it's the right thing to do," the prospector replied.

"You're taking the mule with you," Dan pointed out. "It looks like you don't plan to return to the west."

"It's part of a promise I made to my father 48 years ago," Amos told him. "I have spent the years treating myself and it is time to give back."

Dan shook his head. "There isn't a man I've met that has given more to others than you. For crying out loud, you finally find the mother lode, your life's quest, and you give it away."

"Your words are kind, Dan," Amos said, "but I had no need for the gold. Others did, to be able to live their dreams. Now I realize my dream was just to find the mother lode. Now I need to settle debts long owed."

Mary and Joanie came to the depot platform to wish him well. Amos pulled a peppermint stick from the pocket of his dark suit and gave it to the little girl. "Make sure you take good care of your folks," he advised her.

"She does that," Mary told him, giving the prospector a hug. "You take care of yourself and come back west. We'd be proud to have you stay at the ranch."

The conductor called, "All aboard."

Dan shook the prospector's hand. "Be safe, Amos."

Before getting on the train, the prospector handed him a package wrapped in paper and tied with string. "It's my wolf skin coat, to keep you warm in the winter."

Amos got onto the train as the wheels spun, trying to gain traction. It slowly moved away from the depot, spewing clouds of black smoke. He waved to those standing on the platform. The night before, Angie and Bert had given him a farewell party. Those he had become close to in Casper were all there. Amos wasn't sure if life would allow him to come back, but he would always consider Casper as his home in the west.

The weather was pleasant and the rolling hills around the train were coming awake with spring flowers. Pronghorn looked up from feeding as the train approached, and then bounding away as it got close. Amos had the window open so he could enjoy the sweet smell of the open plain.

Each time the train stopped to take on fuel and water, the prospector would go back to the cattle car and check on the mule. There were two horses and his mule in the car. After some stops, Amos would sit on a bail near Jenny and talk about where they were going. He had a one-day layover in Ohio, so Amos left his baggage at the depot and took the mule for a long ride along the rutted country roads. He marveled at the large fields, plowed and planted with corn.

His train pulled into Houlton, Maine in June of 1898. He got off at an impressive depot. Further down the train, he saw men taking the mule from the cattle car. The ground under his feet felt unstable after the days of riding on the swaying train. Collecting his baggage, he walked down the cinder cover side of the track to get Jenny. His saddle and blanket roll lay next the mule, tied to the cattle pen rail.

He looked around in wonder. The population of Houlton had almost tripled since he had last been there in 1850. Amos had eaten a sandwich on the train a couple of hours ago and now felt an urgency to saddle up and get out of the town. To the east was the St. John River in Canada. To the west was the farm he'd grown up on. He turned the mule to the west, winding through the streets, passing homes and businesses. Folks would wave as he rode past and, mindlessly, Amos would wave back.

As he headed west he recognized the road his father had used coming to Houlton. Many of the landmarks were gone, but enough were left, including a large stone church. Amos almost missed the turnoff to the farm. Much of the land was cleared and the fields put into potatoes.

The barn and sorting sheds were gone and had been replaced by larger and longer sheds., but the cabin that he had grown up in was still there. The roof was sagging. Amos dismounted and stepped up onto the porch. The door hung ajar and he peered in. It was now a tool shed.

"Can I help you?" someone called out, interrupting the prospector's trip down memory lane. He turned and saw a man dressed in denim trousers held up by suspenders and a dirty, blue cotton shirt. Amos walked toward the man. "I'm Amos Mudd. I grew up on this farm."

"I'll be damned," the man said. "My father used to talk about a man named Jacob Mudd."

"That was my father," Amos told him.

"Yep, they said he died right out there," the man replied, pointing to a nearby field. Already filled with guilt, that was something the prospector did not need to know.

Then the man reached out his hand, "My name's Ray Hanson. I'm second generation on this farm. We still grow some potatoes from the original Mudd seed. They are a damn fine potato."

Amos took the man's hand. "I left in 1850 to find gold in California. My father wasn't too happy that I didn't stay and take the farm over."

The man gave him a sideways grin. "Did you ever find any?"

"My friend, I never even made it to California," Amos admitted.

"I'd be happy to show you around the farm," Ray offered.

There was little that still looked like the place Amos had left, and he had no desire to look at the changes. "Thanks, but I'm just here to visit my father's grave."

"I believe it is behind the Lutheran church just a bit more up the road," the man told him.

"If you don't mind, I'd like to buy a bag or two of the taters from my father's seed," Amos said. "I'll come back after I visit his grave."

"I'll have them waiting for you," Ray promised. "They was grown in the same field of the original farm."

Hesitating a minute while staring at the old cabin, Amos then climbed on the mule and headed for the church. The white clapboard building, with an open steeple housing a bell, came into view just beyond a row of maples that the prospector used to play under as a child. It was before his mother had died. Those had been good days. Toward the back of the graveyard, Amos found the stones of his mother and father. He had left Jenny grazing near the shoulder of the road.

"Hello mother," he whispered as he removed the bowler and placed his hand on top of her grave. He said a prayer for her, knowing that she would hear it in heaven. Then he looked at his father's stone. It read: Jacob Mudd 1801- 1851. It was simple, like the life he had lived.

Kneeling at the foot of the grave he said, "I have brought the mule back, just like I promised. It ain't the Jenny I left with, but it's a good mule. I got sidelined on the way to California and never did get there." Tears filled the prospector's eyes. "I am sorry I wasn't here when you collapsed in the field. It wasn't right that you died alone, lying in the plowing. I did finally find gold, but I couldn't keep it. I did bring you this."

Amos reached into his coat pocket and brought out the gold cross from the cave. He dug into the dirt in front of the stone and placed the cross in the indention and covered it over. For several minutes Amos prayed for his father, tears glistening on his cheeks.

Then, clearing his throat, he told his father, "I have never spent the money sent to me from the sales of the farm. I just couldn't until I come back to explain things to you. I hope you will forgive me for leaving. The cross is for you and momma. I hope the two of you are happy in heaven. I think I know now how you felt when she was suddenly taken from you."

Before leaving the graves, he whispered, "I'll be coming to see you soon, momma."

For the longest time, Amos stood with the mule near the graveyard. It was a peaceful place. He wished that he had brought some flowers to put onto his mother's grave. Wiping his nose on the sleeve of his coat, he climbed back on Jenny and headed back to the farm to get the potatoes.

* * *

The train station was crowded in Ottawa. Amos had to wait for 30 minutes before the animals were unloaded from the train. He looked at the name on the front of the train station. It had been called Bytown the last time he had been here.

Before boarding the train in Houlton, Amos had shipped one of the bags of potatoes to A.J. and Lucia, so they could plant some of the same type that his father had. He hoped that the climate and soil in Montana wouldn't change them too much. The second bag he would enjoy during his travels.

After saddling the mule and tying the packs to the saddle, he led the animal past the series of locks along the Rideau Canal in Ottawa. The sun was warm on his face and it felt good to walk. Amos wondered if the farm he had stopped at was still around.

The first thing he recognized was the barn. It was now painted red, with several white board fences enclosing pastures. Several horses grazed and the sight of some playful red ponies reminded him of the red mare that was in labor the night he had gotten to the farm.

He smiled, the small house was still there. A white-haired man came out of the barn. "If you're looking for work, we're looking for men a bit younger," he called to Amos.

"I ain't looking for work," the prospector said. "Just traveling down memory lane and visiting graves."

"Well, that's an awful thought," the white-haired man replied. "No graves here."

"I'm wondering if you know of a man named, Junior?" Amos asked.

"Why, hell, I ain't heard that name in 30 years," the man exclaimed. "I was called Junior until my grandpa died. Now they call me Ralph."

Ralph squinted at the mule Amos was leading. "I remember a rag-tag man that stopped by the farm years ago. I believe he called himself Amos, but I don't remember his last name. He did have a mule."

"Good to see you again, Junior. It is me, Amos Mudd."

Ralph approached the prospector, his hand out. "Me and my grandpa figured you would never make it through the winter."

He shook Amos' hand with a firm grip of years of hard work. "Come on in the barn, I got some cider working from last year's apples."

While they sat drinking the hard cider, the man pointed at the ponies. "They're from the line that you helped with the foal."

"You got more fences and the barn is painted red," Amos replied, "but you still have the same damn fine cider."

Amos spent several days at the farm telling stories, drinking cider, and even helping out with some of the chores. Not wanting to outstay his welcome, he wished Ralph well and headed back for the train station. Walking along the Rideau Canal, he tried to picture people skating along it in the winter. He stopped and watched a lock being opened by the workmen, and three boats passed through. *Someday,* he thought, *the locks will be run with steam engines.*

The prospector caught the train from Ottawa to Mattawa, Ontario. It had a modern station and Amos took his meal there at a small lunch counter before collecting his baggage and the mule. He had a strong desire to see the area where he had spent the winter logging. It was a two-day walk above the Mattawa.

With the packs on the mule he headed out. Every time he stopped to rest, black flies would swarm around his head. The logged-off areas had a mix of poplar and evergreens. He remembered being able to drive a wagon or sledge anywhere between the original tall pines. The new growth was too thick, with brush between the trees.

There was a decent trail along the river. Amos stopped and camped in an area that had been frequented by others. He rigged up a fishing pole and sat, slapping flies, in the late evening. Once he had a trout and a bullhead, the prospector got his fire going and got the blackened frying pan out. He loved the taste of the trout's tender meat and didn't mind bullheads. He drank coffee and smoked his pipe after the meal. Tomorrow he would be in the area they had logged. He remembered that the cook house had been left each year. With luck some of it would be standing to mark the old logging camp.

A cool June rain began to fall during the night. Amos huddled under his blanket with the rain slicker spread over the top. It continued the next morning, making the prospector abandon thoughts of having a hot breakfast. Amos had switched his old wool pants and worn, plaid shirt. His drooping hat and the slicker kept most of the water off him.

As he walked leading the mule, water squished in his low-heeled boots. The only advantage he could see was that the black flies did not like the rain either and he got relief from them. The drizzle had just stopped when he stood looking at the bend upriver. He was willing to bet that the camp had been somewhere between his location and that bend. Old, gray, weathered stumps were everywhere, giving evidence of past activities.

As he had found at other logged-off areas, poplar trees, tag alders and hazelnut bushes had replaced the pine. Suddenly, Amos saw an old building. At first, he thought it was too small to be the cook house. Pushing through the brambles on the edge of the trail, he headed for the structure. The log walls still stood and the rafters rose like skeletons above the building.

Tying the mule to a hazelnut bush, he walked around the building. Sure enough, he found the entrance to the root cellar. The moss-covered logs on that side of the building had fared the worst and were sagging. Continuing around, he saw that the door was gone and any hardware had been scavenged. Looking in, he saw a rusty stove that Chef had used.

Standing back, he looked around. Amos tried to picture that camp. It had been wide-open and had had several buildings. Standing at the corner of the cook house, he tried to remember where they had buried his friend Jake. The wooden marker would have been long gone, but he knew that it was within 50 paces and he felt close to his departed friend. He walked beyond the cook house, knowing nothing would be there.

He spotted an old, moss-covered marker. Another man had joined Jake in later years. Amos knelt near the marker and scraped the moss from the granite face. He felt a cold sweat break over him. It was a marker for Jake. It read: Jacques Larue 1851. Someone from the camp had brought a marker for the grave in the years after Jake's death. The memory of Jake going under the runaway sedge would be forever burned into Amos' mind.

The prospector again prayed over the grave of someone he had known. Jake had convinced him to spend the winter in the logging camp and had saved him from an early death freezing in the Canadian wilds. Amos left the camp with a sense of peace. He had accomplished a good part of what he had wanted to do. There was another grave he still had to pray over, and that one would be the most difficult because he owed her a debt that no amount of praying could offset.

* * *

Amos reached Sault Ste. Marie, Ontario on July 2nd. The Tahquamenon Falls, where he had stayed with Ona, were still two days away. Many had told him while on the train that the Ojibwe had been moved to the prairies of Canada. If that was so, Amos just wanted to sit near the falls where he and Ona had once been. A good amount of his supplies had been used up by now, so the prospector could ride the mule with the remaining packs tied with the bed roll.

Amos spent a week around Sault Ste. Marie in upper Michigan. He enjoyed the celebration of independence. There was a day of revelry and wonderful food to eat. Seldom had he been in a town on the 4th that had such festivities. He talked for some time with an old man about the Council of Three Fires, which had brought the Ojibwe, Odawa, and Potawatomi tribes together.

The man told Amos about the relocation of tribes, of many of the Ojibwe moving to Canada and of the fever that killed many. The old man believed that had they had a Midewinin with history of the origin of the Ojibwe and secret medicines, the people could have been saved. Amos asked about the Ojibwe that lived around the Tahquamenon Falls. The man shook his head sadly. "Many died of the fever. Those that did not moved to St. Ignace or to the west. They have scattered to the winds."

While the celebration had left Amos feeling good to be an American, what he had learned about the Ojibwe left him feeling that finding information about Ona was a hopeless task. Determined to follow any possible lead, Amos rode south toward St. Ignace. He had been told that the Upper Peninsula of Michigan was surrounded on three sides by lakes. He expected to see waters stretching to the horizon when he got to St. Ignace.

Stopping on the high ground near the city, he was surprised. To his left he could see an island, and to the south was another shore after a narrow strait of water. The view was beautiful and Amos decided to have his midday meal on the hill. Ships with tall masts were tied up on both sides of the strait. While he ate, he saw a tall ship with billowing sails come from the east and sail through the channel.

An old man carrying a bag of tools settled down next to him. He nodded at Amos. "I love watching the ships come and go." The man pulled a meat pie from the bag and began to unwrap it. "I like to come up here and eat on nice days."

"I had expected to see large lakes when I got here," Amos admitted.

"Oh, they're big all right," the man said. "To your left is Lake Huron which borders Canada and well down along the lower. To the right is Lake Michigan. It goes all the way to Chicago."

"What I can see from here is a sight," the prospector replied. Then he asked, "What brings you to St. Ignace?"

"I been here since I was a lad," the old man said proudly. "I work on the boats, and with the rough waters of these lakes, it keeps me plenty busy."

"Maybe you can tell me where I can find information on the Ojibwe?" Amos asked. "I am looking for a friend's grave."

"You might want to start with the Mission," the old-timer said. "They got some old records."

The St. Ignace Mission was on Moran Bay, just a short ride to the northeast. Amos thanked the man and left, leading his mule. With luck those at the mission could give him some direction where to look for a grave site.

The single-story, clapboard building was easy to find. There was a modest steeple with a cross on the gable roof. The mission was weathered from the storms coming in off Lake Huron. Amos climbed the steps on the gable end and opened one of the double doors.

He stopped a moment and looked at the murals painted on the walls. A gust of wind slammed the door behind him. Wondering where he should go to find the priest was short-lived as a man came through one of the doors at the front of the church.

"Can I help you?" the priest asked.

For the next hour the Catholic priest talked with the prospector about the history of the mission, while the two of them sat in the front pew. Amos asked about the Ojibwe in St. Ignace and asked about any existing graves. The priest only knew of one where Indians who had converted to Christianity were buried.

"Most of the Ojibwe still follow the old beliefs and are buried in mounds with a spirit house above it," the priest told him. "Unfortunately, these burial places are easily found and are looted by grave robbers. Once done, there is nothing left to find, including who was buried in the mound."

Disappointed by the last statement, Amos stood up with hat in hand. "I would like to thank you for your time."

"Would you like to have confession before you leave?" the priest offered.

Smiling, Amos replied, "We don't have enough hours to do that. I talk regular to the lord and he and I got an understanding. I'd like to think we are even in that department."

"A prayer for a successful quest then," the kindly priest suggested.

"I'd like that," Amos said, bowing his head.

After another day of searching the St. Ignace area without success, Amos was back on the mule, heading for the Tahquamenon Falls. The name of the falls was an Ojibwe word meaning "dark berry" due to the tannin in the water making it brown.

Amos recalled sitting with Ona in the sweat lodge, cleansing their spirits. That was where he had told Ona that he still planned on going to California. She had refused to go and they had parted in the next few days. While he had thought of her often, he'd never gone back to see her.

Arriving at the Tahquamenon, Amos took a seat on the bank of the upper falls and stared at the amber water flowing as though a ribbon over the falls. He closed his eyes and the smell of the air and feel of the area felt very familiar. Memories of going after whitefish in birchbark canoes and meeting her family and friends flooded back. Amos also remembered the warm softness of her body and the wonderful nights they had spent together. The pain he had felt upon leaving her had dulled over the many years, but suddenly it came back as sharp as ever. It was a pain that the little bottle in his pocket wouldn't help.

Slowly getting up, Amos felt all the ache of loss he'd felt when he had first left. Taking the lead rope of the mule, he said, "I was wrong to come back here. I tried to drink her out of my mind once before. I don't have enough years left to do it again."

Suddenly, he felt an urgency to get away from the falls. It was almost like he was running from his past. Amos followed a logging road for several miles before coming to a small building that served as a tavern. Loosening the cinch on the saddle, he left the mule tied to a small poplar tree.

A white-haired, well wrinkled man stood behind the bar. "What'll you have?" he asked in a raspy voice.

"Rye," the prospector told him, in desperate need of the drink.

The rye tasted good, warming Amos' throat and stomach. The next few would be for his head. "I'll have another one."

The tavern had a sour smell of cabbage. It was small, with only four worn stools and a warped bar. Two narrow tables were against the back wall. The floor sloped to one side, telling of a rotting foundation. A dusty plank behind the bar held partial bottles of liquor, and the drink glasses were kept below the bar.

After several shots, the prospector finally had enough drink to blunt the pain he had felt at the falls. It was time to leave, but Amos wasn't sure where he needed to go. The white-haired bartender offered to pour one more drink. Amos told him to pour one for himself also.

"I'm looking for an Ojibwa woman's grave," he told the bartender, more for conversation than anything else.

"Woo," the man said, "that's a tough one. Ain't too many Indians' graves in this area anymore. Most have been dug into."

"Is there a place where they were buried after the fever years ago? Maybe the bastards would be afraid to dig in them," Amos said, trying to jog the memory of the old bartender.

The bartender poured Amos another drink without asking and then another for himself. "You know," he said, "on my trips to Newberry for supplies, I see this old blind woman sitting on her porch. I think she's part Indian. Maybe she'll know something."

"Maybe she will," Amos said, finishing his drink. The prospector settled up with the bartender and was sure that he had paid for more drinks than he had. Leaving the tavern with a bit of a stagger, Amos muttered, "Yes, look over the next hill. It's always over the next hill."

The prospector and mule started down the road, heading for Newberry. It was beginning to get dark and heavy rain clouds were building. Amos wasn't so sure he wouldn't fall off the mule after the stop at the tavern. Seeing a stand of spruce trees, he pulled off the road and set up camp.

Muttering and complaining about having stayed at the bar too long, Amos struggled to cut some of the lower branches and laced them into those above his head. Giving up, he figured it would help marginally should it start raining.

Just after midnight the thunder crashed and it began to pour. Awakened by the thunder, Amos stared into darkness until lightning allowed him to see. The mule was still where he had left it with its tail to the storm. "Hell of a gully washer, Jenny!" Amos shouted to the mule, still feeling the rye he had drank.

Pulling the slicker closer around him, the prospector was having trouble getting back to sleep. Lying awake in the storm, Amos started thinking about his next move. There was nothing but pain for him in Michigan. This part of the trip had given him no closure. It was time to go back, back to Montana, he decided. He could buy a place in Absarokee and be close to his son. Thinking about A.J gave him some comfort.

Sleep finally came and when he opened his eyes again it was full daylight. Amos' mouth was dry, his stomach upset, and his head was pounding. The rain had passed, leaving everything smelling fresh, but this was lost on the hungover prospector. He had a piece of hard bread and a bit of smoked fish to make his breakfast. Amos sat over his fire waiting for the coffee water to heat. He used the last of his grounds to make the pot.

After finishing nursing the coffee and forcing down the meal, his stomach and head began to feel better. Taking his time, Amos started to collect his gear. Much of it had gotten wet. The prospector hadn't taken care of things when he had made camp the night before. He had slept in his dark suit, and that was somewhat wrinkled, but it was dry. Finally, he had the gear ready and headed to get the animal.

"Hey mule," he called. "Don't forget to remind me to get some supplies in Newberry. I bet they got a train and we can start the trip back west. Been years since I've been through the Dakotas." Ignoring the prospector, the animal continued to pull on the tasty leaves of the poplar.

His head and stomach were feeling much better. Thinking of going back west had helped his mood. Amos walked briskly, leading the mule for about a mile to sweat out the rye and take the kinks out of his joints. His desire to be on his way west was stronger than his heart, and he tired quickly. Sitting on the side of the road, he waved at a wagon going by. The driver touched his hat in return. "See that, Jenny, they're friendly folks here, just like in Casper."

Thinking and walking, he continued to plan. His first stop west would be in Casper. He would take up the offer from Dan and Mary and spend a month or two at the ranch. Then, if the body was willing, he would ride the mule to Montana, spending time camping and fishing along the many streams.

Tiring again, Amos climbed onto the mule and urged it on. He had never needed to use a bit on any of his mules. A halter and lead rope were all he used. The smarter ones he had been able to guide with his knees.

Riding and daydreaming, he went around a bend in the road. Amos spotted a large pond, almost a lake. He stopped the mule and admired the sun reflecting off the waves. "I'll bet it got some nice fish," he told the mule. Further up the road, he spotted a weathered cabin. Vaguely remembering the conversation with the white-haired bartender, he wondered if it was the blind woman's place.

Amos continued closer. "If it's hers, it's too bad she's blind," he told the mule. "That is a beautiful view behind the cabin."

A voice came from the front of the cabin. "It sure is beautiful. I can't see it with my eyes anymore, but it is still in my mind."

He had found the blind woman. What he had thought of asking her wasn't as important anymore. By tomorrow he would be on a train heading for Casper. For all he knew, Ona's grave could be lost to time, or on the prairies of Canada.

Amos stopped in front and tied the mule to her fence. Pushing the gate open, he went up the walk. "Does the lake have fish in it?"

"Fish?" she chuckled. "You drop a worm on a hook in that pond and you have to beat them off to get the one you caught." He liked the way she laughed at her own joke.

The woman had a strip of cloth across her eyes. Amos asked, "Do they hurt?"

"Do what hurt?" she asked.

"Your eyes," he replied. "You have them covered."

"No, they don't hurt," she said. "I can't see a fly or a piece of dirt coming toward me, so I wear this to protect them."

The woman was of medium build and had a gingham dress on. Her hair was tied back in a loose braid with a red ribbon.

"I was wondering if you could help me," he said. "I am . . ." Stopping, he said, "I'm sorry, I should start out by introducing myself." Amos took off his bowler hat and then realized that it made little difference. She couldn't see anyway. "My name is

Amos Mudd, and I am looking for the grave of an Ojibwe woman named Ona. I mean, Onaiwa."

The blind woman put her hand to her cheek, and asked, "What was this woman to you?"

"Well," Amos said, "I knew her 48 years ago and we had grown close. I have some things I have to tell her and was hoping to find her grave." The woman didn't speak, so Amos continued. "I went west and kind of forgot about those I loved back here. I visited my folks in Maine and even found a friend who died near the Mattawa. This grave would be the last one."

She shook her head and said, "I'm sorry. I don't know of any such grave."

"I want to thank you anyway," he told her. Now Amos could head west without feeling that he hadn't tried to find her. While in the mission he had said a prayer to her, hoping that her spirit understood how he felt and how much he had loved her.

"I can smell the rye on you," she said, wrinkling her nose.

"What?" Amos replied, confused.

"You smell of the rye you drank," the blind woman repeated.

"I'm sorry," he apologized. "I guess I do. I tried to drown a memory last night."

"Have you eaten?" she asked.

"A little earlier. I plan to pick a few things up in Newberry before catching the train," Amos told her.

"I am hungry," she said. "Would you mind fixing a meal for an old, blind woman? You can join me if your stomach is up to it."

"I'm not in any hurry," he lied. "I have to warn you, I'm a fair cook."

She sniffed the air again. "You've a mule near the road?"

"Yes, how did you . . ."

She interrupted him, "I could hear and smell it. Put it around back near the stable. I don't want it messing my road. I believe there is some good grass back there."

The lady went in while Amos brought the mule around. He decided that the woman had a pretty good grouch on and maybe a meal would mellow her. He saw the cabin also had a back porch overlooking the pond. Amos felt bad that the woman couldn't see it. When he went inside, Amos saw that the cabin was very clean and the kitchen had a layout that would make a chef proud.

The blind woman had no trouble moving around the familiar surroundings. Hearing Amos come in, she said, "Just look around the kitchen. Make anything you want. Just don't move anything."

Amos was hungry for some of his potatoes and eggs. He added wood to the coals in the stove and got the fire going. After putting on water for coffee, he peeled and sliced the taters.

"I like the sound of someone in the kitchen," she said. "A woman comes in each evening and makes my supper. The other two meals I can do for myself."

"I hope my messing in your kitchen doesn't upset her," the prospector warned her.

Sitting at the table, she replied, "Just clean what you mess."

When they were eating, she complimented him on how good everything was. Amos was enjoying the potatoes from his father's farm with the eggs, but even more sitting at a proper table in a nice kitchen. While he was cleaning up, she told him about the fever and how so many of her friends had died. She felt lucky to only be blind. Then she said, "I shouldn't talk of such things. It is the good memories we should remember."

Amos thanked her for letting him share a meal and was about to take his leave when she asked, "Would you do one more thing before you go? Bring me down near the pond. It has been a long time since I've been down there. Your speaking of it makes me want to put my feet in the water."

Anxious to head for the train station, Amos wished that she hadn't asked, but she had provided his meal. "I would be happy to, but then I've got to be going."

He took her arm and they went out the back. Amos hesitated on the porch. "The water and trees back here are as beautiful as any mountain meadow."

"Tell me more," she urged him. "Describe what you are seeing. Tell me about the mountain meadows."

Standing on the porch, Amos talked of the waves and sparkling of the water, of the shades of green leaves and how the wind was moving them gently. She then reminded him of the mountain meadows. Amos closed his eyes, remembering the first time he had seen the high meadows near the Tetons. He described it to her and told her about the sunsets in the west.

"You should see the sunsets here," she said. "I used to love looking at it."

Holding her arm, the two of them continued down the path to the pond. There was a strip of sand near the edge. The woman kicked off her moccasins and stood in the water. "I haven't been down here for . . . it's been too long."

There was a bench near the water. Amos asked, "Do you mind if I sit while you wade?"

"Please do," she said.

Amos watch her in the water as she reached down and ran her fingers, making ripples. The woman then turned and started walking into the pond. "Don't do that," Amos warned. "If you have trouble, I may not be able to help you." Truth was, he didn't want to get wet.

"I've swam here for years. I won't go too deep," she promised.

Still in her dress, she walked in to her waist. Then she removed the strip from her eyes and splashed her face with the cool water. The tightness Amos had seen around her mouth seemed to disappear. "Don't get scared, Mr. Mudd, but I am going to go under water and push myself toward the shore. Just say something so I know which way to go."

"I think you should walk back," he urged. Then the woman dove forward toward shore, floating into the shallows and then stood up, water dripping off her clothing.

"I don't want to slip," she said. "Can you lead me to the bench?"

Amos got up to help her. He couldn't avoid noticing how the wet dress clung to her curves. Suddenly he felt awkward with the thoughts he was having. Taking her outstretched hand, he started to help her when she rushed to him and held him tight. "I thought you would never come back," she whispered. "I prayed every night that God would bring you back to me."

"Ona?" he asked.

"When you said your name, I felt panic. I was afraid you would want to go away. That you wouldn't want a blind woman. I wanted you to go so I wouldn't be hurt again, but something inside wouldn't let it happen. Tell me you will stay," she pleaded.

On the shore, with Ona in his arms, Amos held her close in disbelief. His heart pounded and his legs threatened to give way. "I came back to find you. I thought you were dead and wanted to pray over your grave."

The prospector's throat ached and he couldn't trust his voice. All his planning was now . . . now gone. Breathing deep, he continued, blinking back tears of emotion, "Ona, I found the mother lode in Montana and it could not match what I thought I'd lost here in Michigan. If you will have me, I will never leave you," Amos finished in a whisper.

"Will you marry me?" she asked.

Without hesitation, he said, "Yes." Amos held her close. "I should never have left."

"I should have gone with you," Ona countered. Both were quiet for a moment, as what had just happened sunk in.

"I met our son in Casper," Amos whispered.

"He was angry. I'm glad he didn't kill you," Ona replied.

"He did make me pretty miserable last winter," he informed her.

"Good, it makes up for you going to California," she said, pressing her soft body close to him, her warm breath in his ear.

"I never made it to California," he informed her, "and, our son . . ." He liked the word. "Our son is married."

"He is?" she asked, surprised.

"She's a very nice lady with two children and a potato farm," Amos informed her.

"Potatoes? Now I know why you came back," she said, remembering his talk of why he left Maine.

The couple returned to the bench, enjoying the sunshine and soft breeze. The closeness was very comforting. Amos looked up at the cabin. It had nicely squared logs. "Did our son square the logs for the cabin?" he asked.

"He did," Ona said. "It was built for another family. After A.J. left, I was able to buy it. I had told him stories of you squaring logs in Canada and he decided to try it when building the cabin. He did a lot of wood work before leaving to find you. That was ten years ago." Amos saw sadness on her face.

"We better get you back to the cabin and get you into some dry clothes," Amos said. Arm in arm, they started up the path to the cabin. "Where would you like to go for our honeymoon?" he asked.

"A honeymoon, at our age?" Ona wondered.

"At our age it's not something we should put off," he reminded her. "I would like to take you to Montana to visit our son."

"Really," she said, tilting her head up at him, her sightless eyes smiling.

CHAPTER TWENTY

That first night when they'd gone to bed, Ona snuggled close to the old prospector, and her warmth and softness brought Amos back to their younger days at the shanty when they'd first met and the sparks of their love had been kindled. The shine of western gold had had more brilliance, blinding the young Amos to the treasure that now lay beside him.

He touched her soft hair, feeling the ribbon. "It is the same color as the one I brought you while working at the logging camp," he whispered.

"I still have the original ribbon," she replied. "I have kept it safe for our wedding. I have bought many over the years, wearing one in my hair every day."

The next morning, they sat in the kitchen drinking coffee when Ona said, "When we go to Montana to visit A.J. and his family, we should stay and settle down near them."

Surprised as her comment, Amos set his cup down before replying, "You once told me that if you left this area your spirit would wander among strangers."

"That is no longer so," she said, reaching across the table for his hands. "We now have family in the west. Our blood has become one with our son and, with luck, he and his wife will give us grandchildren."

With the help of Amos, it took two months for Ona to sort through her things and sell her house. She would sit in the room and tell him where each item was and what was to be kept or gotten rid of. Several long breaks were needed by the two, sitting on the back porch or down by the pond.

A letter was sent to A.J., letting him know of their decision to relocate in Montana, and about wanting the preacher in Red Lodge to marry them. Amos borrowed a cart to carry their belongings to Newberry. The prospector and Ona sat for some time on the bench near the pond saying goodbye her home, breathing in the familiar smells of the water and forest. Then they slowly climbed the slope to the waiting mule and cart.

The train ride to Red Lodge took just over a week. Sitting on the cushioned seats, Amos would describe what he saw from the window. They had a berth in one of the sleeping cars for part of the trip. The rest they made due on the seats, Ona using Amos' shoulder for a pillow.

The train platform was crowded with people when they reached Red Lodge. Amos and Ona were on the wrong side of the car to look out. As the brakes were applied, the steel wheels screeched on the rails, bringing the cars to a stop.

Amos helped Ona down from the train, taking care that she didn't misstep reaching the platform. As they turned to search for A.J., Amos was relieved to see him standing only a few feet away. "Mother!" A.J. cried, hurrying to give her a hug. Amos saw the tears in their eyes as the two were reunited. He looked beyond and saw Lucia with Chip and Elly.

A.J. took his mother's hand and said, "Come meet my wife and children"

As the introductions were being made, Amos felt a bit like an outsider, until A.J. moved close and whispered, "Thank you father, for bringing us all together again."

The minister did not disappoint, delivering a find sermon during the wedding. Hoss and his family joined the festivities, showing off their cute baby girl. He had purchased the ranch that he'd wanted and invited Amos and Ona to visit them as soon as possible.

That evening while celebrating the wedding, Amos was surrounded by his family. A warm feeling washed over him. It was a feeling he'd not had since his mother died. To top everything else off, he had also learned from Lucia that he was going to be a grandfather.

While dancing with her new husband, Ona asked him, "Does all the air in Montana smell like this?"

Laughing his replied, "What you smell are the coal fires. I can promise you the air will be fresh and sweet where were going."

The family spent another day in Red Lodge before traveling north. Amos was unsure whether he and Ona would build a place near the stream he had camped at so many times, or continue up to Absarokee and find something there. Either way, he and Ona would be close to the farm. A.J. surprised them with a cabin near the farm, with promises to Amos that he wouldn't have to help in the potato fields if they stayed.

Amos and Ona would sit on the porch of their cabin, her sipping a lemonade and him a glass of rye, while the prospector told her stories of his 48 years of traveling in the mountains. The women he had met and the rye he'd consumed was never part of the story. Ona had never lost faith that he would come back to her, and the stories Amos told her helped her understand what had drawn him to the west and why it had taken so long for him to finally come back to her.

NOTES AND COMMENTS

Thank you for reading this book.